Emmanuelle Arsan is the pseudonym of a young
Eurasian – Maryat Rollet-Andriane, the wife of a member
of the French delegation at UNESCO who had previously
served at a diplomatic post in Bangkok. Her frank,
liberated view of the human sexual impulse has brought
her international fame and has turned her into a
controversial figure on both sides of the Atlantic. Distinguished critic Françoise Giroud of *L'Express* wrote of her
that she 'preaches the "erotic revolution" as seriously as
others teach in today's China the "cultural revolution".'
The bestselling *Emmanuelle* novels have been turned into
films that have broken box-office records all over the
world and set new standards for the erotic cinema.

Also by Emmanuelle Arsan

Emmanuelle Arsan

Vanna

Translated from the French
by Celeste Piano

A MAYFLOWER BOOK

GRANADA
London Toronto Sydney New York

Published by Granada Publishing Limited in 1981

ISBN 0 583 13294 4

A Granada Paperback UK Original

Granada Publishing Ltd
Frogmore, St Albans, Herts AL2 2NF
and
3 Upper James Street, London W1R 4BP
866 United Nations Plaza, New York, NY10017, USA
117 York Street, Sydney, NSW 2000, Australia
100 Skyway Avenue, Rexdale, Ontario, M9W 3A6, Canada
PO Box 84165, Greenside, 2034 Johannesburg, South Africa
61 Beach Road, Auckland, New Zealand

Typeset by Elanders Computer Assisted
Typesetting Systems, Inverness

Printed and bound in Great Britain by
©ollins, Glasgow

Granada ®
Granada Publishing ®

Contents

Life ultimately gives rise to itself
and not to death

YVES BONNEFOY:
(In the threshold's trap)

1 Hieroglyphics Explained

The Root Of Exiles

Hat-an-Shau is the ancient Egyptian term for a palace on the sand. Palace upon sand ... Palace of sand ... Palace in Egypt ... Palace in ... Palace ... Camel on the sand ... Plateau ... Flat sands ... Sand ....

Suspended between dream and reality, Guido gazed at the outlines of the air hostess's breasts, clearly etched against the curved interior of the plane. Her reddish gold hair resembled the *pschent* or double crown of ancient Egypt. The angle of her arms tautly proffering a tray recalled the penultimate hieroglyph on that tablet, which mentions the name of Maât-Ka-Rê Hatshepsout-chnem-Amon.

Since his student days Guido had shown a marked, albeit misunderstood, partiality towards this wise and mysterious queen who had altered the succession of the 18th dynasty. Her brother and husband, when he succeeded her as head of his race, tried in vain to destroy all effigies of her and even to erase her name from the Theban pedestals, obelisks and temples she had built. Such hysterical behaviour couldn't prevent the legend of Hatshepsout's omnipotence reaching Guido, but what was really odd was that the latter had himself rediscovered traces of it on the eve of his departure from Milan – by way of one of his company vouchers.

Fancy being portrayed thus, thirty-five centuries later!

Anyhow, he'd thought, better to be suspect than forgotten.

Would he himself, he found himself wondering, leave behind anything that would so mockingly and for so long foil death? Computers programmed his life, but would these mausoleums know how to preserve within their plastic storage the characters of his name, all too short and common as it was, for three thousand five hundred years?

In the sovereign's indelible shadow, a naked slave held out a jasper goblet from which her own lips had first tasted. She also dipped into it her black tongue and the crimson tips of her breasts. The mistress of Lower and Upper Egypt stared silently at the swollen pubis of her slave and touched her knee.

The knee of the air hostess pressed against Guido's thigh as she was bending across him with a glass of champagne and some crisps. The twin columns of her thighs tightly stretched the reddish-violet material of her skirt. Her eyes, wide open and vacant like those of the little cupbearer of antiquity, gave away nothing of what she felt or desired.

Guido took a mouthful of his drink and let his head fall back against the foam head-rest. Mingled images of women neither time nor space could separate disintegrated and re-formed before his eyes, becoming disembodied cells, stray blonde molecules, warm atoms. His vision blurred, turned into patterns and shapes of stripes and blobs just like a malfunctioning TV.

And what if the very computer's programme also misfired? Neither the machines nor those faceless directors who were sending Guido off into the unknown would feel the slightest disruption of their comfort or their circuits. But he, Guido, would be reduced to nothingness.

He played around a while, varying the possible combinations of those elements which were painting a *pointilliste* picture behind his closed eyelids.

He reopened his eyes without dwelling upon his situation or any further stocktaking. His stock, after all, was high enough! He smiled munificently at the stewardess, whose knee was now back in his orbit. Without worrying about the other passengers, he stroked the silk stocking and the young woman's soft inner thigh. She didn't flinch and said not a word.

The skirt was too tight for Guido's hand to slide further up.

'In my day,' quoth the female Pharaoh of the Two kingdoms, 'my servant women wore nothing about their rounded buttocks. Cats were goddesses: I founded a whole religion for them in Bastet's name. If upon a whim I ordered one of my subjects to clothe herself, she would drape around her haunches folds of some diaphanous material which did not hide her beauty nor make access to that beauty difficult.'

As if she understood perfectly, the stewardess laid the backs of her wrists along Guido's stomach before removing his empty glass and his tray.

'Ah, Giulia!' he sighed.

At that hour she'd still be asleep between those sheets which smelt of lovemaking. Exhausted, like himself. Ready to begin all over again, as he was. Alone like himself. Alone for how long, though? Not as long as he'd be, he was prepared to bet on that! The waiting list must already be prancing about impatiently. Who was first in line or how much importance to give them were simple matters, with which Guido didn't need to trouble himself: the wisdom of his employers and an easygoing life-style had between them taken care of that.

The landscape turned from blue to brown and then from mauve to bronze. Tall palm trees rose upwards, flanked by thin cylindrical spikes of stone and brick. The skyscrapers of the faithful! Towers of Babel for the credulous, Guido thought getting himself ready to get back down to earth.

His taxi swung from the airport motorway to the white avenues of Cairo's suburbs, taking him along the banks of the muddy Nile, carelessly scattering the lethargic early-morning crowds. The air smelled wonderfully of eucalyptus and less wonderfully of dust.

After a last agonized screech of tyres and an Arabic harangue which he pacified with conciliatory nods, the traveller with some relief recognized the fascia of the hotel as it came into view. To him every Hilton was a home from home.

At this particular one, however, the sand-filled spring wind had an unexpectedly disconcerting affect. Impalpable, invisible in the murky room, it somehow managed to penetrate everywhere. Guido felt it under his fingernails, inside his opened cases, and saw shining diamond specks of it across every polished surface and mirror. From time to time an even more violent gust of wind tore at the landscape from which the city's domes and minarets bristled, so clean and crisp that Guido could have imagined their being painted upon the glass of his window.

Despite the air-conditioning, his sinuses were dry and his lungs hurt.

'The *khamsin* is blowing, sir,' the service waiter explained, placing the Glenmorangie which the new arrival had ordered in front of him. He added, whether politely or condescendingly: 'Foreigners often have trouble getting used to the air here.'

'I'm not your average foreigner,' Guido assured him.

That was the time Vanna awoke on a furry rug, by another window in that vast city.

'Well, that's it,' she mused. 'I'm twenty-seven now. Three Cubed!'

Mija was still asleep beside her, huddled up in a ball, like a little tame leopard. Vanna leaned over her friend's face to try to discern those images which while dreaming made her smile. Were they images of freedom?

That night, the night of her birthday, Vanna had for the first time slid her legs between Mija's own, which were soft as lips. And slid her lips, sweet as the delicious Delta limes . . . .

Vanna got up, stretched her slender arms and arched her finely tapering back. Legs spread, hands raised skywards, she stayed like that a moment, crucified nude in the emptiness of her room, motionless, testing out her body, relaxed and watchful at once, inspecting herself as reflected in the copper door – the slightly slanted eyes, whose green irises were transmuted by that metal; the large and sensuous mouth; the narrow, straight nose, quite Pharaonic; sensitive rounded breasts, and thighs which paradoxically combined delicacy with a certain sculptural weight. Was she, she wondered, always two characters – always some duality within herself? She rejected this idea. Why only *two*? The suggestion that something, a number, source or appearance could impose a limit on her was distasteful to her.

She brushed her chestnut hair, restoring it to the softly-moulded upswept style she had selected.

She slid aside the tapestry, opening the window. Youssaf-Mustafa Street was torpid, in spite of the wind which sandpapered and browned the façades of the houses. The day after a night's celebration, all mornings seem to ache.

Still naked, she went through to serve breakfst in that particular corner of the flat which she had earmarked for the purpose.

Mija's huge dark eyes, when she opened them, attested to her astonishment at finding herself once again with Vanna. Her long frizzy hair was in disarray. Her beautiful Coptic Jewess's mouth half-parted as if about to ask what she was doing there and in these circumstances, upon this dun fur rug which accentuated the pallor of her skin. But she changed her mind, and giving Vanna a roguish grin, declared: 'I no longer have any shame!'

'Prove it!' Vanna said.

With one bound the girl leaped forward. Unknowingly she took up the very posture of crucifixion which Vanna's body had earlier assumed. Then she licked a fingertip and moistened her sex with it. Her wedge-shaped fleece almost reached her navel while clearly defining her clitoris and the crease of her vulva: these she stroked, standing upright, and began groaning almost at once.

'Keep going – right to the end,' Vanna ordered her.

Mija sank the wet finger into her vagina and gasped that she was about to come. Vanna couldn't wait, and kneeling between her friend's legs, pulled Mija's hands down into her own hair. Mija opened herself as wide as she could. Vanna took her entire sex into her mouth, not letting her go until Mija had bent her knees and collapsed to the floor.

Then Vanna gripped her thighs, thrust a couple of fingers inside her, plunging them back and forth. When Mija could no longer cry out nor jerk convulsively even, Vanna lay down on top of her, head to tail, so that each of their cunts was level with the other's mouth. For several minutes they hit upon a mutual rhythm. Together they came, continued, came again, went on again.

Prolongation had become an integral part of their pleasure. Neither wanted to be the first to come. All the same, it was Mija who lost control. Even then Vanna wouldn't stop until she herself finally exploded into orgasm.

16

She remained where she was, lying over Mija, one cheek resting on the younger girl's pubis, dreaming and, since it was her birthday, taking stock of her life. The stocktaking satisfied her. She had friends and lovers: enough of them to be free of them and other people. She earned her own living and lived well, happily, not ruled by her work, but on the contrary, moulding it to her own tastes and ideas. She was capable, if she so wished, of changing it just as confidently as she might move from one place to another.

To move to a different place sometimes entailed depriving herself of those she loved. She missed her mother. She no longer knew where her father was hiding himself. It was quite beyond her to find him again. At least that way she would be free of having to look for him.

Her mother ... Vanna smiled to think that that untypical Catalan woman would recognize herself, seeing this naked girl under her daughter! It had taken Vanna a long time to realize that her mother was quite capable of following some beauty glimpsed in the street and of coaxing her back home with her, undressing her and teaching her to love as she did. Vanna was surprised to find herself following her footsteps, even there, probably in much the same way as she had chosen to read archaeology so that their professions would be related.

Yet Vanna had still known how to escape, leaving Barcelona after gaining her degree. She left Iñez behind there – the mother she only revisited once or twice a year. Had she chosen to settle in Cairo because Egypt was the land of archaeology, or was it because it was her father's native land? That father who had left them both without explanations or good-byes almost twenty-five years ago and whom they'd never seen again!

It was one thing for him not to be able to stand sharing his wife with others, even if those others were the opposite sex to his own, but why did he also reject his only daughter? Did he secretly resent her Spanish blood? Couldn't he accept the fact that she was only half Egyptian? If that was it, why had he brought her into the world by coupling with a foreigner? Wasn't he, in this, being the first to affirm that bodies have no country?

Vanna had followed his example by wanting to be cosmopolitan. Did she really know what language – Arabic, Spanish, French, Greek, Hebrew, German – was her true mother-tongue? Did she check out the nationalities of the men and women she loved? It wasn't possible, she considered, both to love and to belong. Love provides human beings with new roots: it is the changing fatherland of exile.

Replacing the telephone, which had scarcely stopped ringing after Mija (who didn't want to take the whole day off school) had departed, Vanna ran herself a bath with lukewarm water, sprinkled in bath salts and lowered herself into it, resuming the thread of her reveries.

'Mother seduced young girls, too,' she told herself. This thought, no matter how often she formulated it, excited her more than any other. As usual when she bathed or showered, her hand involuntarily strayed towards her sex. The fact that hardly an hour ago her coltish lover had made her come in no way altered her solitary desire.

'I was much younger than Mija when I learned to make love to myself,' she recalled. 'And right from the start I did it several times a day.'

As far back as she could remember, back in childhood days, she couldn't recollect ever having had a bath without an orgasm. Of course masturbation was much more satisfying if accompanied by some new fantasy. So today she quickly gave up her imaginary quest for a young girl with a downy pubis and budding breasts to whom she'd teach what she herself had already known at that

18

age, and let her mind wander towards the stranger who had just telephoned her.

She liked Renato, the bearded Lombard architect who'd given the man her name. The stranger said they'd seen each other only a night or so back in Milan. And yes, Renato still dreamed of houses shaped like roses! He was still shy and overworked, still fanatical about good wine. Renato the connoisseur it had been who'd insisted that she alone could supply a newcomer with the necessary information about the country's sights to see and its marvels, she who could guide him round the desert.

After he'd rung off, Vanna reflected that the stranger had really picked an awkward time for his suggested projects. True, every so often she'd double as a part-time guide to supplement the wage paid her by the UNESCO archaeological mission for which she worked, but her current plans already included a tour of Upper Egypt. Was she to change these arrangements just because a friend of a friend wanted her for a girlfriend on a trip up the Nile?

Even so, she had agreed to meet the interloper. But that, as she reproached herself, was only before her bath had assuaged her curiosity! Now ... Ah, well, dinner at the Hilton was always agreeable.

'It's not even the end of the month and I'm broke already, as usual,' she thought. 'One day I really must learn not to throw money down the drain.'

Where did it all go? Certainly not on clothes and knick-knacks. Books, yes. And on antiques for which she paid exorbitant prices instead of budgeting properly to be able to afford them, taking advantage of sales and special offers meanwhile. But then nobody in her circle worried too much about making ends meet either. Iñez's instruction had borne fruit!

She put on a thin cotton dress of pale blue with a dark pattern, and a chunky, heavy silver necklace she had brought back from Ethiopia. She used a whitish-coloured lipstick and ringed her eyes with a tiny amount of *kohl*. She knew it made her look like a certain character in antiquity – not that this Maât, goddess of Justice and Truth wholly appealed to Vanna. She was, however, attractive; she led the powerful a merry dance, and the men of her time constantly fell in love with her. The statuette of her, gracefully seated, and incorporating the ostrich stylus that had inscribed her name upon the old scrolls, the carved goddess holding upon her knees the *ankh* or ansate cross which is the sign of eternity, was one of the treasures Vanna had ruined herself to acquire. She winked at it before departing.

There was only one good-looking man in the Hilton Bar. Vanna made a beeline for him. He rose casually to his feet and introduced himself as Guido Andreotti, delighting her with a display of admiration out of the most refined Italian repertoire: 'I really must say, Renato Bombo wasn't having me on!'

'Well, I play it straight with him too,' said Vanna. 'How is he? Is he thinking of coming back here?'

'He asked me to give you a kiss on his behalf.' Guido said.

He was surprised to see Vanna offer her cheek, but kissed it suavely. She let him know her first impression:

'You're not at all like him.'

'Do you hold that against me?' Guido inquired anxiously.

'Of course.'

He looked crestfallen, adding:

'Won't you suspend judgment until after dinner?'

'First let me have a good meal,' she said, 'I'm always more susceptible after eating well.'

Just then she didn't feel inclined to put herself out: the guy seemed something of a snob to her, rather insipid and too sure of himself. Her intuition even suspected him of worrying about creasing his new alpaca suit and messing up his nice dark hair.

'Well, what have you got to say for yourself?' she teased him, after she had made her order.

'I know nothing about Egypt, except for one queen I think I must be the only one to like – who goes by the name of Maât-ka-Rê Hatshepsout-chnem-Amon .... '

'Hatshepsout was a slut,' Vanna exclaimed, interrupting him, 'but Maât's my goddess! Where did you encounter her?'

'The goddess? Nowhere. Nor the pharaoh, either. I tend to picture her carried aloft by naked slaves.'

'We couldn't have lived in the same era,' Vanna decided. 'We'll never meet again.'

'Let's settle for the future,' Guido suggested. 'I confess I'm no history buff. But I've lots of time to learn about it.'

'From me?' said Vanna, astonished.

'Isn't that your speciality?'

'No. I'm a digger, a navvy. I collect broken pots.'

'That's the same thing. Renato calls that being an expert.'

'Renato's sweet but he knows nothing about it. Would you help me on a dig?'

'On a ... Sorry, yes ... But I'm more interested in men than what's under the earth.'

'Men?'

'Man, I should say. Human beings.'

'Bully for you, but is it a profession?'

'I write,' Guido explained.

'Ah!'

Vanna didn't seem favourably impressed. For a while she stopped asking him questions and responded half-heartedly to his own. She avoided telling him about herself. Then she retrieved the shawl she had draped over her chair-back and covered her shoulders with it once again. Guido felt he was losing ground. He pressed on:

'Obviously I don't measure up to Renato. But I *am* his friend. Wouldn't you want to do for me just a little of what you've done for him?'

'A little?'

'I meant – you took him around everywhere, into the Sudan even. For three months you never left him . . . .'

'Longer: ninety-nine days.'

'Don't you want to be my guide and mentor, even if it involved not taking me so far and spending less of your time with me?'

'I'm not qualified to escort secret agents.'

'What? . . . Ah, I see!'

He burst out laughing, which pleased Vanna.

'There I assure you you're absolutely mistaken. I've nothing at all to do with that sort of thing.'

'So much the better,' Vanna said. 'Because I'm warning you right away that I don't get turned on at all by that kind of dirty tricks league.'

'Nor do I. It's all right, though: the truth is I'm just a dilettante. A bit obsessive, but harmless. I do like mysteries, but gratuitous ones.'

'I hope you won't mind my saying that I haven't understood one iota of this conversation. And as for mysteries, they give me no buzz whatever.'

'You're a positivist, Renato told me. Or was it a materialist I can't quite recall. A rationalist, maybe?'

'I'm not an-ist. Not even a tourist. I didn't accompany Renato to see the countryside, nor even because I wanted to sleep with him, but because I needed the money. I'm a worker and I do the dragoman bit to earn my livelihood. Not to *lose* it. I don't do anything and everything, not at any price.'

'I'm hardly asking you to guide me gratis,' Guido replied with some irritation.

'Unfortunately my engagements book is full. I'm sorry to have misled you.'

'I didn't expect you to let me know what you yourself already knew,' he persisted. 'I did think that we could learn something else together.'

'Something else?' said Vanna, nonplussed.

'Something else new. Unknown.'

Vanna just stared silently at him as he continued:

'It's not your occasional guide-interpreter role that interests me in you, it's your archaeological side. You're a real archaeologist and the choice you've made proves that you have the passion for exploration. You're not content with knowing what others know, you try to find out what no one before you has known.'

Vanna smiled, this time sympathetically and Guido took heart and went on:

'If you found an ancient relic of which there were several others, or even a single museum copy, I'm sure you'd derive no satisfaction from that. You're only really happy when you uncover something whose significance no one yet suspects, something you have, in a sense, invented.'

'And you really think we have a chance of inventing something together?' she joked.

'I don't know. I'd just like to try.'

She thought for a while and finally said:

'It's weird. What makes you think we can get along with each other? Don't tell me it's my eyes, nose, or tits: you'd wind up throwing away what you've almost salvaged.'

'I don't want to play these games with you. All I know about you is via Renato. And I'm under no illusion that such knowledge is definitive. But it's enough for me to want you desperately to take up my offer.'

'Are you aware of something, Mr Andreotti?'

'No, what?'

'That I haven't the slightest idea what your offer consists of?'

His attention was suddenly drawn to a group of men and women – the latter stunningly elegant and beautiful, wearing very lowcut dresses with tight slit skirts, their necks and arms bare and bejewelled – that had just made a noisy incursion into the bar. Vanna was not in the least put out by the interest he was taking in this unexpected fashion show: she shared it.

One of the young women (the best-looking of all was Guido's snap decision) spotted Vanna and hailed her delightedly. Then she broke away from the arm which held her, glided between the tables and came across to kiss Vanna. Her movement when bending over towards the young woman's lips made the front of her dress hang forward, completely exposing her breasts.

Vanna embraced her thus, keeping her in this position for some moments. Guido immediately knew she was doing so for his benefit, so that he could feast his eyes at will upon the spectacle.

When the visitor rejoined her companions for the evening, Vanna asked Guido: 'What do you think of her?'

'Superb,' he acknowledged. 'You choose your friends well . . . . '

He added, before she had time to suggest to him – as he was sure she was going to do – that he might like to get to know the woman better:

'You see, we share the same tastes, that's a good sign.'

Vanna's gesture took him by surprise. Instead of answering him, she suddenly leaned heavily against his shoulder. He was about to put an arm around her but restrained himself just in time. He let several minutes elapse without saying anything. Vanna seemed to be dreaming. She finally sat up, looking him straight in the eye: 'Well?'

'Do you know of a palace in the desert here?'

'*Hat-en-Shau,*' she said. 'It's not here. It's far away, a long way off. At Siwah. A lost oasis at the end of nowhere.'

'That's one of the places I'd like to visit.'

'No one can get inside there,' she said.

'Doesn't that make *you* want to go there?'

She thought for a while. Her answer seemed quite ingenuous:

'Yes, maybe. But why should I want to go there with you?'

Guido sighed wearily. 'I see it now, in the long run you don't really like me,' he said.

'Instead of trying to impress me with catchpenny analysis,' Vanna pointed out, 'you'd do better to tell me – and a bit more honestly than you have so far – *your* reasons for wanting to get to Hat-en-Shau with me.'

'I told you,' said Guido, shrugging.

'No you didn't. There are plenty of other, better guides and interpreters than I in Cairo. Better historians and archaeologists too.'

'What do you want me to say?' Guido grumbled, as if he had to all intents and purposes given up trying to persuade her.

'Right, let's talk philosophy, since that's what you like!' Vanna jeered. 'Does our society seem honest to you? When a man invites a woman to dinner, is it in order to exchange ideas or chatter about geography with her? If its for something else, why doesn't he come straight out with it and tell her frankly? Is it that he's ashamed of his intentions? Not even that! It's because he doesn't have the appropriate vocabulary. We're often hypocritical simply because we don't know how to talk.'

He looked at her with something of his former good humour.

'That's obviously not the case with you!' he declared. 'Why then didn't you say all this to start with? Maybe because you only wanted to finish your cognac and leave.'

'Right. But just now I feel like dancing. What I'd like later I don't yet know.'

The discotheque was packed, of course. The *sofraghi* trying to resemble Travolta found them a corner, however, into which they wedged themselves. Unusually, that evening the sound system hadn't been turned up full blast, so by dint of repeating everything several times they could just about make themselves heard.

Even so, they kept conversation to a minimum. After a few dances, Guido took advantage of a moment's exhaustion during a brief lull to comment to Vanna, who, since space at their table was still limited, was practically sitting on his lap, and had just offered him a paper handkerchief with which to mop the perspiration off his brow:

'With sensitive hands like yours, you must caress yourself often.

'Drunken logic!' she laughed. 'And therefore quite correct.'

Vanna's thighs jammed against his own were relaxed and yielding and he felt himself giving in to an erection which was fast beginning to overwhelm any previous sense of propriety. With his free hand he raised his companion's skirt until her legs were wholly bared. Vanna seemed not so much affronted as content. Guido's prick hardened.

He raised the skirt a fraction higher and this time Vanna's dark pubic thatch was clearly exposed to view. Guido's first thought, naturally, was: Ah, she doesn't wear knickers. He could have kicked himself for not guessing earlier – he prided himself on being able to tell at once if a woman belonged to one or the other of the two categories ruling the world just like Good and Evil in bygone times – those who wear underclothes and those who do not.

'Let's dance some more!' Vanna requested.

Reluctantly Guido led her back into the throng gyrating to the Bee Gees on the dance floor, but this time he made sure the lower halves of their bodies were pressed tightly together: too bad about convention! She adroitly complied with this gambit of his. A bit too adroitly perhaps, he reflected after a while. And he pulled away slightly from Vanna's control over him, for her effect at close range was only too predictable.

This retreat didn't seem to please Vanna, who decided to sit out once more. Guido, hoping to make her smile again, unbuttoned the top of her dress, baring her breasts: Vanna actually stopped sulking.

Then he began caressing her breasts, legs and sex. The show wasn't lost upon their neighbours, either. For her part Vanna squeezed Guido's prick, through his trousers at first, then trying to pull it out of his flies, which she had now opened. Guido stopped her and she protested:

'You're less logical than I thought. This isn't the way you'll ever be accepted at Siwah.'

'I don't want you to toss me off,' Guido said. 'I want to fuck you.'

The dry click of the latch, even more than Guido's hotel room door closing after them, completed their separation from the conventions and habits of their world. He didn't even feel obliged to get a bottle of champagne from the refrigerator, as was his wont at the hotel before undressing a woman.

Without saying a word he pulled Vanna's dress up and stripped her himself. Only after he'd stared at her

27

nakedness to his heart's content did he open his mouth to ask the most dated of questions:

'Don't you ever have any use for underwear?'

She shook her head. He took her in his arms.

'Really never?' he persisted. She kissed him.

'Never, absolutely never,'

'I saw that at once, the moment you arrived in the bar,' he lied. She smiled, and keeping her lips against Guido's, asked:

'Was that why you desired me?'

'I can only love women who don't wear knickers.'

'That's what you should have told me straight away, instead of spouting so much crap.'

As she had done earlier while they were dancing, she rubbed her belly and pubis so irresistibly against Guido's erect prick that he had to avoid the too rapid conclusion she seemed to be wanting to provoke.

'What did you mean about Siwah?' he asked, talking in order to resist the temptation to come immediately, there and then against Vanna's warm and compliant skin without even penetrating her.

'That they aren't ashamed about their inclinations there.'

'And what's your inclination?'

'It's never the same, and never the same as anybody else's.'

'Don't you have preferences?'

'That'd be a way of depriving myself.'

'Isn't there anything you don't like?'

'Yes. I don't like people being ashamed of the body. Or of their sex. Or being ashamed of their desires.'

'In your book is everything permissible?'

'Everything that makes one happy without making others unhappy.'

'How can I know in advance if what gives me pleasure also gives you physical pleasure?'

28

'You can't know in advance. Nor do I. One has to try.'

His erection continued to grow and this conversation was anything but detumescent. He led Vanna to one side of the bed and made her kneel down and bury her face in the quilted silk coverlet. His hands gripped her waist, forcing her to straighten her back still more. This way her buttocks jutted out and took on a statuesque splendour. He leaned against them until Vanna's thighs rested on her calves.

He bent forward and licked the downy hollow of the small of her back, especially the deep twin dimples just above her buttocks, either side of the crack. He licked that too and then her sex and then returned to the cleft of her buttocks until that became moist. Vanna was moaning with pleasure. Then he introduced his prick with so little difficulty that he thought she must be used to the practice.

The idea pleased him although he wasn't absolutely sure that it was correct. Often he liked to imagine that a woman (even if he himself had actually taken her virginity) was a whore all along, just as on other occasions, equally dishonestly, he would fantasize that he was deflowering one of his conquests, even if she were, say, a friend's wife.

Guido could only make friends with men who had the good taste to marry beautiful women. At the precise moment he was buggering Vanna he told himself – and it amused him so much that he almost laughed out loud – that if he was in fact taking her in a manner unusual for himself also, it was doubtless because she didn't fall into the category of his usual mistresses: those women who seemed to him so much more delightful to possess when newlywed and hence devoted to their husbands.

He wanted to tell Vanna that he was proud of having not one friend whose wife he hadn't fucked. Not one, he murmured in ecstasy. Not a single one! But he didn't reckon that they were yet intimate enough to justify this sort of confidence. At present, he was better off taking advantage of this splendid arse and deriving as much pleasure from it as possible. And, maybe, introducing Vanna to new pleasures as well.

Was she still unmarried, in fact? It was true that when Renato knew her she hadn't been, but she could have got married since. Surely she must have! Otherwise Guido's cock would certainly not have felt so at ease inside her . . .

'Ah, how I'd like her husband to be watching us!' Guido privately fantasized: 'I'd like him to know that I've only just met his wife and here I am buggering her! I'd like him to see me come into his property!'

This fantasy excited him to the point at which he could no longer hold back. Yet he didn't want the experience to end just then. He stayed still until the imminence of the spasm had receded. Only then, with an intuition so finely timed that he marvelled at its intimate abandon, did Vanna, who had hitherto been motionless, begin gently contracting her muscles and moving her pelvis left and right, up and down . . . .

'That's good,' he gasped, 'go on!'

He himself was rotating his hips without yet picking up the motion to and fro.

'How about you,' he asked, 'do you like that?'

She didn't answer, so Guido's hand moved to her clitoris and began tickling it. Vanna moaned.

'I'm coming,' she murmured, then cried out again as she did so, and with the climax lost consciousness.

She regained it when she felt Guido withdraw. Had they been sleeping, still coupled, without realizing it? She turned, first kissing her companion on the cheek and then took into her mouth the penis which had just transfixed her.

Later the next morning he wanted to fuck her cunt. It would have been the first time. She forebade this, however.

'No!' she said. 'No. Do it the other way.' He did as he was told.

2

Three Interlocking Rhombuses and A Black Nebula

Upon rush mats – whose texture and shape had probably not changed over the fifty centuries during which they had been gathered and woven throughout that triangle of obstinate earth gripped by the seven-fingered Nile – Vanna and Mija laid out red-lacquered bowls in which jasmine and frangipani blossom floated. Their scent wafted over the savoury odour of kebabs and fritters.

The young women drew the curtains and lit the lights. The large room like a trapezium with concave base, that with the copper- and mosaic-decorated bathroom comprised Vanna's whole flat, seemed to sway about them, dappled with shadows and embossed with carvings illumined by fitful candle flames.

Next to an armless and headless sandstone torso the gentle curves of whose breast, eroded by time, might have been those of man or woman, a papyrus plant with serried stems and gleaming leaves, which had been sent to Vanna from Trinacria (since it has disappeared from the Nile Delta and Valley), sprouted from a willow-green bowl and sprayed out like a petrified fountain of green to the ceiling itself.

The lady of the house removed from its position – for she liked to change objects around as much as she enjoyed changing herself – a terra cotta statuette with a tiny head, flat chest and immense phallus, which had been lovingly carved on some Greek island today no longer existent.

The library took up two of the four walls; some of its shelves containing only books, while others were almost empty save for here a single medallion or there a lump of blackened bronze shaped like a vulva; elsewhere there was a piece of white coral, some marine fossils or a gypsum flower large as a Persian rose; the dog Anubis; Horus in his hieratic headdress; Maât, of course; and another vulva, this time a model of Vanna's own.

On the other walls were photographic blow-ups of sand dunes, high seas, skin, green and golden elytra, naked girls. Vanna's photographic apparata, fine, black expensive equipment and lenses which from their reflection one might have mistaken for amethyst or topaz were themselves laid out upon thick glass shelving like *objets d'art* – which actually they were.

Three huge interlocking rhombuses: one black and white, another red and white and the centre piece black, red and white, took up one whole side of the room. She refused to attribute any mystical significance to this enormous contemporary triptych constructed by a Venetian friend – she might well have preferred an erotic meaning, but was it necessary to ascribe to an artist's work any other sense than that of bringing into the world a beauty which without the artist would never have existed?

There are certainly other beauties, anyhow! Quite near the gypsum flower there was a large panel which depicted the night sky millions of light years distant, with a black nebula imploding, sowing the curved space of the room with the petals of dead stars.

There was no furniture other than the bookshelves, thick cushions and a fur rug on the floor. Vanna had no bed, chairs, table, or chests. When she wrote, she did so lying full-length upon the rug. She never cooked at home, getting food in from a cheap restaurant nearby. In one corner of the bookcases stood an electric hotplate for preparing tea and coffee. Her clothes hung in a narrow cupboard in the bathroom, which also contained the thing she used most, her overnight bag.

The lighting, perhaps by way of homage to Edgar Allan Poe was crimson-hued – that of candles and from the glow emanating from lamps of perforated brick placed on the floor.

From an unseen tape recorder issued a muffled chanting, a sort of counterpoint for four or five voices, subtle and full of complex harmonies.

'Pygmy music,' she explained to Guido on his arrival. 'Would you like some *kif*?'

He accepted, looking Mija over without saying anything.

'Nikos is arriving later,' Vanna said.

'Who's Nikos?'

'Someone from your Embassy, though he's Greek. He seems to be quite influential.'

Mija was wearing that flimsy veil of a hundred diaphanous folds which Guido had wished upon the air hostess during his flight from Italy to Egypt: it was swathed round her thighs and bust, gathered over one shoulder with the other left bare. The young girl's heavy breasts were separated by a lozenge-shaped pendant of gold links, and their nipples seemed to be piercing through the fabric. Each time she passed a candle the flame stripped her and emphasised the line of her legs. Strangely slender and savage legs at that: the legs of a savanna animal rather than of a woman.

Vanna's legs when she walked were clearly visible to the groin, through her long slit skirt. The billowy yet clinging cheesecloth dress supplied a different sense to the word immodesty than Mija's see-through style: but both approaches were more aesthetically pleasing than merely sensual. To understand Vanna, Guido was thinking, you first had to fathom her amazing and almost obsessive feel for the beautiful: that, he inferred, she had not derived from artistic theories of the past but from a morality of the future.

'No, not a morality,' Vanna contradicted him when he voiced this hypothesis, 'all morality scares me. I'd prefer your calling that intuition a sort of science.'

'An occult one?' he joked.

'Not in the least! I hate everything sacred and secret.' Pressing her groin close to his she continued: 'I like *you* to expose yourself too, Guido. I don't like your hiding things.'

'You've just been using a word you condemn: "prefer",' he teased her again.

'Are you going to deny me the freedom to contradict myself?'

He realized that during the few days he'd known her he had had difficulty categorizing the many facets of the complex character he was discovering.

'I wouldn't want to be someone complete, rounded,' she had told him herself in an area of town due for demolition. 'Till my dying day I want to be a constantly altering choice. A reconstruction without a plan.'

Another day, she had taken the subject up again, while together they passed basalt statues whose noses and foreheads were worn away, broken tablets, fragments of birds, indecipherable intaglios and sphinxes with sightless eyes.

'You see, their eternity is finished. They leave us free today to invent another.'

'I thought that time, even that of eternity, didn't exist for the gods,' he had joked. 'Aren't they still living at Siwah? Like the men who believe in them – out of time?'

'Time exists for no one except those it carries off in its course,' she had replied.

'My bosses have another idea of the future.'

'Do you have bosses? Then you're a slave. So don't rush, slave! If your time doesn't belong to you, waste it!'

'Don't waste time, you man-in-a-hurry!' she said to provoke him, turning on her heel before he could kiss her. 'Kiss Mija at once!'

The young Copt offered Guido her mouth, which had the alien sweetness of some African fruit.

Perhaps because he'd begun to be even more attracted to her than Vanna, he tried to find fault with this young body he was holding for the first time: her breasts were too full for too slim a waist and shoulders that were too slight. Her skin was too pale and she had too much hair framing too small a face. Nonetheless, he couldn't help having an erection.

Vanna put her arms round both their necks, slid her face between theirs kissed their lips in turn and nibbled at both their tongues simultaneously.

Vanna's hands pulled out Guido's prick and Mija's hands stroked it. The two women both slid to the floor together and their mouths were reunited around the erect phallus.

He was unsure whose mouth he entered first. In due course the second swallowed him and he got used to plunging swiftly from one to the other.

Each supplied different pleasures, one silken-smooth, the other moister – but he could not have said which mouth he preferred, if indeed he he had any preference.

Oh to be able to come inside both at once!

There was shouting from the street. He thought he heard: Amon! Allah! . . . .

He leaned forward, a breast each of Mija's and Vanna's squeezed in either hand. But he didn't want to hold back any longer. Wasn't it time now to act like a god, for the eternity of a mirage? Vanna sensed it as she sensed everything. Her hand tightened around the protruding shaft, sliding up and down from tip to base. Guido was glad she was no longer caressing him tenderly but specifically to bring him off.

Her free hand rested on Mija's nape so that the prick would sink deep down the young girl's throat when the climactic spasm shook it.

Later when they had all recovered and were crunching pistachios while they waited for the other guest, Mija plucked at the strings of a small flat zither-like instrument, intoning softly:

> 'My god, my beloved,
> How sweet it is to swim,
> To bathe myself before you.
> I'll let you see my beauty
> In my royal linen tunic
> When it's soaking wet.
> I enter the water with you.
> I come with you.
> A splendid red fish
> Wriggles through my fingers.
> Come with me! Behold me!'

The young girl cupped a handful of water from the bowl and sprinkled the top of her ruched blouse, which was sticking to her skin.

'That poem's 3,000 years old,' Vanna explained. 'The priestesses of Amon sang it in the temple, they always sang it at Siwah while the faithful exchanged kisses. Man with man. Woman with woman. Man with woman. Woman with man. Brother with brother. Sister with sister. Brother with sister and vice versa. Mother with son or daughter. Father with son or daughter . . . .'

'Vanna . . . ' Guido was about to question her when the doorbell rang.

'Nikos at last!' she exclaimed, leaping to her feet.

Guido could gladly have done without this intrusion. He

studied the new arrival boorishly: his white shirt and jeans gave no hint of that status which Vanna ascribed to him. He had a dark beard and grecian features. He was certainly handsome, maybe even too handsome. Guido did not like him.

The newcomer kissed Vanna fulsomely on the lips, then Mija, then Guido also, who let him do so, somewhat disconcerted.

At table they exchanged banal small-talk about the Italian's first impressions of Egypt, complimented the two women on their appearance, and talked of current affairs and bygone times. Guido studiously avoided any mention of Siwah. It was Nikos who brought up the subject. He also held forth about homosexuality and incest being highly regarded in the desert. He declared these practices to be 'natural'.

'Nowhere and never,' he claimed, 'can love be unnatural. Nothing, after all, can be – not bodies nor ideas. Even when mankind tries to pervert itself through its beliefs or achievements it contributes to, rather than opposes, nature. One universal god alone would have the power to deny nature, but such a god has never existed – only bodies have, and ideas of divinity. The people of Siwah have known this since the beginning of time. That's why they are simultaneously sceptics and believers, visionaries and fanatics, religious and atheistic. Our limitations and categories have no significance for them in the limitless desert where they live free.'

After they had finished dessert, coffee and liqueurs, Nikos joined Mija upon the cushions where she lay. Vanna was standing in front of Guido, who planted a kiss on her buttock – a chaste kiss, as if trying to delay matters.

But the Greek was not the man to spin things out. He

temporarily forsook Mija, grabbed Vanna by the waist and pulled her down on to the fur rug. He kissed her mouth, taking his time, and drew up her skirts, presenting the lower half of her body to Mija, who at once began tickling her friend's sex with playful little laps of her tongue.

Guido, quite sated, yet unable to resist the desire beginning to overwhelm him, gradually undressed – hesitant, finally, then grimly decisive. He slid down along Vanna's back and slowly rubbed against her.

A rhythmic piece of music provided the accompaniment to this game whose rules he was haltingly seeking. But his tool's friction against Vanna's inner thighs cheered him considerably and the harder his prick the fainter his apprehensions. Vanna, who was playing with her own clitoris, gasped in climax, then positioned herself to take Guido's prick in her mouth.

Without transition, Handel's *Largo* now succeeded the music that had gone before.

Guido realised the game had no rules and that it'd be a waste of time to look for what did not exist.

He seemed to hear the singer's voice intoning: 'Life has no rules, happiness no rules, freedom no rules, ecstasy no rules ...' Ah how good his prick felt, free and alive and about to explode wildly, not caring about rules, right into Vanna's incomparable mouth!

He was aware of Nikos's weight against his back and the handsome Greek's breath hot upon his neck. It was the first time anything like this had happened to Guido, the first time a man had touched him in such a way. His whole body contracted but he made himself relax gradually, let things happen and find the intimacy pleasurable.

In turn Vanna kissed Mija, Nikos and Guido himself, sharing with them equally the sperm she had received upon her tongue.

It was dawn when, after other caresses and carnal permutations, all four of them slept.

The oasis of Amon was no longer very far away.

3

Opinion The Colour, Sweetness, Bitterness

'In my childhood days,' Guido bantered, 'if some fuzzy-wuzzy or other happened to get it into his head to vent his spleen in front of one of Her Britannic Majesty's subjects, or dared refuse him access to the family archives, all the explorer had to say was "I'll complain to my Consulate" and the native would grovel in the dust begging forgiveness and offering him his wife and daughters.'

'Were you British in your younger days?' said the Embassy secretary quizzically.

'No, but I used to read Jules Verne and I knew what was what.'

'I hope nowadays you read the newspapers,' the civil servant observed wearily. 'The sirdars in shorts of your schooldays have been replaced by colonels trained by the CIA. And Italian consuls allow agents access to their files, if you see what I mean.'

'Well tell me if you can, without talking out of turn: what use are Embassies?' Guido enquired.

'To give their personnel a living,' the functionary admitted. 'It means I can support a large family. I like children, do you? Are you married? Radical? Christian-Democrat, maybe? You don't much care for this new Polish Pope, I take it, nor for the Egyptians? You ought to be able to get on with them, though.'

'In short, are you handing me over to the tender mercies of the barbarians?'

'I haven't that much rank to pull,' sighed his host, stubbing out his cigarette prematurely. 'I'm only going by what Nikos told me. You're in luck, he liked you. So go and look up Nesrin Adly. If you don't mention me to him, he should be reasonably civil to you. When you've done that, there'll be no more you can do except wait patiently. And I *mean* patiently! You'll need a great deal of that virtue: patience is the thing, here. Everything's impossible here but nothing's really difficult. Patience doesn't require exceptional talent.'

'I don't like waiting,' Guido informed him.

'In that case it'd be better for you to take a plane back to Milan. It's a nice city. Quiet. Straightforward. Contemplative.'

'It's Siwah I'm going to,' Guido reminded him.

'If this country's bureaucracy warms to you, you'll go further still. It all depends on your ingenuity, charm, and social graces.'

'And upon . . . what did you say his name was?'

'Nesrin Adly.'

The secretary drew towards himself with seemingly as much effort as he might have employed had it been a lump of lead, a square notepad on each sheet of which was embossed the Fiat emblem, detached the top sheet with deliberation, and upon it inscribed the name of the Egyptian he had just mentioned, together with the address of his Department: MINISTRY OF FOREIGN AFFAIRS. Cultural Relations, Scientific and Technical Co-Ordination Dept. // Orientation & Programming Division. // *Section for International Research Studies.*

He added various telephone numbers after riffling languidly through a grubby green directory.

'Good day!' he concluded, passing Guido this handwritten document. 'And don't forget: make no mention of me. These American air-conditioning systems are pneumonia-traps – don't you think this room is devilishly cold?'

'All this palaver just to get authorization to visit an oasis!' the visitor jibed, pretending not to understand the significance of his trip.

'Having to repatriate your coffin would mean far more work for myself,' his interlocutor remarked. 'And you can see I'm snowed under already.'

Guido hung his head.

'Yes, I can see how tiring this sort of futile small-talk must be.'

'Goodbye Mr Fornari,' said the Embassy secretary, putting out his hand. 'Nikos is my best friend. Try to get on as well with Adly. *Tante belle cose!*'

Before leaving, Guido had time to add:

'My name, dear sir, is not Fornari but Andreotti. It's there on my card, right in front of you.'

In the taxi Guido was blind to the teeming spectacle of the street, deaf to its clamour, indifferent to its smells. He was recalling how things were back home – those gleaming premises of his firm, all steel and glass: its quite transparent obviousness and its deviousness; how in his absence someone must be trying to do his work and fill his shoes – as if that work could be done or that place taken, by anyone but himself! He was irreplaceable.

Was he though? he suddenly wondered. At the same time he realized that had he been in Milan just then, with all the cogs of the machinery revolving around him, he would never have experienced such a doubt. Should he assume that he needed them as much as they him?

'Absurd!' he muttered indignantly.

Or was the corrosive, unsettling effect of the desert wind already in action? Is there a disorientation in lucidity of judgement as there is said to be in love?

One minute a sense of loss – the next, doubt . . . He was no longer sure . . . .

'I'm far away from it all,' he decided, 'but I haven't yet

managed to distance myself. If only I could become sceptical, useless, irresponsible like that diplomatic creep! Not to bother about what's going on in the lousy firm, just be a stupid prick on holiday. Take my time. Get fucked.'

The taxi, however, was getting fucked up: it was only crawling along, but somehow contrived to do so dangerously. Guido felt a new surge of exasperation. He only just restrained himself from giving the driver an earful.

'Fucking me about like this!' he exclaimed.

He felt his cock absently.

'Like a fucking cunt!' he continued, raising his voice. 'Bugger. Cocksucker. Wanker. Arse-bandit!'

With one hand upon his new duck trousers he played with his growing erection, swelling it rapidly. He wanted to come there and then, all over that eunuch of a driver. But the thought of the resultant damp stain, probably all too noticeable when he got out, deterred him. He leaned forward.

'Change course, kid!' he yelled.

He gave him Vanna's address.

'That arsehole can wait,' he grumbled.

The arsehole being Nesrin Adly.

Vanna wasn't in.

'Probably stoned or fucking somewhere with that Mija of hers,' he cursed. 'Two fuck-artists are no better than one.'

He returned to his hotel, deciding to ring Adly. An operator who spoke some indeterminate language connected him with a secretary who seemed able to speak them all. She informed him with exquisite and well-chosen phraseology that the gentleman he wished to see would be pleased to receive him in a week's time, and Guido could do nothing to persuade her to advance the appointment by one hour, even when hinting that he'd be prepared to pay for such a favour.

'Little slut!' he remarked after hanging up. 'What a bunch of wankers!'

Vanna rang. Yes, join her right away. It would be OK to visit the citadel tomorrow, the bazaar at Khan Khalil the day after, and the day after that the al-Azhar Mosque. Then they'd play it by ear. There was plenty of time, she reassured him. She'd been wondering what he'd been up to.

He lay down on his bed, rang for room service, ordered a whisky and undid his trousers.

'What a beauty,' he congratulated himself, looking with the necessary impartiality at his prick. 'A fine one!'

His fingers stroked the entire length of the swollen vein; ran from root to meatus, and he sighed blissfully. He gripped the shaft in his palm, pulled up the skin towards the tip, then back towards the pubis, then began again, still sighing.

He told himself he should pay attention to the rhythm, not to rush it, avoid the pleasure ending prematurely. But not to hold back too much either. Not to make heavy weather of it.

'Don't act like a woman!' he admonished his trusty tool. 'A woman always complains that lovemaking finishes before it's started.'

He masturbated energetically for several minutes, his eyes half closed. Then he took a break, reflecting that to wank was to make love without high or low, forward or backward, inside or outside. It was just the orgasm from start to finish.

He started stroking the tip of his prick again, squeezed its head, cupped his balls, and slid his forefinger slowly up his anus. He stimulated his sphincter, emitting a low moan.

'All the same, I won't go so far as getting to like this!'

he said, astonished at his lewdness. 'Being gay isn't my scene.'

The thought so excited him that he gripped his prick in his clenched fist and began moving rhythmically again. Neither he himself nor his hand were controlling this movement: it was his sex dictating it. This sex was somehow so knowing that it invariably succeeded in finding the most suitable rhythm, the one to make Guido groan in ecstasy without, however, leading to premature ejaculation. This sex was master of space and time, of body and mind. It was worth living for, serving, gratifying, worth giving it all it desired: sometimes a hand or vagina, sometimes a soft deep mouth, sometimes a tight velvety arsehole. Or even a warm belly upon which to ejaculate, breasts between which to come. The fine sand of a beach. The clean sheet of a hotel room. The intimate interior of a car in the night, while listening to stereo cassettes of plainsong, alone or accompanied by a girl in evening dress whose breasts and legs you stroke while she jerks you off; or sucks you off. Or while you watch her boyfriend fuck her . . .

Guildo couldn't stand any more physical and mental pleasure. He devoutly wished that the waiter (or waitress it didn't matter which) who was bringing him his drink would enter the room before he'd finished masturbating. He would continue wanking in front of them. He wouldn't ask them to join him, nor touch him, just to watch. He'd come before their very eyes.

This image was so delightful that it quite overwhelmed him. The air-conditioning murmured reassuringly, congratulating Guido for knowing so well how to make himself come.

'This evening I'll go to bed early and do it again,' he resolved. 'And after that two or three times more?'

He'd tell Vanna he had a business appointment.

He took a shower, put on some clean clothes and went

out to meet her again, sprightlier than he'd been for hours.

Cairo wasn't so bad after all!

No one brought him his whisky.

Vanna was scrutinizing herself in the mirror.

'What are my weak points?' she asked herself, and she would always provide the same answer: 'None, I haven't any.'

Just the same, she tried highlighting her hard little nipples and the areolae of her breasts with lipstick.

'More like the image one might expect of a courtesan in olden days,' she mused. 'A well brought up Oriental doesn't disillusion the charming stranger's dreams.'

The next moment she rubbed off the make-up with some cotton wool.

'I'm not Oriental, nor am I well bred,' she told her nude reflection. 'And he's no stranger, he's the man I love.'

The expression made her heart miss a beat.

'That's all I need!' She felt astounded. 'Can I really be in love?'

She wasn't thrilled by the prospect, and said so out loud:

'I was quite happy as I was: what idiocies am I letting myself in for now?'

She tried to take stock of the facts she was sure of: 'He, of course, doesn't love me. That's all right. The most annoying thing is that I myself don't know any more what I want or what I'm doing. I'd just decided to marry Mija!'

She laughed heartily, cupping her breasts sensuously. Then, tickling her clitoris, she watched herself as she spoke: 'Two women living together is just the opposite of the usual domestic *ménage*-cum-menagerie.'

She quizzed her double, who replied with a pout of criticism.

'Who do you think you're impressing, with these deep utterances?'

'Myself!'

'And are you succeeding?'

'Not at all.'

'Meanwhile, what would become of your ex-wife-to-be?'

Vanna sighed, genuinely concerned, and asked the naked girl in the mirror:

'Will I end up like all the others, maybe like Mija too one day, in the hopeless, banal daily routine of the heterofuckingsexual couple? Or shall I opt out of all that shit in the nick of time?'

The ringing doorbell cut short this closed-circuit exchange. With one rapid movement she flung on some very thin Saharan cotton jeans which barely did more than change the colour of her skin from amber to pale blue. Her breasts exposed, she opened the door.

'I really do love him!' she inwardly grieved as she kissed Guido on the lips. 'It's pathetic!'

He apologized vaguely for being late. Vanna looked at him delightedly. 'Pathetic!' she repeated, this time aloud. 'Are you taking me out?' she asked him directly. He seemed somewhat embarrassed by her being half-naked.

'Like that?'

'Are you ashamed of me?'

She gave him no time to protest, but pulled her jeans down past her buttocks, hoisting out each of her long legs in turn. Then with a single kick she sent the superfluous garment flying across the room. Using two fingers, she fluffed up her fleece.

'You're right,' she said. 'You'll be prouder of me if you can show off all of me.'

She slipped her arm through Guido's and tugged the Italian towards the door, asking: 'Where are we going?'

Guido took refuge in digression: 'If what they claim at the Embassy is correct, I might well find myself stuck in a regular shitpile here and have a job extricating myself.'

'What are they saying, then? That Egypt is a police state? If only they spied on us a little less they might know a bit more about it.'

'You see – you've caught the germ too! As things stand, it's not surprising that your less informed compatriots think I've "come in from the cold", as it were.'

'It's up to you to prove that the only icy thing about you is your glass of scotch and that your burning motivation in life is nothing more incendiary than hot pants.'

'An excellent idea. Put me to the test immediately.'

He drew closer to her, twirling a curl of her pubic hair round one of his fingers until she protested:

'Ouch! I can't judge you here. Every trial needs witnesses.'

'Summon them,' he said. 'You must have a little black book of phone numbers.'

He sat down on the low divan, both hands around Vanna's waist, and then began caressing her stomach softly, playing once again with her short hairs.

'Do you like whores?' she asked him.

He pursed his lips, somewhat perplexed by this.

'Not particularly,' he declared. 'Depends who.' He pretended to be moving on to truth games:

'I particularly like other people's wives.'

'How can you recognize a whore?' Vanna went on relentlessly: 'What do you mean by other people's wives? What's your view of property? And in which precise area of marketing do you place love?'

Guido glanced at her in discomfiture.

'For heaven's sake,' he said. 'I'm not qualified to discuss feminist dialectics.'

'Fine. Are you strong on religious history? What do you think of St Jerome and his teachings?'

Guido's snort of laughter in no way distracted her.

'That old anchorite,' she expatiated, 'classified three sorts of probity – in decreasing order of merit. First the virgins, then the continent, and finally the married couples. Fifteen centuries later, we haven't got any further than that.'

'You're dramatizing. Virginity is outdated and out of fashion.'

'Where and when? Whatever has a price tag and attracts the customers is always in fashion.'

'As for continence, do you know many people who practice it, apart from ourselves at this very minute?'

'Continence has never been a practice. It's a power principle – meaning it's confined to those other than the powerful. And it's dangerous, like all faiths.'

'*Va bene*! Well, let's get to the couple. Are you denying that young people marry less and less and live more and more from one liaison to the next?'

'But are they, any more than their elders, capable of simultaneous loves? Loving and living as a couple, whether married or not, invariably remains the sole theme of song and the universal stumbling-block of the ballads.'

'Yet do you who talk so glibly really know how to love? Before you go collecting men and women in droves, have you ever loved one alone? Of either sex?'

Vanna broke free of Guido's embrace.

'How boring you are!' she jeered. 'When a punter chats to a prostitute he inevitably asks her to tell him how she got started on the game. Whereupon he's amazed that a nice girl like herself could have sunk so low.'

'But what's all this about? Why all this constant talk of prostitution this evening? Have I said or done something that makes you think . . . .'

50

'No no, relax! I'm asking *myself* the question: to be or not to be a whore?'

With a gesture she cut short a new protest.

'The answer is no easier today than it was in Hamlet's time,' she said. 'So I've no intention of resolving the problem today. My real concern is what we're going to eat. I've no food to offer you.'

'I'm not hungry.'

'But I am.'

She wriggled once more into her skintight jeans.

'As you don't like my breasts –'

And she put on a blouse.

'Come on, get moving!' she ordered. '*Primum vivere!*'

On their return from the restaurant Guido appeared to hesitate while opening the taxi door for Vanna. She anticipated him:

'Don't feel obliged to make love to me. I feel like making love to myself.'

At this he seemed to regain interest.

'If you like you can watch,' she suggested.

He followed her without needing further encouragement.

During dinner he had been distant, not to say absent. So much so that Vanna had silently reprimanded herself: 'I'm not going to let myself be taken in by this oaf, if my company bores him already. It was a narrow escape! One more like that and I'd turn into a silly old biddy!'

Yet she had found it impossible to swallow the oily, spicy soup which she was usually crazy about. She had a lump in her throat.

'I've lost my appetite,' she said by way of excuse, without his taking her up on her self-contradictions or displaying concern at this sudden indisposition.

So she had talked about Mija, in order to see whether

he might be (of all things!) jealous. That experiment also
fell flat. In desperation, she had invited him to tell her
about his travels and his conquests of women only
recently married. Didn't he make love with their men
too. No? Ah! She almost dropped off to sleep from
boredom.

'Do you want to dance?' he asked her at the end of the
evening. She no longer wanted anything any more. She
inquired:

'Do you like dancing for its own sake or only as a means
to an end?'

'I like to get a hard on while dancing.'

'When you're dancing and feeling up a girl, does the fact
that people are watching increase your pleasure?'

'I couldn't care less.'

'Pity,' Vanna considered. 'Luckily you're not telling
the truth.'

'Why? Do you think I'm an exhibitionist?'

'I don't judge anyone by such stupid criteria.'

He had forgotten to repeat his invitation.

Now they found themselves back at her flat, as ill at
ease with one another as if they had never fucked. Vanna
made an effort:

'I'm going to get you drunk,' she announced.

He did not reply, but drank the mango cocktail she'd
mixed, at one gulp. It went to his head almost immediately.

'I'd rather you raped me,' he commented, sprawling
across the cushions.

'Sorry,' she said, 'but I've a date with myself.'

She went and shut herself in the bathroom. Guido either
didn't see her leave or else he didn't mind talking to
himself; be that as it may, he launched off on a leisurely
and rambling confession: 'It's true I didn't tell you
everything when you asked me if I was an exhibitionist.
One thing I greatly like when dancing with a girl is for her

to wear a full, flowing skirt – a sort of *crêpe de chine*. So I can lift it up while dancing and expose her thighs and arse. In Milan these days there are lots of girls like you, who never wear anything under a long skirt, especially not in the evenings. You're one better, because you never have underwear on at any time. But what can one do to see your arse if you wear slacks while dancing? I hate jeans, to tell the truth. I'd really appreciate it if you don't wear them any more.'

When he roused himself a moment later, Vanna was lying upon the fur which served as a rug, a foot or two away from him. She was wearing a sort of light, almost transparent white kaftan fastened in front by a row of tiny silk buttons.

'There must be about a hundred,' he calculated aloud, without her answering him. 'It must take you quite some time to do them all up.'

She was reading. Or rather, slowly turning the parchment-thick pages of some book. He leaned over to see what it was. A collection of prints.

'I see,' he muttered. 'Your Japanese stamp collection. Who posed for it? Fujititi and Akhenamoto, I presume?'

'You're not with it at all, are you? In your honour I'm refreshing my memory of Roman erotic art. Don't you recognize it? They're reproductions of reliefs.'

'Relief,' he said, nodding with sudden tolerance. 'Why not, if it helps.'

Then he learnedly identified the work Vanna was perusing.

'Yes, *De Figuris Veneris*, the erotic illustrations to Suetonius's *Lives of the Twelve Caesars*.'

His head and his mood lightened. He smiled affectionately at Vanna, asking: 'Are you reading this as an art-lover or to stimulate yourself?'

'Would you call art something which didn't stimulate you?'

He slumped back on to the cushions.

'Which position do you think the most artistic?' he questioned her.

She passed the book across to him: a man was standing upright, sodomizing another, who was fucking the vagina (or was it the anus?) of a woman lying on her back. Guido turned the page and passed the book back to Vanna:

'Don't you find this one even more appealing?'

This time the woman was between the two men, who were taking her simultaneously fore and aft.

'I don't really know – is that possible?' Vanna queried. Guido appeared to be astonished.

'*A fortiori*, since this combination is also very well-known!' he remarked after riffling through the volume.

In the illustration he was indicating, one of the two men was taking the woman orally. Vanna nodded appreciatively.

'And here, of course, we find logical perfection,' Guido went on, pointing out a new plate.

Here three men were taking the heroine simultaneously, penetrating mouth, vagina and anus at once.

It was now Vanna's turn to leaf through the worn pages, pausing at one whereon a young woman with rounded breasts and prominent pubis was tossing off with expertise and zest the impressive prick proudly sprouting from the sinewy loins of a naked athlete.

'That's what I've done most of,' she revealed.

'Mostly when you were a little girl, I assume?'

'Not only then.'

Guido realized that this last reply was arousing his own sex, where the previous conversation had left him cold. He carried the line of questioning further:

'Do you mean you still make men come with your hands more often than with another part of your body?'

'Yes.'

'Which part of you, other than your hands, do yo
most readily?'

'My mouth.'

'More than your quim?'

'I think so. To tell the truth, I don't keep count.'

'And what about your arse?'

'You were the first, there.'

He exclaimed in disbelief. Yet at the same time he had
a definite intuition that Vanna wasn't lying. Appearances
are deceptive, he reflected.

'Did my buttocks seem so expert to you?' Vanna, who
had guessed what he was thinking, asked him with some
amusement.

'They didn't seem altogether inexperienced.'

'One shouldn't trust one's senses too much,' Vanna
lectured him. ' "Opinion the colour, sweetness, bitterness
. . . ." '

Guido identified the quotation:

'Democritus. You have strange tastes in reading . . . .'
She went back to examining the Roman engravings. After
a while she undid her kaftan to the groin, just far enough
for her to slip her hand inside. Guido reckoned he was
entitled to take similar liberties, and, pulling out his cock,
felt its pleasant warmth upon his palm.

Vanna opened her legs as wide as the kaftan permitted
and with half a dozen motions brought herself to climax.

Guido wanted to suggest that she try out that preferred
talent on which she prided herself, this time upon *him*, but
before he could phrase such a suggestion appropriately
she had got to her feet and gone back into the bathroom.

When Vanna returned, she was carrying something he
didn't really catch sight of. She resumed her full-length
sprawl upon the fur. She had also brought with her a small
jar of beauty cream, with which she gently lubricated one
end of the unidentified object.

'A dildo?' Guido inquired.

'"In reality, nothing else exists but the atom and the void"', she explained, completing the aphorism by the philosopher Plato hated.

'That contraption is certainly not the work of nature,' Guido observed.

'Art was invented to fill the void,' Vanna declared.

'I'm not criticizing you,' Guido assured her. 'Who created your artificial phallus?'

'The scribe Nakhim. Don't you recognize his touch?'

Then Guido did recall the finely carved writing implement tapering to a lotus bud, which Vanna had shown him on his first visit. It was this lotus which she had warily inserted within her sex after opening her kaftan still wider.

The ivory petals, then the whole stem slipped right into her vagina. Vanna left it in this position while with her eyes closed she slowly worked her haunches and thighs, her heels braced against the edge of the fireplace. Very soon her back began to arch, its curve ever more pronounced. Several times she contracted the muscles of her cunt and cried out in orgasm. With the hand which had been stimulating her clitoris and whose fingers she now kept outspread like a golden butterfly's wing, she brushed the tips of her nipples through the kaftan and reached climax yet again.

Guido tugged briskly at his sex, wanting to come but unable to do so.

'Let me have your anus,' he begged her.

Vanna, biting her lip, shook her head. She worked the lotus stem in and out of her vulva. Establishing a regular rhythm her moans became louder and louder. She sobbed, wept, screamed. In the end she sank the ivory handle more violently than ever deep into her cunt, lapsing suddenly into silence and immobility, as if dead.

Guido got up, went over to her and unfastened those

countless buttons one by one, lifting the hem of the kaftan so as to admire her at leisure – the roundness of her breasts, the gentle swell of her belly, the tapering thighs, the plump curve of her pubis and the cushioned gash which the antique implement seemed to have slashed open. He seized this spike and extracted it with as much care as if it had been a weapon and the vagina a wound.

Vanna did not shudder, nor did she make a sound.

Guido inserted his prick – thicker than the pen's bud, longer, and seemingly harder still – between the lips of that vulva at which he liked to stare quite as much as Vanna liked to display it.

He thrust home until he touched the neck of the womb, enjoying the sensation and trying to pierce still deeper. Not succeeding in this, he pulled back to gather momentum and sink back more forcefully, recommencing the sequence of thrusts and withdrawals, advances and retreats, for what seemed an infinite length of time, crying out with pleasure at each jab, each backward tug. His prick had never felt so thick, long, powerful. No cunt had ever given him this sensation of tightness, elasticity and softness; none had ever had just the right moistness and heat; none had ever been so perfectly attuned to the ecstasy he sought.

He lay above Vanna's nude, spreadeagled body, bearing down upon her outstretched arms. In order to penetrate her yet more deeply he brought his whole pelvis into play. He was skewering her without consideration as if he really intended opening her up more than ever, disembowelling her. Why should he be considerate? She seemed to feel nothing – insensible, inert, as if she had swooned away.

He no longer knew how long this act had lasted – the best fuck, he told himself, the most wonderful, loving fuck he'd ever known.

His mouth met Vanna's.

'I love you,' he murmured. 'I love you!'

Vanna's lips also moved against his, but he did not hear what they were saying to him.

4

Solitary Eternity And Transient Love

What with his well-trimmed, pointed beard, benevolent smile, warm expression and Savile Row suit, Nesrin Adly inspired confidence. His serious deep voice resounded agreeably in the opulent setting of his high-ceilinged office. Guido told himself that he'd have difficulty himself speaking Italian as correctly as this foreigner. On hearing him address his secretary a moment or two earlier he had noted that the diplomat was quite as fluent in English – which he spoke like the Oxford man he no doubt was.

This affable fellow passed his guest an engraved gold cigarette-box.

'You're very welcome,' he said. 'The more so since you've been highly recommended to me by my good friend Gatto, first secretary at your Embassy. Him I can refuse nothing.'

Guido looked aghast at him, suddenly remembering that creep who had insisted that his name not be mentioned to Adly.

'Oh him,' he heard himself stammer, 'he ....'

'Yes?'

'Oh nothing. I beg your pardon.'

His host scrutinized him for a good few seconds with evident amusement. He carried on: 'I know your Cultural Attaché, Professor Andreou also holds you in considerable esteem.'

'Who?' Guido blurted out, more and more bewildered.

'Nikos Andreou,' his host supplied, continuing to observe him with some curiosity.

Guido experienced that growing sense of unreality which had plagued him since entering this particular Ministry. Once more he spoke out of turn:

'His name's Andreou?' he murmured almost plaintively.

'Isn't he an old friend of yours?' Nesrin Adly asked.

'That's right. I see you're well-informed about all my relationships.'

Adly smiled in satisfaction, continuing:

'I also know that you're a close friend of the daughter of my old schoolmate, Selim El Fattah. A great administrator! In our country we need many more like him. Unfortunately I've not had the pleasure of meeting his wife – they say she's a wonderful person. Pity she doesn't visit us more often, but it seems her work keeps her in Barcelona. You know she's Curator at the Gaudi Museum there. Interesting job. She's written the definitive work on the subject, at least according to admirers of the architect.'

He smiled pleasantly, as if giving Guido to understand that they themselves were not to be numbered among such freaks. He leaned towards Guido as if to emphasise the confidential nature of what he was about to say:

'Do you think our Vanna's also going to startle us one day with some marvellous archaeological treatise? She's certainly capable of it.'

He sat back once again in his seat:

'So much the better for our libraries, eh?'

Our Vanna? thought Guido. And why this wealth of family allusions? To make him understand that Vanna wasn't just any old scrubber? Really, it was an absolute obsession in this country!

'I know neither Vanna's father nor her mother,' he revealed with irritation, at once regretting having played

60

his adversary's game. Because the man, he sensed, wasn't really on his side – and of this he had immediate confirmation:

'Anyhow, would you be good enough to let me know why you're so keen on going to Siwah, Mr Fornari?' Adly asked, suddenly curt.

'Andreotti,' Guido complained.

'Pardon?'

'My name is Andreotti. Guido Andreotti, engineer.'

'Really? Apologies. And you were telling me, I believe, about your interest in Siwah.'

'I'd like to prepare a study,' Guido explained. 'That is, to research a monograph I'm doing on this amazing place in all its aspects – locale, vegetation, riches, civilization.'

Nesrin Adly affected astonishment:

'Its civilization? What do you mean by that? How does it differ from that of the rest of our country? We're all Egyptians – have been for centuries! – in this ancient Nile land and its deserts. You know that as well as I do, you're an educated man.'

He offered him another cigarette from the gold box. Then Adly asked:

'And did you say treasures? What sort of treasures or riches do you mean?'

'Cultural wealth, that is,' Guido answered, recovering his composure. 'In spite of what you said, the people of Siwah represent – as far as Egypt and the rest of the world are concerned – a culture apart. It's said that they still adhere to the religion of the Pharaohs, continuing to uphold the worship of Amon. You'll agree that this is interesting material for ethnological research.'

'Yes, but is there in your view something rather more specific about Siwah's culture which rates a visit from someone as well-qualified as yourself?'

Guido was losing ground again.

'Apparently the people of Siwah live within a homosexual community structure. Which seems to me of universal interest.'

'Oh yes?'

Nesrin Adly let a long interval elapse, during which he simply took long drags from his strongly-scented, gilt-tipped cigarette. When he spoke, finally, it was with sudden and evident weariness: 'And you're a sexologist too?'

Guido felt as weary as his interviewer of this conversation. Was it worth sustaining? He settled for just a sort of unintelligible grunt.

'Well, I'll see what I can do to accommodate you,' Adly said.

Guido began an effusive peroration:

'I'd like to see with my own eyes the site of that temple, the one with the oracle, where Alexander the Great is reputed to have summoned the Beloved of Amon. My ambition is to publish a book – because to my knowledge there are none – on the history of this oasis. A book about something other than the Pyramids, the Sphinx or Abu Simbel, for a change.'

Nesrin Adly rubbed his broad forehead, as if his thoughts were elsewhere. Absently he picked up a fresh cigarette, sighing:

'You should have been informed that this part of the country is at war at the moment. One isn't allowed to wander about there as though it's the Appian Way. Though there are just as many tombs there, in fact.'

'Yet you still let dozens of archaeologists, ethnologists, and journalists traipse round there all year long.'

'Not as many as you think, but too many, actually. Anyhow, they only go if escorted.'

'Can you see me setting off in search of Jupiter-Amon stuck between two cops?'

'There are better compromises, perhaps. A more informed and congenial escort, less expensive and better

62

suited to your requirements. I'll need time to think about it.'

'I can't wait indefinitely: I'm not the rich playboy you apparently seem to take me for.'

'I take you for no such animal. To assuage your impatience, why don't you have a browse through some of our excellent libraries? The documents you'll find there will be proof against mirages.'

'Do you think I'm given to seeing things?'

'Not you maybe. Those who sent you.'

Nesrin Adly rose to his feet, extending his hand.

'Don't worry, everything'll be all right. Trust me, I'll arrange it. Thank you for your visit, Mr . . . . '

'Andreotti,' Guido was quick to interject.

Adly raised an eyebrow, indicating that he was mildly vexed.

'Of course. And as you told me, you're an engineer. The humanist engineer, Guido Andreotti.'

What if I punched him in the teeth? Guido pondered. But the gesture would have been misplaced at that hour of the morning and between such well-dressed people.

Returning to the hotel, Guido rang Nikos on impulse. The latter answered in such affectionate and intimate tones that Guido, to his amazement, felt his sex throbbing.

'Am I going to wank because of a man?' he asked himself. 'It'd certainly be the first time I've ever done that!'

He concentrated on talking about less emotive topics, recounting his interview with Adly.

'The whole time I had the impression he was pulling my leg. What does he take me for?'

'Naturally he doesn't for one moment believe in your interest in the history of Hat-en-Shau. Nor in your scholarly thesis. Who would? But that doesn't matter. You aren't asking to be believed, but to be left free to go

63

where you please and do what you want. Why would Adly be opposed to that? He's only keeping you on a string to get his kicks. He's a sensualist, you must have noticed?'

'Huh,' Guido grumbled. 'Not really.'

'Sure he is. Don't tell me you don't know how to recognize what passes through men's minds?'

Guido made no attempt to regain his bearings amid all this deviousness, which was lost upon him. He inquired shyly:

'So what must I do?'

'Nothing. Nothing at all. Let things happen. And they will.'

The line was silent for a moment. Neither spoke. Guido touched his prick, undoing two fly-buttons. He had masturbated so often while telephoning women that it had become a sort of habit for him. He refused to dwell upon the fact that Nikos was a man. Nikos was talking to him again, so softly, warmly, tenderly: 'It's not the attitudes of the Cairo authorities which worry me. I'm more concerned about the sort of reception you'll get at Siwah. People out there are positively allergic to indiscretion.'

'They'll soon see I wish them well.'

'I hope you'll succeed in making them understand that. I wouldn't want them to harm you.'

'One must take risks in order to be happy!'

'You won't be very comfortable. There isn't a Hilton in that oasis. Nor any soft beds.'

'I don't expect such amenities. I'm sure I'll find others.'

'Oh yes, of course. You'll like a lot of things. You'll forget us.'

'You talk as if you were sure I'll get permission to go there.'

'Do you doubt me, Guido? Don't you trust me as a friend? Do you think I won't go on caring about you?'

The only thing Guido cared about just then was for the

conversation to last until he reached climax. No doubt Nikos knew that: his voice went on soothing Guido for as long as it took for the sperm to swell his prick to bursting-point, until it gushed copiously into his clenched fist.

He hung up reluctantly, lay down on his bed, and, as happened each time he masturbated, had the urge at once to start all over again.

'The engineer-cum-sexologist,' he sighed. 'Engineering hand-tooled orgasms . . . .'

'Vanna?' Nesrin Adly was on the telephone. 'It's ages since we met. Let's have dinner together. I've something to tell you which I think you'll be pleased about. At least I hope so.'

She didn't need asking twice. She recalled with perturbation the almost perverse pleasure she'd had when this man old enough to be her father had taken her out one evening, at least two – no, three, years ago now. She remembered (she was then twenty-four) that after paying her a courtship worthy of some romantic novel and exercising a charm which moved her more than she liked to admit to herself, he had spent the night with her.

It was a night that disappointed neither of them. Yet they had never repeated the experience. Had Nesrin felt guilty? Did he never make love more than once with the same woman? Or quite simply, did his official duties take up so much of his time that he could find none left to pursue a liaison?

Vanna, for her part, had had other infatuations, but she had good memories of this one. And she regretted its brevity.

Had he invited her out in order to start things up again? The tone of his call hadn't given her that impression. She herself was so preoccupied with her unexpected love for Guido that she wasn't feeling in the mood for additional amatory complications. She hoped Nesrin wouldn't be too eager. Above all, though, if she were not to reciprocate his advances, finally, she did not want him to think she bore him any ill-will for having so long neglected her. She would hate to be taken for that sort of woman.

So much so that the moment she saw Nesrin again, sitting at the Turkish cafe behind the mosque, her initial coolness completely melted away: now she felt in the mood to offer him her body even before he bothered to ask her for it.

He kissed her rather formally, complimenting her on her appearance and looking at her breasts scarcely concealed by her blouse. She sat down and crossed her legs, so that her slit skirt opened to crotch-level, revealing sleek naked thighs.

'Your father's at Siwah,' he said.

For a moment she seemed paralysed. Mechanically, she re-covered her legs with the folds of her skirt. Her knees alone remained bare and these she stroked, more as if they had been bruised than out of any teasing coquetry.

'At Siwah?' She repeated, incredulous then suddenly amused. 'What's he doing there?' She began laughing uproariously. 'At Siwah of all places!'

Then she turned serious, almost wistful.

'What could have got into him? Why has he disappeared like this?'

'He hasn't disappeared.'

'From me and my mother he has. He never even let us know of his existence. Mother was sure he'd been killed somewhere, secretly. I never believed that. I felt he was alive, but I didn't know where. For years I tried to find him again. Why didn't you tell me where he was?'

'I didn't know.'

'Oh!'

Vanna pouted, brooding and somewhat sceptical.

'Anyhow, I'd have found him on my own. Surely I can't

66

have had this sudden urge to go to Siwah myself, just by chance.'

'Ah, you had a sudden urge, did you?'

'It's an intuition, isn't it? Telepathy. Even though I don't believe in telepathy!'

'Do you love Selim so much?'

'I don't really know. Of course I've probably idealized him. Anyway, since he left us, I became obsessed by him. I know very well it's silly, but I'm not perfect!'

'When did you last see him?'

'Last? I've never seen him again. I was two years old when he left.'

'Then you can't really remember him.'

'But I'm sure I'd recognize him immediately.'

'He hardly concerned himself with paternal obligations, so why do you feel any filial ones towards him?'

Vanna smiled a fine bright smile without illusions. Impulsively she rested a hand on her companion's.

'Nesrin,' she said. 'You know quite well I don't assume pointless obligations. I'm aware of having few rights, so I feel myself bound by equally few obligations.'

'My civil servant's ears are tactfully sealed.'

'The liberties I allow myself don't harm my country. I think actually that they do her a service.'

'Words are sometimes more dangerous than deeds,' Nesrin warned. 'True, words are important. Anyhow, I set great store by words, whether they refer to things or name people.'

'You changed yours. I remember when you were a little girl . . .'

'And was called Vanessa? You see what I mean, then. The attachment I felt towards my parents, though they were both fickle, didn't stop my considering that I had even more right than they to choose my own name. A butterfly's name, I thought, would have given me butterfly characteristics . . .'

67

'You always were keen on language and languages. How many do you speak?'

'A few. Not Italian.'

'Is it in order to learn Italian that you're always with that goodlooking fellow who arrived here recently?'

'What sense is there in life if it's not a perpetual learning process?'

'You already have a good deal of wisdom. You're a good archaeologist. A woman of ideas.'

'I've no vanity on that score. I'm careful not to become an intellectual.'

'We're all ruled by specialization and the jargon of our professions. We're becoming the prisoners of our privileges.'

'I do my best not to be taken in by the idiocies, fakes and pretensions that abound in my kind of work. I try to stay outside its petty intrigues and office politics. I think I've managed quite well up to now not to *belong.* That's probably the reason why I like my work. I devote to it the only interest that isn't deceptive – a relative interest.'

'By constantly dealing with beautiful objects aren't you running the risk of preferring things to people?'

'The real risk is treating men as things. That's what I try above all to avoid doing.'

'Shouldn't you yourself be easy to deal with?'

'You want to make use of me, don't you, Nesrin? Is that why you wanted to see me again?'

'Not exactly to make use of you. Enlist your services, yes. But don't worry about your independence, however. Our views and beliefs won't be at loggerheads.'

'You want *me,* my body? I know it's not on your own behalf. Government business, then?'

'Are you available?'

'No. Or yes, that depends. Do you want me to escort Guido to Siwah in order to keep an eye on him? Are you offering to find my father for me in exchange?'

'I've made a bet. Actually I'm not at all sure whether Selim wants to see you again.'

'What a loyal bet. The main thing is that *I* want to. I wouldn't have any chance at all of being authorized to go to Siwah if I didn't agree to your bargain, would I?'

Nesrin made a vague, polite wave of a gesture.

'What's my father doing down there?'

'He's the governor's assistant. One of his duties consists in keeping foreigners at arm's length.'

Vanna once again chuckled delightedly.

'You must admit, life's a scream!' she gasped.

She leaned across to kiss Nesrin, unconcerned about the policeman hovering nearby – Adly's official body-guard.

'Here are my terms,' she said. 'I'll go with Guido to Siwah. I'm not at all embarrassed to prostitute myself to someone I love. But I won't report on him if it might harm him in any way. I'll only keep you informed of what doesn't concern him personally. I'm not wild about a multi-national petrol-dominated society, nor do I want him to be. OK? When do we leave?'

'Not for a while. First I need to examine this project. In the meantime, show your friend around, tell him to be patient. If you need transport I'll arrange it. Do you want some money?'

'Do you know any prostitutes who make no charge?' she said cheekily.

He smiled in his debonair fashion.

'You enjoy playing this role, don't you? Who knows, you may secretly have dreamed of it at some time or other.'

'What about you, Nesrin, come clean. Isn't it one of your private fantasies to be pimp to the State? By enlisting the services of the only daughter of your childhood friend, as a high priced whore?'

'Why high priced?' Nesrin asked pleasantly. 'You see, you're not proof against the temptations of vanity.'

'Tomorrow,' Vanna said, opening her door to Guido, 'we'll visit Giza.'

'May I remind you that it's Siwah I'm interested in?'

'You have to go through the customary channels. I'll decide what's what. Since yesterday I've been your official guide.'

'Who appointed you? Nesrin Adly? To keep an eye on me?'

'Correct. And don't imagine I'll let you out of my sight, even in my sleep.'

'What do I have to do in return for such protection?'

'Learn. You want to play at being archaeologist, historian and sexologist, it seems. Well, learn about these professions. Do you want me to be your teacher?'

'Are you versed in all these sciences?'

'The purpose of science isn't to know, but to ask questions. The right questions.'

'And doesn't the answer to these questions interest you?'

'A potsherd, a hewn stone, a bronze or an alabaster sculpture don't provide answers. Besides, what interests me isn't finding but seeking.'

'These fragments still tell you something about a vanished civilization.'

'No civilization has quite vanished from the earth: civilization hasn't yet been invented.'

'Don't you rate the pyramids you want to show me as works of civilization? Do you consider those capable of planning and executing the technical wizardry that such edifices required, as savages?'

'Worse than savages: men of power.'

'Then why visit them and make others visit them, if they seem to you so monstrous?'

70

'Because they can make one want to understand.'

'What's there to understand?'

'Which do you reckon is the main aspect to get straight: the material means by which these gigantic stone blocks could have been transported and precisely placed, or the religion and politics thanks to which the Pharaohs, their ministers and priests succeeded in compelling millions of their subjects to suffer and die like animals in order to produce that perfection?'

'Don't you think that faith played its part?'

'Who spread that faith? Let's get back to our era: is it more scientific to investigate the connections between the original cubit measure and the dimensions and positioning of the pyramids in relation to the constants of the solar system, or to seek the reasons why the forced credulity of my ancestors has led to the servitude and wretchedness of my contemporaries?'

'Has the government really given someone like you the job of spying on me? You seem more likely than myself to end up in one of the regime's dungeons.'

'I haven't the taste for treason. I'm as frank with my country as I am with you. If I've stayed free, that's because I'm not afraid.'

'All things considered, I'm not so badly off having you for a bodyguard!'

'Do you imagine that Egypt would entrust you to me if she didn't like you?'

He tried to take her into his arms but she lithely wriggled free, out of his grasp.

'There is a time for everything under the sun, as Ecclesiastes has it. A time to leap across the centuries and a time to leap upon the guide. First things first. That way you'll understand the pyramids at Giza better, if you first see the one with steps, built by King Djoser. We'll start with that first, and today.'

He did not enquire whence came the comfortable

ir-conditioned limousine that awaited them, complete with smart black chauffeur. He could guess. After an hour's drive they reached Sakkara, near the place where Memphis was constructed. The mausoleum of the first king of the third dynasty dominated a rugged desert which seemed thoroughly depressing to Guido.

They went through the only entrance, walked along the colonnade and great courtyard, and found themselves on the jubilee dais.

'The architect's name was Imhotep,' droned Vanna, mimicking the tone of official guides. 'Before becoming high priest of the sun god's cult at Heliopolis he was the king's physician, chancellor, chief archivist, keeper of the seal and, most important, treasurer! In the end he became a god.'

'Good for him,' Guido pronounced.

'Since you're a believer, note that the origin of stone architecture – and this gentleman was one of the very first craftsmen in that material – is closely bound up with the concept of the *Ka*, the desire for immortality.'

'Absolutely,' Guido agreed.

'Less known is the belief, still extant today, which has it that Djoser's *Ka* wanders invisible throughout the area, dwelling in the underground chambers, promenading along the ceremonial path within the great courtyard of Heb-Sed, closing the open doors behind him or passing easily through the false exits carved in the exterior wall.'

Guido didn't take up any of these points. He was interested in what he saw. He particularly liked a certain funeral chamber whose lower walls were decorated with tiny squares of gently convex turquoise pottery. Their colour seemed to shimmer deceptively like that on a butterfly's wing. The whole pattern was of rush mats framed within columns.

'We're now in the private precincts of the *Ka*,' Vanna revealed.

He unbuttoned her tussore shirt-waist dress all the way down and fucked her standing up, her back wedged against the ancient tablets; took her in slow and leisurely manner, contemplating eternity.

The next day, on the edge of the Libyan desert, which stretched as far as the eye could see in the direction of Siwah, Guido tried to imagine whereabouts the oasis might be. Vanna however left him no time to daydream. She instructed the chauffeur to park the car in front of a tent where camel-drivers sipped their teas or their Coca-Colas.

'You have a further lesson to learn,' she announced. 'On the back of a camel. You'll find this necessary later on.'

The camel-driver she chose made his beast kneel and beckoned to them to sit upon the narrow wooden saddle.

'What? Only one saddle for both of us?' said the astonished Guido.

'I am a woman,' Vanna said, as if her sex explained such economy of means.

The Arab motioned to Guido to sit behind Vanna. When the animal rose to its feet, the saddle began to tilt crazily backwards and the Italian was panic-stricken: at this rate he wouldn't stay on for long! And a fall from that height could do you an injury, not to mention covering you in ridicule. A fine initiation!

'You'll feel better in a couple of minutes,' Vanna promised.

In fact he quite soon acquired a sense of equilibrium. But another anxiety replaced the earlier one: the camel's undulations and lurches had unexpected results. Unexpected, that is, for himself, though clearly not for the camel-driver, who was giving him a series of lewd winks.

The way Guido was sitting, with his pubis jammed against Vanna's buttocks, the rhythmic pitching served to massage his sex with relentless inevitability. In a few minutes the trainee dromedarist once again had an erection hard as gypsum.

The camel-driver made the beast canter, thus accelerating the process of frottage.

'I told you,' Vanna commented, 'that women here have to be useful in some way.'

'I really have no desire to have it off in the air, perched up here,' Guido protested.

'You've still got to go through with it,' Vanna said. 'It's the custom. And didn't you tell me you were interested in the local traditions?'

'It's ridiculous! Not even pleasant.'

'Come off it! Folklore has its virtues.'

'And what if you weren't here?'

'The camel man's son would consider it his duty and pleasure to take my place.'

'I wouldn't have agreed to that.'

'Oh yes you would! You'd have enjoyed it.'

'Vanna . . . . '

'Darling?'

'I can't hold back!'

'I know. Come then, my love. Come with all your sperm and all your soul.'

'What the hell will I look like with my trousers all stained?'

'What can I do about it? Would you hang on to your virtue for longer if I recited multiplication tables, complete with errors, or the gospels backwards?'

'It'd all be too late,' he prophesied glumly.

She felt him trying to hoist up her skirt. She leaned forward so that he could expose her buttocks. At the same time he was feverishly trying to undo his flies so as to come against Vanna's skin. A final twist of the camel's flanks anticipated his intention.

He closed his eyes while his steed, as if aware of his potency, strove to squeeze the last drop of seed from him, by means of some sly corkscrew motions.

Guido had scarcely spent himself when the camel-driver said something in Arabic.

'What's he say?' Guido asked, afraid the man was mocking him.

'He's asking if you want to continue the outing. If you think you can make it again, that is. If so, of course, you'll have to pay extra.'

'Thank him. That'll do fine for a preliminary ride, today.'

'Skinflint!' Vanna teased.

In front of the pyramid of Cheops, Guido experienced the mixture of emotion and disappointment which is the general rule. Luckily they were spared the additional indignity of hordes of tourists: on that day and at that hour they seemed to be the only visitors. The Italian braced himself to repel the onslaughts of various vendors of trinkets and mementoes, of pickpockets and self-appointed guides, ready to use oaths universally comprehensible, when to his surprise he saw Vanna grab one of them by the hand and drag him forward as if about to kiss him, pulling him towards Guido in order to introduce him proudly.

He was a remarkably good-looking youth of about eighteen. His impressive eyes regarded Guido with easy-going indifference.

'Today it's his turn to guide us to eternity,' Vanna joked.

After climbing some steps they followed a descending

passageway. A dry heat almost overcame Guido, who had to halt a moment before following their youthful guide. Vanna was just behind them. The three of them remained silent.

The passage described a sharp bend and led on to another, this time ascending. Guido felt prey to a vertigo unlike anything he had ever experienced before. He was relieved to be able to stand upright when they reached the centre of the pyramid. According to the tradition, their guide demonstrated that not even a needle or a hair could be inserted between the joins in the walls.

After leaving this room they moved into a new low corridor, then an ante-chamber, and finally into the King's funeral chamber, made out of granite and forty metres underground.

At the north east corner of the chamber, laid out according to the cardinal points, was the Pharaoh's sarcophagus. This was simple, without inscription, and, its container originally having been found wide open and lidless, mysterious too. Vanna explained the symbolic implications which some numerologists and other experts had ascribed to the dimensions of this cavern and those of the stone coffin.

'Isn't it extraordinary?' she concluded.

'It'd be extraordinary if it were true,' Guido said.

She gazed at him happily. Meanwhile he had been observing the youth, who hadn't said a word since they'd met and whose bearing was admirably upright and dignified, like that of a statue.

Vanna smiled, putting her arm round the young Egyptian's waist and hugging him affectionately. He let her do so, his expression becoming suddenly tender, but revealing more embarrassment than alacrity.

'Have you ever been married, Vanna?' Guido asked.

She burst out laughing.

'Do you think this lad might be my son? Do you think he looks like me?'

'Yes, but you'd have had to bring him into the world aged about ten. You seem to know him.'

'We know each other very well, but like brother and sister.'

'Would you have me believe you incapable of incest?'

'I was waiting for you to commit it with us,' she remarked.

She kissed the boy right on the mouth and he let her do so a long time without turning a hair. Then with one movement he half opened his djellaba, his prick jutting out in its full, tapering nakedness.

Vanna grasped it in one hand, without ceasing to kiss the young man. She caressed the phallus until it had hardened almost to the point of being vertical.

Then she left the lad's lips and knelt down so as to take his prick in her mouth. But he uttered some Arabic phrase in an urgent, peremptory tone. She broke off, unbuttoned her skirt as far as her groin, and lay down inside the yawning tomb, assisting the dark cock to pierce her vulva. The boy arched his back, then sank into her with frenzied haste. She gasped in pain, but he took no notice, and after burying himself inside her to the very root of his prick, began to thrust to and fro with a violence that Guido had never in his life witnessed.

The Italian wondered whether to come to his friend's assistance or if indeed she would get used to this treatment. He settled for *laisser-faire*, because this spectacle was making him horny, giving him such a hard on that he would never have imagined that only a short time ago upon the camel's back he had felt completely drained of desire.

The young Egyptian sobbed raucously. At that very moment he pulled out of Vanna and reached his climax.

Guido pushed the boy aside and his own prick replaced the Arab's within Vanna's cunt.

She grunted with pleasure. Guido squeezed her nipples, at first through her dress, then ripping at its material so brutally that he pulled off the buttons. With one hand he succeeded in stripping her, tearing off her robe and excited by the thought that everyone would see them like that, tattered and scarcely detumescent when they emerged from the pyramid.

If they emerged ... For as he was energetically screwing her, his prick in exquisite agony, he had the fantasy that they might stay buried there for ever, all three of them and that these might be their last throes.

'God you know how to do it to my tits!' Vanna exclaimed deliriously, reaching orgasm yet again. 'I'm thirsty,' she groaned, 'fuck my mouth!'

He withdrew and she knelt down. Guido straddled her, gripping the nape of her neck and jamming his cock into her mouth. He did not want to feel the softness of her lips, but to explode in the back of her throat.

The boy drew closer to them once again. Guido had almost forgotten him. He noticed that the Egyptian was wanking with insistent strokes, rigid already.

Guido's hand met his. The Egyptian must have known that Guido was an expert manipulator for he let go of himself and surrendered his weapon to the foreigner's discretion. When the latter decided that the organ was hard enough, he raised Vanna's haunches without himself withdrawing from her mouth and pulled the young man's prick up against her magnificently sculpted buttocks.

The youth smiled so winningly that Guido's own erection tensed as if suddenly galvanized by an electric shock. Then the Egyptian spat into his palm, wet his prick, and with a single thrust had sodomized Vanna.

5

A Husband Who Loves His Wives

Guido was lying between Vanna and Mija in his hotel room. The two women had decided to stay all night. Mija had promptly fallen asleep.

'Vanna, you never answered my question, the day before yesterday,' Guido said, 'when I asked you if you'd ever been married.'

'The idea is so grotesque!' Vanna guffawed. 'Do I look like the marrying kind?'

'I used to boast about it too. I even stuck a piece of paper over my bed. It read "I'll never marry". Net result – I've been married twice.'

'That doesn't surprise me.'

'It does me. But I did keep my promise till I was thirty. Anyhow in both cases, it wasn't I who got married, *they* married *me*.'

'Is your defence so flimsy? True, you like to be controlled.'

She began to caress him again and he let her do so, warning her however that on this particular night he did not feel up to making love any more.

'So Mija exhausted you, eh?' Vanna teased. 'You're not used to youthful naivety.'

'Your pupil is a savage,' he sighed. 'But I'd be quite happy myself to return to that sort of savagery. Perhaps it'd help me understand civilization.'

'From time to time I found myself wondering if it was going to end badly for one or the other of you: would you disembowel her first, before she tore off your cock? I've never seen a horse treated the way she was riding you!'

'Well, we both came to mutually satisfactory conclusions. And now, as the ancient poet once remarked, to me even the recollection of those frightful torments has its charms. Mija doesn't seem to have any hard feelings ... '

'I don't either, even though at her age I wasn't as good at it as she is.'

'If you could make that sort of comparison you wouldn't be with me here now.'

'How little you know me! Of course I can and do! Imagine me fucking as a young girl: all the more reason for you to feel me when I'm "in" Mija's body – it makes me come even more strongly than when you're really fucking my actual body. And I'd also like to enter the bodies of your women, all the women you've made love to. Those you fucked while thinking about others. Those who fuck while thinking of you. Those to whom you were unfaithful but haven't forgotten. And since you've told me about their existence, I'd like to be inside the bodies of the women you married. I'd like to *be* them, the times you fucked them. To be you when they were fucking you. Tell me about them, my love, while I wank you very gently.'

'My first woman,' Guido said, 'was inherited.'

'From whom?' Vanna smiled. 'A wicked uncle or a ruined gambler?'

'From an American friend I knew at Caltech.'

'Where?'

'An American university.'

'What were you doing there?' asked Vanna, surprised.

'I'll tell you about that later. The friend I mentioned was called Allan Levi and he was the same age as myself. He was Professor of Molecular Biology, something of a genius. One day about five years ago I had a phone call from Los Angeles. It was some lawyer I didn't know telling me Allan had just died of a brain tumor, leaving me his books, his Jaguar, his two pedigree Dobermann Pinschers and his half-Hungarian, half-French-Canadian wife.'

Vanna clapped her hands delightedly.

'Marvellous! Only you could have such luck.'

'That wasn't my original view of it. To start with, I was stunned to hear of my friend's death. Since I left Caltech the previous year we'd written to each other regularly. He'd never even mentioned his illness or his marriage.'

'Didn't he even have a woman when you were in the States?'

'Not casual lays. I think he liked boys.'

'Especially you. Otherwise, why would he have given you these posthumous presents?'

'We were friends, not lovers.'

'Same thing,' Vanna claimed.

'Not quite. The proof being that I'd hardly left Caltech before he got married.'

'On the rebound, no doubt. He missed you.'

'Don't fantasize without the facts.'

'All right, give me a better explanation.'

'Love at first sight is a rare phenomenon, but it has been known to happen.'

'Did you know the woman he married?'

'Never saw her, never heard him talk about her. He only met her after my departure.'

'But he never told you. Nor did he tell you he was dying. Yet he knew it when he got married. He didn't get married for himself, he married for you. For love of you, Q.E.D.'

'As you might have guessed, the legal eagle was quick

to inform me that the clause whereby Allan left me his wife was legally absolutely null and void. Which didn't invalidate the rest of the Will. So I could take possession of the car, dogs, and books whenever I wanted. That is, as soon as I sorted out the death duties, of course.'

'Which you did.'

'I told that miserable pen-pusher what he could do with his legalities and duties. That's how I missed out on several thousand interesting books, a powerful sports car and some supposedly fierce and faithful animals.'

'But not the woman.'

'Two days later I was woken up at six a.m. by someone knocking on my door. It was her.'

'In Milan!'

'She'd taken the first flight out and there she was at my door, between two big trunks like coffins. She was tall and thin and wearing a multicoloured fur cape, and her own long hair seemed to be everywhere – over her cheeks and temples, upon her shoulders and down her back almost to her waist. She was watching me with that green stare panthers have when you look into their eyes.'

'She can't have been bad-looking, because you've suddenly become as poetic as my ancestors who invented animal gods.'

'I'd never seen anyone so beautiful in my life. I stood there gaping at her, my pyjamas undone, quite speechless. Especially as I hadn't the least idea who she might be.'

'Didn't she introduce herself?'

'Yes, but only after a moment or two. She said: "I'm your legacy".'

'In what language?'

'French. It took me a while to understand.'

'Didn't you speak French in those days?'

'Before dawn, on a winter's day, French isn't too comprehensible ... Even less so when someone resembling a far superior version of Marilyn Monroe is doing the talking.'

'You fucked her straight away, though.'

'Without even waking up properly.'

'And you married her.'

'As soon as her papers were in order.'

'You must have had to pay the death duties, though?'

'No. That was the lawyer's problem.'

'And how long did the idyll last?'

'It's still going on. I'm still crazy about Maika and she is about me.'

'From what you told me earlier, I though she'd been replaced.'

'Don't interrupt. The main thing to remember is this: for two whole years we not only shared a perfect physical and mental love-affair, but Maika never once set her cap at any other man. Other men, I promise you, positively drooled over her. They tried like safe-blowers to crack her, all in vain ... She stayed absolutely rock-solid, unyielding – where they were concerned, you understand. She only opened up to my hands. And then, believe me, she was perfection.'

'Let's have a moratorium on superlatives! You, of course, were unfaithful to her all the same?'

'Yes, but with her agreement and blessing. So there was no apparent reason why this blissful episode shouldn't last for ever. I loved the most beautiful woman in the world and she loved me – only me – and because she did, she offered me her prettiest girlfriends.'

'Until ....'

'We took a short trip to Barcelona.'

'My home town! To visit the Gaudi Museum. And my mother stole Maika from you, did she? Good for little Maika! Life's just great. Things are looking up, just for a bit.'

'Stop talking crap! Neither Maika nor I had the bad taste

to go and look at such dreck. Nor did we have the opportunity of meeting your famous mother. But what with Spain (as you know) trying to shake herself from her torpor, we did go and see a film we'd missed during its Milan run. I wasn't expecting very much of it, but it had been produced and directed by friends of mine. It was called *Madame Claude*.'

'I saw it. Also in Barcelona. Maybe we were in the cinema together, that day, No, we can't have been, I'd have noticed your wife.'

'Thanks. Anyway, she came out of the movie in a state of shock. When I returned to the hotel that evening I found her note. There were no cases or furs to be seen. Maika had left for Paris. She'd gone looking for Madame Claude, to ask her to employ her. "I'm better than her most beautiful girls," she explained in her note, confusing the film's actresses with the famous brothel keeper's real girls! "So I can do just as well."'

'And you never saw her again.'

'Oh yes I did! I see her every time I'm in Paris, which is very often. Or when she's in Milan.'

'Working for Claude?'

'Not quite, but almost. A week after her disappearance she phoned me to say Claude no longer existed, or rather was no longer in business. She'd been elbowed out of the scene. But Maika had fallen on her feet, happily. She told me about a fashion designer who was nice, elegant and beautiful and who had at once recognized Maika's potential and aptitude. So she'd hired Maika without even a trial, to model dresses for a select clientele, taking as long as she wished for changing between outfits, in order that what she was wearing underneath could be appreciated.'

'Nothing, you mean.'

'That's what sells the gear to those of only limited

means. The model is thrown in when the buyers' resources aren't so restricted.'

'And was Maika happy to be highly-rated?'

'More than just happy – overjoyed and over the moon. And in three years her contentment has increased. These days, at a yes or a no, she takes off from one continent to another – the reward of presidents, consoler of monarchs, consort of commissars, secret weapon of arms-dealers and promised providence of prelates. You can't count her suitcases any more, while her fur coats are even finer than the one which enraptured me.'

'Furry outfits beneath which, of course, she's stark naked?'

'Not invariably, but often. Especially, she tells me, when travelling by plane.'

'Which must give the crew and half the passengers quite a treat.'

'If they can afford her. She's only free for me, just like when we were married.'

'Yes, quite. Why are you no longer married? Didn't you want a whore for a wife?'

'On the contrary, I was thrilled by the idea. But her boss was jealous. She insisted we divorce. Maika didn't want to cross her, so . . . . '

'Dear Guido, always accommodating! So much so that you found yourself the eligible bachelor once again. You're really a dab hand at marriage!'

'The next time, too, was out of the ordinary.'

'Go ahead. I've started yawning, but I'm all ears.'

'So Maika and I stayed married for two years. She was nineteen when we met, twenty-one when she left me. A year went by, during which my friends' wives kept me happy, on the whole. Whereupon I decided to leave the firm that employed me.'

'Which was?'

'You really should think about making your living as a

spy, sometime. Otherwise you'll have a hard time with your own employer. My boss was none other than Gianni Pecori. You know him.'

'No.'

'What! With agents like you, the secret services would go out of business.'

'I've never been interested in industry, nor in Italy.'

'They even know that guy in Patagonia. Don't bother to take down his name, your bosses cultivate him assiduously. To cut a long story short, I ditched that creep and his crew, glad to be unemployed again.'

'Did you have any savings? Or did Maika send you a little something every once in a while?'

'I live frugally but it's harder to remain independent than one thinks.'

'Harder for whom? Wage-slaves?'

'That was how I fell into the clutches of another guy, even richer and more powerful than Pecori, if that's possible. Before I had time to make the sort of excuses you set such little store by, he made me an offer I couldn't refuse.'

'You're too mercenary, what's more!'

'I see myself right. But the best thing about it was that (over and above an increased subsidy from the lady who'd been supporting me at that time) the guy offered me a woman by way of a bonus. And not just any old slag either, but an heiress, to marry.'

'Outrageous! Your apparent propensity towards inheritance will send you back to second childhood yet.'

'That's life. The fact remains that the lady in question was no widow but a well-known stockbroker's daughter, her virginity actually guaranteed by contract. Aged eighteen. As you see, I was rapidly moving back towards second childhood but wasn't, please note, quite at the point to which you've brought me with Mija.'

'Stick to the subject. What did the spoilt brat look like?'

'You probably won't believe me, but I promise you it's true. She was as attractive as Maika, black-haired rather than tawny, however. Their faces were quite different, naturally, but though it may seem surprising, their figures were somewhat similar.'

'Don't tell me they resembled mine, or I'll sling you out.'

'Sorry to annoy you, but all three of you do have something in common. Anyhow, Maika never needed my telling her to wear as few underclothes as yourself. As for Giulia (the memory gives me gooseflesh and I still blush for her), when she was first introduced to me, she was wearing not only a petticoat but a bra.'

'Did you undress her in front of the solicitor, to check up?'

'No need. You can tell these things at a glance. An informed glance, that is.'

'Still, this secret vice didn't outrage you to the point of calling off the deal.'

'You must realize that my belief in a person's potential tends to outweigh my rejection reflexes, even the most justifiable ones. You can guess my delight, however, when on our wedding day – which was fashionable and well-attended – I saw her among her parents and posh relations who were all togged out in tails and the full gear. Yes, my bride to be was wearing only a skin-tight wedding dress that enabled myself and everyone present to count the number of public hairs on her virginal pussy.'

'Was she still a virgin then? You married her without even making it with her first?'

'Right. I played the game absolutely according to the rules.'

'You disappoint me. But I trust that she at least, unlike

87

your previous spouse, didn't prove as suspiciously monogamous – I mean before the latter saw the light in some obscure moviehall in my native Catalonia?'

'In no time at all Giulia proved herself quite as sensually gifted as Maika, and just as Maika had done remained exclusively, uniquely, mine. Such fidelity was, I think, an integral part of her erotic talent rather than out of any sense of duty. Every day since she appeared almost naked at that gathering of her relatives – who knew her only by her strait-laced finishing school image – she continued her defiance of convention. The first favour she asked of me was to take her to nudist beaches. There and wherever else she got the chance to sprawl naked with arms and legs akimbo (always in my company, of course) the beauty of her twat became legendary. From St Tropez to Taormina, half Europe licked its chops, yet no stud but myself laid a finger on it.'

'No woman either?'

'Yes. One. Maika.'

'Bravo! Did you all make love together?'

'I'm going to have to disappoint you again! When Maika visits Milan, Giulia and I waste no time calling on her in her hotel room, but separately. Not behind one another's back, mind you, yet not at the same time.'

'I'm sorry for you! You're abnormal. You're crazy.'

'If you don't mind my cross-questioning you while I have the opportunity, where do you get your fanaticism about troilism from?'

'It's not fanaticism, it's a premonition.'

'Do you think that's the formula of the future?'

'If the world wants to go on evolving, yes. In the beginning there was one Being, who was therefore alone, whether mortal or divine, and whose name was Yama (as the Zeud Avesta has it) or just the Self, according to the Upanishads, or a fat Androgyne, or as in the early days of Egypt, the god Khnoum. The first progression in all the early stories was the division into two of these creators or their creations. Thus Eve was taken from Adam's body. Thus we have the Vedic twins, Yami and Yama, whose incest produced us. Thus Apollo cut the Hermaphrodites or Androgynes into two and sewed up the halves again to make male and female as we know them more or less presentable. (Less, in my view.) So Khnoum fashioned Chou and Tefnout, those distant parents of mine. And all these "halves", since that avatar, are struggling to reunite with each other, mostly only succeeding in aggravating their loneliness. This state of affairs has lasted long enough. We ought to be able to do better than our old gods did, and instead of contenting ourselves with two sexes, to invent three, four, five, ten, sixty-nine, all different! And while waiting for the biologists to spring these mutants from their test-tubes, let's at least try to enlarge the concept of the couple. One day let's give a woman two men. Another time, offer one man two women. Without, of course, confining ourselves to these combinations and limits! Or else the trio would soon become as irritating as the couple.'

'What erudition and staying-power, for this time of night! My own practical observations, I'm afraid, don't lend themselves to such eloquence. I've been in quite a few of those laboratories in which you place your faith, but alas, so far I've only met professors as jealous and possessive of their retorts as of their wives. Or lab assistants who prefer cosy chats to resolving the sort of unfamiliar equations you posit. And I myself – here I have to disillusion you yet again, though I'm ashamed to admit this to you – until you and Mija put me up to it, I'd never made love with two women simultaneously.'

'Surely you didn't doubt your abilities?'

'I'm more sentimental than you think. I was worried that the attention I'd be paying one lover might hurt the other. If she were there too, that is.'

'That's nice, but silly. The pleasure you give Mija gives me pleasure too. Particularly when I'm watching.'

'You're not like most people.'

'From what you say, though, your wives are supposed not to have been possessive or jealous, Or was their tolerance conditional (as society likes it to be) upon your doing whatever you wanted provided they didn't know about it? I have difficulty reconciling this with Giulia's and Maika's pleasure in displaying their bodies. Do you see what I'm getting at?'

'Not really. Especially since they didn't resemble each other in everything, and not in that. Maika, certainly, was born without a jealous bone in her body. But Giulia was jealous in the early days.'

'It didn't stop you sleeping around, though.'

'No, but I hid that from her. With considerable guilt.'

'Did you succeed in changing her outlook just the same?'

'It was Maika, not I, who brought about her conversion. The day Giulia learned from her how to love women she also learned that I might be capable of desiring other women too. Or, more precisely, she understood that I could go on loving Maika.'

'Logical, yet not logical.'

'Normal.'

'What's normal is generally petty. Did Giulia herself also acquire the taste for whoring from Maika? Or anyway, for variety?'

'Oddly enough, Maika never breathed a word to her about her principles and practices, nor her principalities and powers.'

'Didn't you say anything to Giulia either?'

'No. She thinks Maika is just a model, with no other connotations, and that's it.'

'How did they meet?'

'I arranged that. In fact I had to drag Giulia, who was

almost in tears, to meet Maika. An hour later, it was all smiles and kisses.'

'So actually *you* taught Giulia to love women. You see, you're not such a bad teacher as you make out!'

'I'm afraid I didn't explain myself properly: when I said just now Giulia learned to love women, I meant she learned to love Maika.'

'No one else?'

'No one else.'

'Then making love to Maika didn't give her the urge to make love to other women, just as loving you didn't make her go off and fuck other men.'

'I suppose that's it.'

'Then I take back the compliment I just paid you. You're a very bad teacher. And Maika an equally worthless instructress.'

'I'm going to amaze you yet again. Before she got to know Maika, I tried several times to get Giulia to go to bed with mutual friends. Friends we both knew. Men. She didn't want to. After the success of her little scene with Maika, I tried to get her to make love with women I thought she'd fancy. No dice there, either.'

'That's weird,' Vanna complained sceptically. 'Really weird!'

After a moment's silence, she asked:

'Didn't you have children by either of them?'

'*Porco dio!*' Guido exclaimed.

'No metaphysical excuses now,' Vanna pronounced sternly.

'*Porco Madonna!*' her bedmate lapsed, apparently genuinely shocked. 'Making babies! Don't you feel there are quite enough people on the planet who think only of that? Might I ask if that's your obsession too?'

'It's got nothing to do with the human race, nor mine,' Vanna corrected him again, 'but with that of you and your wives.'

'What can I tell you that you don't already know? Neither they nor I wanted children, but that's an even longer story . . . .'

For some time Vanna asked no more questions. Guido wondered if she had fallen asleep. In fact, when she continued her voice had taken on something of a sleepy tone:

'Do you think Giulia is waiting for you now like Penelope?'

'I don't think any such thing,' said Guido.

'Well, what then?'

'Giulia and I have been married two years. The time has come for her too to have a change.'

'This biennial cycle seems really eccentric to me,' she giggled. 'Why two years, rather than three, ten or one?'

'I'm not theorizing,' Guido retorted, 'just stating what happens.'

'Have you been feeling that Giulia's begun to tire of you?'

'No.'

'Are you getting tired of her?'

'It's not that either. It's wiser not to wait for one or the other to become bored.'

'So you want to divorce in order to see if you can fuck Giulia on your return with as much pleasure as you fuck Maika?'

'Exactly.'

'Will you stick to your customary practice of separate assignations or will you use the experience you've gained with me and Mija to liven up the daily grind a bit? Once she's not hitched to you, Giulia may become less naive. Even if the game Maika bets on has stakes too high for a financier's daughter, I trust she might at least increase the amount of players to three.'

'If only out of consideration for you, I'd hope so too.'

'And would you remarry as soon as a new Maecenas gives you a third donation?'

'For the time being I'm determined to do nothing of the sort.'

'But do you have any say as to who your successor will be? Or don't you care any more about who'll take your place in Giulia's bed than you do about selecting those who currently swarm under Maika's furs? Yet perhaps you in fact already know your successor? Or who he might be – since the day you caught the plane and came to see me.'

'No, I don't know him. Giulia and I both agreed when I left Milan not to exchange our news.'

'As you were leaving, did she have anyone in mind at all?'

'I'm sure she didn't. Luckily, those who fancy her are legion, so she should be spoilt for choice.'

'Why "should"?'

'Because she wouldn't have to decide for herself. Any more than she did the first time, when she was offered to me. My boss is still there.'

'And will he designate – or has he already done so – Giulia's new husband? For I assume that a girl from such a good family won't be sold off to any old vulgarian. Free love doesn't enter into it.'

'In his desk,' Guido said, 'my boss has a divorce petition signed by myself. He'll fill in the date himself, or maybe he's done so already, as you imply.'

'Won't Giulia have any say in it?'

'She's already said yes.'

'I didn't expect a country so enlightened as your own to preserve a system which I don't even like to see still operative throughout most of Egypt.'

'The measures I'm telling you about don't amount to a system. They stem from private erotic arrangements which Giulia and Maika have in common with certain other women and quite a few men too: they like being controlled. That's all there is to it.'

'They actually like being "willed" and having a price and being transferred as chattels? You're saying, in other words, that they enjoy being objects. Valuable objects, sure, but objects just the same.'

'You remember our first conversation, Vanna, when you teased me for amateur psychologizing. Well don't *you* start using that very jargon now. The clichés about woman-as-object, the old chestnut of reification, served their turns as thought-fodder for a generation that's still in process of collapse: people of our age ought to be capable of less tautological analyses. They should be content to state that in someone's cerebral make-up the synapses are so regulated as to make him or her relish the prospect of being bought or sold, while those of other individuals would under the same circumstances induce a state of revolt or despair.'

'Is this synaptic structure innate or acquired? Changeable or irreversible? Expanding or regressive?'

'I'll tell you a secret, which I'd be obliged if you kept to yourself ... In the current climate of opinion, no one really knows if there's an answer to your questions nor what that answer is! You see we're far from the certainties of bogus knowledge.'

'Well please tell me how you know that no one knows.'

'Because I'm that "one", and because nobody else knows more about it than I do.'

'Yes, I see ... Or rather I don't at all. It'd probably be better for me not to know too much either.'

'So let's have no more talk about my wives.'

'Oh yes, let's! I find the subject exciting. My synapses aren't sleepy any more.'

'Well then let's go on. What else do you want to know?'

'How Maïka and Giulia make love.'

'I told you – the same way'

'Yes, but?'

'Their cunts suck like mouths and vice versa.'

'And I only score over them in one particular way?'

'Yes. Which is why I do it that way.'

'And to think I knew nothing about it!'

'You too were waiting for me in order to know what you were really capable of. Like them!'

'That's it then! You've managed to lump us all together in the same boat. Happy?'

'Yes. I never even envisaged comparing another woman to Maïka and Giulia. Except you. You shouldn't be ashamed of that.'

'I'm not. I've finally grown to like those two bitches! I even think I'm beginning to know them better than you.'

'Better than you know me?'

'Better than you know them.'

'Oh!'

'Don't get cross with me if I disabuse you, Guido. Contrary to appearances, neither Maïka nor Giulia nor I were found for you by someone else. We ourselves decided that you suited us. You imagine that if we give in to you it's because sometime during gestation or early childhood our neurons made nodes. How very wrong you are Guido! Your drug-pushers came too late to influence our synapses. And, in one sense, our parents also. We're the product of age-old conditioning which the climactic spasm that decided our sex can scarcely change. This conditioning – what a paradox! – makes us free. Contrary to what she led you to believe, Maïka was free to choose you: she it was who drove her first husband to bequeath her to you. You were the necessary ladder by which she could climb when the time came to the heights she wanted to attain: happy hookerdom. Giulia too, although I could have taken the piss out of her just now, has always known the various directions of the road to freedom for one of her background. In order to be free of her family she had to go through the public auction of her virginity as befitted her station in life. Yet she herself had to find out what her body was really worth. To make her own judgement on that and find out her true worth she needed to learn, educate herself, make experiments, undergo training. And you were the best instructor in the vicinity. In hiring you she did well for herself, though you thought you were doing all right. Work it out: who gained most? You, whose orgasm isn't all that different whether coming into the mouth of a Hungaro-Canadian or the cunt of a Milanese? Or this stockbroker's daughter who would have been reduced to speculating on credit had not your special form of spending turned her on? Today she's so skilled in lovemaking that to find any better you yourself have had to come this far, to be taken in hand by younger girls from a civilization older than that of Italy.'

Throughout this tirade Vanna had gradually substituted for the gentle rhythmic pressures she'd earlier employed upon Guido's sex a firmer stroke, which he knew she would not relinquish nor slacken until he came. Now they were both silent while the sperm of which Guido thought he had been thoroughly drained, welled once more within his prick.

'Suck me off!' he finally begged her.

Vanna acceded to his request, then remained with her cheek upon her companion's belly. He was amazed to hear her speak yet again.

'Cheer up, you man of hidden talents,' she said. 'Even if you have less to gain than your partners, you lose nothing. You also – whatever you bet on, whatever the game may be – will always get back your stake! And you'll find it's increased.'

'Vanna,' he sighed. 'Now *I* don't understand a word of

what you're driving at. You must have swallowed my last drop of spunk! Or are you talking in your sleep?'

'I'm pretending to sleep,' she answered. 'Just as you yourself pretend not to choose your wives and to let others choose them for you. Other people and chance. Yet those other people and that chance, you know, really stir things up! They procure for you exactly the sort of women you like, the ones you lust after without admitting it. Without admitting it, for you dare do more than you dare say: that's your weakness.'

'I don't have your luck.'

'It doesn't matter! You'd never have taken on the women Allan or your boss or Renato offered you if they hadn't been the ones you'd dreamed up in a masturbatory trance. The ones whose fictional existence satisfied your reverence for facts. Those you loved before meeting them, sure in advance that you'd find them. Those you seek knowing you're seeking them.'

'I'm not as clairvoyant as you make out,' he again protested.

'Yes, you are, Guido, when your desires enlighten you. You see so very far when your intuition and imagination guide you. But, true, I'm perhaps mistaken when I say you seek. You're not seeking: you're dreaming of the marvellous discoveries you want to make. And it's those dream discoveries which wake you with a hard-on at six in the morning. They're the ones! You confessed as much to me: you didn't get an erection when you saw Maika and her mythic furs: you already had one when you opened the door of your apartment. You don't get horny for the loved one, Guido, but you love what arouses you. And one thing only gives you a hard-on.'

'What's that?'

'A certain form of power which you call a certain kind of understanding.'

'What about you, Vanna?' asked Guido. 'What gets you aroused?'

'Curiosity, just like yourself. But my curiosity's different from yours. I don't know whether or not what I want exists. And either way I don't mind.'

6

The Rosetta Stone Will Never Be Decoded.

'*Niké!*' Vanna's voice exclaimed so piercingly that Guido, out of self-preservation, held the telephone receiver away from his ear.

'Really?' he said finally, with deliberation.

'When I'm talking, you have to believe me,' she scolded him. 'And when I shout Victory you must give me credit for it.'

'I leave the choice of triumphal formulae to you.'

'No, you must get out of that habit!'

'What habit?'

'Of leaving me the choice.'

'I don't know how to choose, myself, although you try to make me believe I do.'

'Don't let's start up that argument. Be content to hand over to me.'

'I'll do just that.'

'I treat every promise as binding, you know. Which is why Nesrin has kept his: our permits are ready. He's even insisting on giving them to us in person. He, you see, doesn't delegate his obligations. To mark the occasion he's giving a small reception for us at his place. Go to the hairdresser and smarten up.'

She guessed from Guido's reaction that he had suddenly become moody.

'What's come over him?' he reflected. 'Is he now going to start publicizing our trip all of a sudden?'

'Don't get worked up,' she reassured him. 'On the contrary, Nesrin lectured me on the need for you and me to be discreet. Apparently the only reservation there might be in high places could be to do with favouritism and setting precedents. In Egyptian planning, Siwah doesn't figure as a holiday resort, not even for tired business-men.'

'So why the shenanigans tonight?'

'There'll only be a few close friends of his.'

'I'm surprised that guy is capable of friendship,' Guido blurted out.

'You're not omniscient. What sort of outfit should I wear, decorous or indecent?'

'Whatever pleases your master most.'

'My master?'

'Have you forgotten you're in Adly's employ?'

'Whoever pays me doesn't possess me!' said Vanna sharply, and hung up leaving Guido free to reflect upon this maxim at will.

When he called by at the agreed time to collect her, she was wearing a long white full-length dress which was not actually see-through, but made of such delicate fabric that it gave the impression of transparency. In the taxi she pulled it up to the tops of her thighs, and Guido told her he liked her style.

'I'm not showing my legs for your particular benefit,' she commented. 'I do it out of habit. Perhaps every habit is a sickness.'

'A sickness is something which hurts you,' Guido remonstrated. 'Are you in pain?'

'No, doctor. But sometimes others get hurt. My schoolmistresses could scarcely abide my mania for hoisting up my skirts. Nor could my mother, especially when I would do it in church.'

'What were you doing going to church?'

'You don't have to be a believer to like the works of art which the faithful dedicate to their particular gods,' Vanna reprimanded him. 'The *Sagrada Familia,* for instance ... Oh sorry, I'd forgotten that Gaudi's buildings turned your stomach.'

'They're just not my kind of thing, that's all. What amazes me is that you like them.'

'My mother helped me understand their special qualities. And it's not every day you find a church that makes you want to come.'

'You came, inside the *Sagrada Familia*?'

'Yes, whenever I sat under the dizzying curve of its vault, completely surrounded by the phallic cluster of its slanting columns.'

'Did you know what a phallus was when you were a little kid?' he teased her.

'I didn't need experience to know that.'

The taxi dropped them in front of a large house with a wide, stone front staircase, imposing but devoid of ostentation or outward opulence. Vanna rearranged her dress, kissed Guido's cheek and declared: 'But I'm not nostalgic about my childhood devotions. One must know how to change temples!'

Guido's eyes never left Nesrin, trying to work out what made him tick. He recalled their original meeting and how the Egyptian had played dumb. Guido had had a hard job keeping abreast of such gamesmanship. Judging by the outcome, their duel of feigned stupidity hadn't been unproductive. A safe-conduct to Siwah was, like Paris, worth a Mass!

That evening Nesrin seemed neither bored nor boring. He was even jovial and had trimmed his beard, which suited him better. His white tuxedo was quite as elegant, it must be admitted, as his afternoon suits.

None of the fashionable women who fluttered around the flower vases was introduced to Guido as the lady of the house. There probably wasn't one, or maybe she was kept under wraps. Guido wanted to ask Vanna about that, but the constant circulation of the guests had now separated them. By the looks of it, Nesrin's idea of intimacy was on the grand scale. Several dozen champagne drinkers and canapé-crunchers were already present.

Everything was most formal. Guido felt rather as if he had been duped. Yet what had he expected? He resolved to make up for his confusion and disappointment: 'This diplomatic scene makes me ill at ease. I don't find it relaxing,' he confided to his host, adopting an unashamedly shifty manner. 'I'm not used to mingling with the mighty.'

'The rabble is, I agree, more colourful,' said Nesrin. 'But I would have had to redecorate my house. I'm obliged to match my friends with my chairs.'

Guido nodded solemnly.

'Real Louis Quinze!' he said with appreciation. 'Ideal for bogus occasions.'

'As you see, I exaggerated nothing,' Nesrin modestly agreed. 'It all has a touch of *Huis Clos*.'

'So your cultural relations number also leaves you time for reading,' Guido retorted, sullenly persisting in his oafishness.

'I draw on my reserves of youth,' the master of the house said.

'How old *are* you?' Guido asked, aware of overstepping the mark.

Nesrin Adly let him know it: 'The Oriental, as you know, tends to be vague upon that subject. Come on, I'll restore you to your own age-group.'

He took the Italian's arm and led him towards a young couple systematcially depleting the buffet. Guido turned his back on the undernourished duo and shook hands with an enormous man wedged against a thin woman. Nesrin smiled and introduced them: 'Mr Andreotti, the engineer,' he said. 'The Hon. Alistair Barret and Mrs Aurora Barret.'

He bowed and went off to find Vanna, while Guido asked the Englishman why he was honourable.

'Yes boss?' Vanna quipped.

Nesrin patted her cheek by way of an amiable reprimand.

'Come with me!' he ordered.

She followed him into a much smaller room, where he produced a small envelope from his jacket pocket and passed it to her.

'Your papers,' he explained.

Aware of the ambiguous nature of her question, he became worried: 'Your bag'll be big enough to hold them, won't it?'

Vanna felt in the mood for some casual teasing: 'In Louis XV's court, a courtesan so graciously rewarded would have pressed this royal favour between her breasts. Unfortunately mine aren't large enough to keep your papers in place. May I entrust them to my colleague?'

'The envelope also contains a cheque,' Nesrin said.

'Are you scared I might share it with him?'

'You have other means,' he smiled condescendingly, 'of keeping your admirers.' And then, affecting a laboured gallantry at odds with his usual manner: 'Sometimes my memory is excellent.'

She looked seriously at him.

'Nesrin, you're not the man to live in the past. What exactly do you have in mind? I don't understand the role I'm playing in your project . . . .'

'Believe me, I'm not in the least calculating. I live from day to day.'

She didn't take him up on this and they returned to the huge drawing-room. Guido looked somewhat hangdog and out of place. Vanna went over to him. He pocketed the envelope without saying a word, glanced round to see if he could catch Nesrin's eye to thank him, then, not seeing him, shrugged: 'Funny old boy.'

He asked Vanna: 'Doesn't he worry you at all?'

'Of course not!' she laughed.

'Then let's hope he's no threat,' Guido concluded. 'I'll trust your intuition.'

They joined the other guests moving around the table, sampling the various dishes and drinking glass after glass. Time passed slowly and drearily.

'What a crashing bore,' Guido observed. 'Only one thing for it, let's get drunk.'

'Right!' Vanna agreed.

A very tall, gangling redfaced fellow whose grey-flecked fair hair was cut in Renaissance pageboy style approached Guido, holding out his hand. He spoke English with a rather pleasant German accent.

'Werner Weiner,' he announced. 'We're colleagues.'

'Oh really?' said Guido coldly.

'You're and ethnologist aren't you? Well so am I.'

'Why are you here?' Guido said, more polite now.

'For the beer, of course!' the German stared.

'I meant, in Egypt. What are you researching?'

'I? Nothing. I'm on holiday. I go on holiday as often as possible. Anyway, what's left in this country to discover? The bazaar-keepers have cleaned it out.'

'He's OK, eh?' Vanna commented to Guido.

Guido assented, and just then felt an arm around his shoulder. He turned to find it was Nikos.

'You again!' Guido pronounced.

'Dear chap, how happy I am that everything's concluded so splendidly for you,' the Greek said, more expansive than ever.

'Concluded? Nothing's even started yet.'

'Tut tut,' Nikos reprimanded him and, calling Vanna to

his aid: 'Dear girl, you must teach our friend to be more trusting.'

Guido felt his head beginning to swim.

'Shall we be moving on?' he suggested to Vanna and the two men. 'Apart from ourselves, the place is full of creeps.'

Vanna linked arms with Guido and Werner, leaning forward to kiss Nikos on the lips.

'One day,' she announced, 'your busts will be on show in a museum, and I'll be dusting them reverently. But that'll be in my next life.'

'Shall we have been sculpted for our looks or our remarkable achievements?' the German wanted to know.

'For neither,' said Vanna. 'You'll be immortalized simply because I like you.'

A Turkish band took the place of the Egyptian musicians.

'Let's go later,' Vanna decreed.

She danced in turn with all three of her statues-to-be, tried unsuccessfully to make them come, and then, reproaching them for their moderation, ditched them outright and went over to a tall, incredibly thin Nubian woman with huge intense eyes. Vanna talked to her in her own dialect and at once had her in fits of enchanting laughter.

'What do you find so amusing?' inquired Nesrin, joining them.

'Ourselves,' Vanna replied. 'Don't we seem rather out of place?'

'Out of place you may be, but you're causing a sensation,' Nesrin smiled. 'Some of my friends are falling over themselves trying to engage you in conversation.'

Vanna eyed him scornfully yet impudently:

'To whom did you promise us?' she demanded.

He assumed an expression of pained courtesy, protesting:

'I do not dispose of my guests like that.'

'Why not?' said Vanna, surprised. And she turned towards the young African woman: 'Wouldn't you like being disposed of with me, Kemi?'

The latter laughed again, the effect being of exotic birdsong. Nesrin stared at Vanna with an insistence which implied volumes before making a pronouncement evidently to do with altogether different concerns than the present ones: 'I'd like everyone to place their own bets.'

She met his stare for a while, shrugged, and looked away. She saw Guido dancing with an ambassador's wife, an affected, cold-looking platinum blonde. Vanna slyly pointed them out to the Egyptian, remarking: 'Don't you have anything more appetising to offer your guest of honour, kind sir?'

'I see my dear that you're not always the best judge,' he retorted, grimacing with polite irony.

Vanna pouted back and hugged Kemi ostentatiously.

The guests were starting to leave in small groups, thanking their host at the door. Soon there were only about fifteen of them left amid the thick odour of scent and tobacco smoke.

'Is that it?' Guido asked hopefully.

'Not yet,' Vanna informed him. 'What do you think of Kemi? Do you know what her name means? Black Earth. That's what ancient Egypt was called, because it was black and beautiful. Have you also heard the saying that all freedom is black and therefore confused with the freedom of sex, which is, for some obscure reason, also black? Who worked that out? But anyway, first tell me if you like my black sister.'

He looked the Nubian up and down.

'I like her hair,' he finally answered, holding in his

fingers one of the innumerable tiny pigtails surrounding the young woman's face. 'How can I assess the rest of her, she's got too much on.'

'You're right,' Nesrin agreed. (He had appeared without their being aware of him.) 'A steam bath or *hammam* as we call it will set off her beauty more than the finest brocades. And it can't do us any harm either, can it?'

'Now?' Guido stared at him in amazement. 'Where though?'

'Here at home, of course! It's high time I showed you round the more interesting parts of my house. Let's start with my garden – the pleasure of the chaste night, before the pure pleasures of the *hammam*.'

Guido was scarcely eager to sample either. He only wanted to go away and sleep. But Vanna unhesitatingly followed their host, who had taken Kemi by the hand. The remaining guests followed them: Nikos Andreou, the two Britons, the lazy Werner Weiner, a young Frenchman, the ambassador's wife Guido had danced with, her husband, and four or five others. Feeling disgruntled, Guido brought up the rear, reluctant to admire the rare plants whose incomprehensible names Nesrin was listing. The formal tour of the lawns and flowerbeds once completed, everyone entered the green dome of the *hammam*.

Still sullen, Guido wandered into a shower cabin, was soaped by a lad he brusquely rebuffed when he felt a hand lingering at his testicles. After a rinse and rubdown he put on the tiny loincloth provided and emerged to find the other guests similarly attired and enveloped (more flatteringly) by thick bluish clouds of steam: even the Honourable Briton himself, Guido observed, looked slimmer, surrounded by it.

Uncertain of how to behave in the circumstances, he sat down on a bench. The Ambassador – the country he represented unknown to Guido – came to sit beside him.

n't you think this a splendid example of Muslim icacity at its most captivating?' the diplomat launched forth. 'It was at Granada I first really understood the culture.'

Guido confined himself to nodding sympathetically and the other man continued: 'Seen from the exterior, one building in the Alhambra isn't particularly different from any other house of the period. They're all tasteful, modest, enclosed. Only after entering can one appreciate the difference in style and scale: the splendour of the palaces, their incomparable comfort and decorative elegance.'

The young Frenchman joined them. He interrupted, wanting to add a dimension of polemic to the conversation: 'Just like today, the wealthy didn't want to excite the jealousy of the poor. And since the poor never went inside the homes of the rich, they could then assume that the palaces resembled their own humble shacks.'

'Are you a Marxist?' the ambassador questioned him keenly. 'Islam has a somewhat Communistic angle to it, also.'

'Oh come on!' Guido sighed.

'Even in Italy, well, the Vatican . . .' the Ambassador pursued.

But Guido got up and left him to his revelations.

The women had gathered together at the far end of the *hammam*, and he made his way determinedly towards them.

'Are you talking politics?' he asked Vanna.

'We don't talk it,' she replied, 'we indulge in it.'

'What is your line of action?' he inquired.

'Physical struggle.'

'I'm for that,' Guido declared.

He was pleasantly surprised by Aurora Barret's figure. He'd never have guessed how well-proportioned it was, under the layers of her evening dress. She responded to his appreciative scrutiny with a smile that left him in no doubt as to her reaction to a more specific proposition.

He took Vanna aside to ask her: 'Is it the custom for Nesrin's parties to end with an orgy?'

'Why worry about custom? Do as you please.'

He caressed her breasts, but she pushed away his hand.

'I don't feel like conforming to the usual customs, either. You and I have got too used to fucking together. Let's have a change just for one evening.'

Guido frowned, either from frustration or anger, and she assumed an air of contrition: 'In my country, if you anger somebody, even involuntarily, you must seek their forgiveness by giving them a present. I have a nice one for you. Guess! Right, I'll tell you – wouldn't you like to try out Kemi?'

'No,' he grumbled, stubbornly.

She wouldn't give in, and went on: 'Why not?'

'Because you selected her for me. If you really wanted to make amends, you'd have let me choose for myself.'

'Isn't that priceless?' she laughed delightedly. 'We're evolving in opposite directions! I really think I love you more and more.'

She kissed him on the lips long enough and skilfully enough to hasten his erection. Having achieved this, she left him abruptly and ran across to mingle with the men's group.

Guido promptly approached Mrs Barret. Without a word she flung her arms round him and glued her mouth and belly against his. After a moment he pulled his head back to look for some spot to which to take her. A nearby bench was vacant. The young woman herself took off the flimsy piece of towelling covering her breasts, stripped Guido of his loincloth and lay down on the bench, drawing him on top of her.

He felt disinclined to waste time upon foreplay. She felt

the same way, for she seized his prick unceremoniously
and guided it towards her cunt, at the same time raising
her pelvis so as to facilitate his entry.

Guido had resolved to come selfishly, quickly and
without any trimmings. Yet scarcely had he penetrated
this woman than he felt she was close to her own orgasm.
So he enjoyed a good long minute or two while she came
and came again, displaying a sensuality and staying power
which his partner greatly appreciated. He didn't withdraw
from her until she had finally climaxed with a sudden
sharp spasm, as if having a fit.

Quite absorbed in giving her the lengthiest orgasm
possible, he had held off and was still erect. He went to
look for someone with whom he could complete his
unfinished business. He seemed to be out of luck:
everyone was occupied, strictly in couples. Even Vanna,
whatever her principles might be, was making love with
one man only, the German ethnologist, as Guido had
expected. She'd warned him she needed a change.

Kemi, after all, whether Vanna had paved the way for
him or not, was worthy of a king. But where was she
hiding herself? He found her in the end, glued to Nikos in
a *soixante-neuf.* Not very far away from them, the
putative French Marxist and the Alhambrologist ambassador were kissing sloppily and indulging in mutual masturbation. Guido thought their haste indecent and vulgar. He
preferred the spectacle of the ambassador's wife, locked
in a graceful Rodinesque pose with a young blonde girl
whose nipple the ambassadress was sucking while simultaneously stroking her clitoris. Guido was about to fuck
one or the other of them, for his distended cock felt as if
it would burst.

But before he could assuage his lust, a black giant
emerged from the steam, also holding his prick in his hand,
a prick, moreover, in proportion to his great height, and
as hard and erect as Guido's own. The new arrival

immediately thrust his dark dick against the Italian's, gripping Guido's loins with Herculean arms. Without further delay he began a rhythmic motion as expert as it was persuasive. Guido realized that this *frottage* didn't really turn him on, although it was something of a novelty. Yet he couldn't extricate himself from the Negro's grasp. Fortunately the roving phallus wasn't long in spitting its contents all over Guido's belly. Relieved, the colossus grinned, let go of Guido's waist and at once disappeared in the mists whence he had emerged.

'There's a man,' the Italian said in admiration, 'who knows how to simplify communication problems!'

'What was that you said?' a voice he knew asked anxiously. It was Alistair Barret, who was looking even more doleful than he'd been at the start of the party.

'Not a single woman free!' he moaned.

'Come on, what about her?' Guido reassured him, pointing out Aurora who, having recovered from the fray, was lounging voluptuously along her bench.

'Thanks,' said the Englishman, going swiftly over to his wife, who opened her arms and legs to him with devoted tenderness.

'What if Vanna were to see that!' Guido chuckled, in excellent spirits now.

He left the Barrets to fulfill their conjugal duties and retraced his steps.

'Maybe I'll bugger Nikos,' he murmed.

But he ended up stretched out along the Nubian's back. He caressed her shoulders, loins and buttocks, sliding a finger into the anus. She struggled, contracted, and protested chokingly – for her mouth was plugged by the Greek's prick.

'OK!' Guido muttered. 'If she doesn't like it . . . .'

He therefore placed his own prick to the young woman's cunt which was being lubricated by Nikos's tongue. But before Guido could work it into her this same tongue lapped at his organ and started dividing its attentions equally between it and Kemi's hot wet cleft. Guido let him do so, rapidly acknowledging that Nikos was not a whit inferior in oral expertise to Vanna herself nor even to the exceptional artistry of Maika and Giulia. Then he came, grunting wildly, continuing to think of Giulia's and Maika's amorous mouths, their wildcat pussies, their goddesses' breasts, their firm rounded flanks whose deepest secrets he now regretted not having fathomed.

Kemi, with an agility and decisiveness that compelled Guido's admiration, turned round and straddled Nikos whose enormous prick at once sank into her vagina. Then she rode him with that same frenzied vehemence that Mija had displayed two nights earlier in reducing Guido to a worn-out wreck.

When the three of them were at last lying side by side, abolutely exhausted, Guido asked Nikos: 'Are they all like that, in this country?'

The Greek replied with a weary gesture. Kemi raised herself on one elbow and gave each in turn a little kiss of friendship.

'Have you retired from the fray, my lovers?' asked Vanna, who was accompanied by Werner. 'And I was going to ask the three of you to fuck me all at once. Just my luck!'

All five rested.

No one seemed concerned about Nesrin's disappearance, which wasn't a sign of lack of interest in his guests. He never lost sight of them from the cabin where he had installed himself.

From the *hammam*, the smoked glass seemed to screen off the guests from the master of the house, but from the other side, within the cabin, he could watch the orgiasts and their exploits with remarkable clarity.

The special characteristic of the two-way mirror set in its porthole ensured that the pictures being taken continually by the hidden automatic cameras were of similar quality. Extremely sensitive microphones had also been in operation, but these Nesrin had disconnected because he found the endearments and intimate noises of all those people boring.

When the last guest had gone, he returned to his private office on the first floor. It was a good time for serious matters: the hour when subordinates are asleep. Nesrin's business was keeping the leaders awake.

He consulted the jotter on his table – *President of Ottoman Bank, Japanese Envoy, Cardinal B, Rais*. They could all wait. He turned to the intercom connecting him to the Ministry, gave a brief command and closed his eyes until the buzzer sounded.

He listened to what his assistant had to say to him and raised an eyebrow.

'Isn't Selim El Fattah home at this hour?' he asked with some surprise. 'Well find him then! And call me back. No, wait, you talk to him yourself. Tell him I've authorized a foreigner to see Siwah, who will be accompanied by a young woman I consider trustworthy. He is to allow them to wander at will around the oasis and to give them a free hand to see whatever they wish and ask anyone any questions they want. Yes, and he's to let them get to know any of the locals. He doesn't need to bother to keep them under surveillance, nor report back to me. I'll ring him back myself in a few days and give him further instructions. Ah Mehdi, one more thing, make sure he extends them his personal hospitality and entertains them himself, as befits distinguished guests. Better still, like old friends. They won't object to that – quite the contrary.'

Nesrin smiled to himself and went on: 'Tell him the

Italian's name, nothing more, and say that you don't know the female guide's name. Understand? I dont want to be disturbed now.'

He lit a cigarette, drew on it only once before stubbing it out, and as he often did when he felt the need to sum up a situation for his own benefit, commented to himself: 'All in all, just another day!'

But he knew he'd said this because in reality he had to take various steps which were somewhat more unusual than he made out. Well, not *so* extraordinary, anyhow. He smiled and carried on talking to himself.

'The man in the street really has such a partial view of the workings of power! If only he knew . . . .'

He pulled out the carrying handle of the portable TV set on his desk; extracted from it a short metal rod that looked like a simple plug, and went over to one wall of his office that was covered by a mosaic.

He pressed the palm of his left hand against a spot that appeared indistinguishable from any other. A tiny circular area hardly larger than a pinhead, the diameter of the metal pin, changed colour next to the point he had touched. With his right hand he inserted one end of the pin, which promptly entered the wall, without trace. The dot of colour itself was no longer visible. Once again Nesrin pressed his hand flat against the wall, but this time where the mark and the metal pin had been. Simultaneously he murmured a code in a language no one living or dead would have recognized, for it had never been transcribed or spoken anywhere in any previous age.

A section of wall pivoted upon unseen hinges. It was in fact a steel panel as thick as the door to a bank vault. Nesrin went along the corridor, and the room he entered lit automatically as the air-conditioning started up. The door closed behind him without his touching it.

Taking no notice of any of this nor even glancing at the

machinery filling the room, the official installed himself comfortably in a dark brown velvet armchair, facing a console of switches and buttons.

On a keyboard like that of a pocket calculator he tapped out from memory a very long set of figures which lit up on a liquid crystal display. Then he waited.

A moment later a tune was relayed from a speaker and repeated with a very slight variation. Then it ceased. Nesrin pressed a switch, tapped out a new series of numbers on various other keyboards, and leaned back in his chair, musing.

This time he waited far longer, maybe five or ten minutes. He was not aware of their passing.

'I hope at this hour no one's on the job,' he murmured. 'And when I say on the job,' he smiled, correcting himself, ' I mean fucking around! That Selim! At his age too . . . .'

A voice boomed out at pointblank range from the loudspeaker:

'*Si?*' it said with a very slight Piedmont intonation. '*Cosa succede?*'

Nesrin replied in his purest Tuscan accent: 'Good evening my dear fellow! Your government isn't listening in, is it?'

'No. Nor is yours.'

It wasn't a question or a joke remark but an affirmation. The speaker, one felt, wasn't given to doubt or error.

'Remember that guy who resigned from your lot two years ago?' asked Nesrin. 'The sex-life of rats, and all that?'

'It was I who no longer required his services.'

'Would you like to reward him for his trouble anyway?' Nesrin suggested.

'I'm interested neither in harming nor pleasing him,' the voice retorted. 'I've other fish to fry.'

115

'How does he get on with his wife?' Nesrin went on imperturbably.

'What's that?'

'Come on! Have I by any chance woken you up or something, *carissimo*? Walter Mauro's daughter.'

'I can't keep track of all the stupid gossip on this peninsula.'

Nesrin sighed loudly enough for the microphone to relay the tone in which he did so, and said mildly: 'Gianni, maybe one day you're going to need me again.'

There was scarcely a moment's pause before the loudspeaker voice asked: 'What do you want?'

'That you send me the little Mauro girl,' Nesrin replied stolidly.

'Send?'

'In the correct sense of the word: that she's brought here to me.'

'For your personal use?'

'You know me better that that.'

'Well then, what do you want with her? I'm sorry Nesrin, but this sort of abduction would cause a hell of a row. Italy's already in turmoil.'

'Quite. So such a minor occurrence wouldn't be noticed. It'll be attributed to the Right or the Red Brigades or whatever . . . The perpetrators can, if it suits them, be paid during the journey, provided they behave like gentlemen and do it the old-fashioned way – leaving no mark.'

There was another distinct pause before the unseen interlocutor commented: 'You're not being absolutely clear, my friend! Do you want her dead or alive?'

'What?' said Nesrin, appalled. 'Alive of course! And well. You ask some strange questions, Gianni. Do you take me for a killer?'

'Your compatriots are sometimes even more incomprehensible than mine, Nesrin. You have a short memory: if

116

your people had been a bit more discreet, you know when, I'd be president of my country right now.'

Nesrin was sure his smile must have been almost audible, as he replied: 'Aren't you better off the way you are, where the *real* power is?'

'Who's going to get the tape you're recording at this moment?' the voice with the Turin accent said scornfully.

'I'm taping nothing. I'm not concerned with you at present, Gianni. It's one of your arch-rivals I'm interested in.'

'That I'd already gathered. But I can assure you that he doesn't give a damn about the Mauro girl either.'

'I can well imagine. Yet he's *very* interested in her husband. So I can count on you then?'

'I'll see.'

'Thanks. Goodbye Gianni.'

When dawn broke over Cairo, Nesrin Adly did not see it. He remained immured in his strong-room, tipping back his chair, staring ahead without seeing the controls and switchboard panel in front of him. He was deep in reflection. Indeed, he was not to go to bed until he understood the real significance of the question he was asking himself.

2 A Desert Without A Mirage

1

Detours In A Straight Line

'As for the pyramids,' Guido announced when their Land Rover passed Giza, 'I only want to see them again when they're turned upside down on to their tips. Flat on their arses those over-rated bone-boxes are just too camp,'

Vanna didn't even smile. Since leaving Cairo neither of them had spoken a word. They were dwelling on their respective bad moods. Loading up the car had been the pretext for their first real quarrel. Perhaps it was really because they'd got up so much earlier than usual, rather than through any irreconcilable ideas about necessary baggage under the circumstances – anyhow, Guido was thinking, it was high time to put an end to the argument. Since his witty outburst hadn't succeeded in cheering up his partner, he went straight to the point.

'We agree on so few things,' he said. 'We're completely different. How can we love each other?'

Vanna melted at once: 'I love you *because* you're another person,' she explained. 'If you were me, how should I love you?'

Guido tried to clarify matters.

'You talk in extreme terms about equality and freedom – between sexes, classes and races. How do you work it so that people's differences can also be fairly respected?'

'If every human being were born identical,' Vanna said, 'there'd be no need to fight for equality. Love, though, is a freedom we must take, because men and women aren't by nature made to understand one another.'

'Do you think they'll succeed one day, anyhow?'

'They already listen to each other when they've a mind to do so. It's not easy – this world is so noisy! And what's more intimidating than noise?'

He took her hand, more out of friendship than reconciliation as yet.

'I'm lucky to have met you,' he said. 'Sorry I've been so bad-tempered.'

Vanna smiled at last.

'You remember that American best-seller *Love Story*, which fed its readers rubbish like "Love is never having to say you're sorry"? Isn't it just the opposite, though – that one best understands what love is when one asks, or hears the other ask, forgiveness?'

'I don't know. More than anything it seems to me that loving is taking sides. Taking the side of the one you love, right or wrong. Not letting them be blamed, or even judged.'

'You move me, Guido. I'd thought love was a game to you.'

'What would be interesting about a game whose outcome one knew in advance?'

Vanna did not reply. They stayed silent a long time, but not because they were moody. They were both looking at the desert, that game they were approaching together without knowing what might transpire – loss or gain, enchantment or disillusion.

Though still so near the city whose life-style was familiar to them, they were already in a new world. After the crowded chaos of the suburbs, the Siwah road opened out into wide open spaces where the only rule was that of the void.

'Are you afraid?' Vanna asked, later.

'Not yet, but I certainly shall be,' Guido confessed. 'Or

rather, yes, I'm already scared. Quite simply, I'm only worried about the little things: problems on the road; breakdowns we might have; creatures that will sting us or eat our rations. That sort of trivia. I can't even imagine the main risks. What about you?'

'I've been assured that we can drive the whole way. We're both good drivers. All this sand shouldn't change the skins we're used to, not really.'

'Skins?'

'Don't you get the feeling of moving over a vast naked body?'

'A body of dunes with changing breasts? And the oasis we dream of will be its sunburnt pubic hair.'

Vanna smiled approval. She said: 'The sun's already in this valley we're passing through, but soon it'll dazzle us.'

'I'm afraid it will tire us, more than anything. I don't like tiring things. I live to a plan: plans are rarely tiring,' Guido joked.

'Be careful not to end up one day saying: "I lived according to plan and so never really lived".'

'Don't you yourself sometimes feel the need to go further than you do?' he asked.

'As of now, I'm probably there already. I sense I've travelled here before: maybe the desert is a journey into childhood.'

'Do you feel you're retracing your steps?' Guido asked, baffled.

'No, because walking backwards is pointless. But it sometimes happens that you do the same thing twice.'

'I don't see what you're getting at when you talk of a childhood journey. You grew up a long way from here.'

'I was thinking of a much older journey, the foetal voyage.

What did I do on entering the world? I switched from my mother to my father. I left a body I knew to look for the unknown, because I couldn't know who this gentleman was, the one I'd someday have to call father. Of course that didn't happen to me alone: every newborn child goes on this voyage. What worries me is the thought that I'm about to undertake it again.'

'When did you actually know your father?' Guido asked.

'When I lost him. I remember him as someone who left my life at the same time as he entered it.'

'The rediscovery you'll make of him in a few days' time won't, though, be repeating a former experience. Only now will you be experiencing what others experience as small children.'

'I'll take up that point where we left it: that's just why I get the impression of an advance into childhood.'

'What are you going to say to this rediscovered father? "You began me, you must complete me"?'

'That'd be naive. Anyone can start us off in life, but we alone can complete ourselves.'

'Don't be ungrateful: your inherited genes programmed you so you could talk . . . . '

'But *I* learned the languages I speak,' Vanna interrupted. 'I'm not being unfair, just trying to protect myself from this mania for belonging which stultifies us. We cling to our parents so much because we desperately hope to be *like* someone else – to be a particular type, with recognized duties and ready-made rights – and to enjoy fortunes less random than those of pure chance.'

She waved, cutting short the conversation as if it had become tiresome. Guido understood and kept quiet.

Hours passed. The sun was almost vertical above them. The road cracked as if badly baked. Stones and potholes forced Guido to grip the steering wheel tightly.

'I'm going too fast' he declared.

'I'll take over,' Vanna decided.

She drove in more relaxed style. They passed the rotting

carcass of a camel, and then the wreckage of an old truck. A few ruined shacks appeared in a hollow of the dunes, around what seemed to have been a well. It had obviously run dry long ago. No one lived there any more. Vanna stopped the car just the same.

'Better than nothing,' she concluded. 'Let's take a break.'

They looked for some shelter that was neither too dilapidated nor dirty, but none of the shanties (which stank of the droppings of scavenging birds) were bearable. They ended up making do with the burning shade flung onto the sand by a wall that seemed to be crumbling to dust by the minute.

'It'll hardly last till we've finished our siesta,' Vanna joked. 'Siesta!' Guido exclaimed indignantly. 'We've no time to spare.'

'We have to eat, anyway.'

They made short work of the thick sandwiches from the ice-box, drank their fill and almost simultaneously fell drowsing where they sat.

Guido awoke when his back hurt too much for him to continue dreaming. The groan he uttered as he got up did not even rouse Vanna from her uncomfortable doze.

'You don't intend spending the rest of the day here, do you?' he grumbled, shaking her.

'Oh it's not so bad,' she protested, yawning and stretching languourously. 'And everyone says it's very nice.'

'What is?'

'Making love on hot sand.'

'Are you kidding? With scorpions to add to the enjoyment!'

'Too bad, we'll say no more about it then!' Vanna said, pulling a face. 'Let's get back to our old jalopy.'

Guido licked his dry lips, complaining: 'Why didn't we just go straight to Siwah by plane?'

'Why?' she replied brightly. 'Because we're down to earth people, we know our way around. And because Nesrin left us no choice.'

'What's it got to do with that cretin? I didn't ask him to pay my fare.'

'Are you sure we'd have found a car to hire, out there?'

'Your father would have lent us one.'

'Go back to sleep,' she suggested, shrugging before concentrating once more on the driving.

He sighed a few times, now and again, and then lapsed into silence. An hour later he was just in time to warn her: 'Look out! The road forks.'

Vanna braked, stopped the car and consulted the map, her brow furrowed. After a moment she smiled.

'In the desert,' she said, 'two directions equal one. Our first mirage! There'll be more. The plane would have deprived you of that experience.'

All afternoon, in fact, they recurred. The illusions didn't vanish instantly, but retreated, faded, changed shape for as long as the travellers journeyed onward.

'Tomorrow,' Vanna informed him, 'we'll be crossing the Quattara depression, which is below sea-level. The heat of the sun there is really ferocious: we aren't through with mirages yet, not by a long chalk. You have to go across that place to learn just how to see.'

'Where'll we sleep tonight?'

'Under some real date-palms, at Abou Marzouk, provided we don't lose our way.'

But they did, and night fell without their reaching the expected village. They took this in their stride: they'd pick up the route again at daybreak.

Vanna refrained from pointing out that she had not been so wrong after all to pack sleeping bags, fill the thermos with hot coffee, and include extra food – all of which had prompted her companion's sarcasm at dawn. As one good turn deserves another, he in turn stifled any witticisms about his guide's talent for navigation.

After all, on the map Siwah was only 700 kilometres or so from Cairo and they'd already covered a third of that distance. On an Italian autostrada Guido's Lamborghini would of course have done the whole trip in a few hours, but if one must make comparisons, what daughter of the desert was capable of making love like Maika and Giulia?

That night he fucked them one after the other without Vanna's body – which he was using in order to make his reminiscences materialize – being so indiscreet as to utter any word that might have exorcized their presences. He did not know if Vanna herself recognized in him the man who was making her come or whether she too was silently exchanging mirages.

Next day they needed the rising sun in order to pick up the correct route. Vanna admitted that the skeletons of rash travellers were often discovered thousands of metres away from landmarks. The stupidity of people capable of wandering about lost in such simple, straightforward countryside made them laugh, however forced thier laughter. The desert is as dangerous as the sea, but when one manages to reach the shoreline one's previous fears seem ridiculous and shameful.

They both felt cold, despite the sleeping bags. They'd slept badly, neither being used to sleeping rough. Guido had spent hours listening to suspicious noises, rustlings, footsteps, prowlers' whispers and the hisses of imaginary reptiles. He told himself a hundred times it was a pity he was unarmed, and had sworn just as often to get up, grab the car jack or the spade and set up watch – but he never budged. Morning found him stiff, sheepish about his panicky obsessions and ready to take it out on his partner.

But she never gave him the opportunity. She also looked tired, yet she was calmly good-humoured. Whatever devilry goaded Guido into trying to pick a quarrel with her, he did not succeed.

The broiling they endured while passing through the arid depression did not make them any more talkative. At nightfall they passed a small tribe on camels, which must have been heading back towards Cyrenaica. Two other caravans crossed their path, then a packed lorry from which hands sprouted to wave at them. Guido thought they'd reached the outskirts of a village, but they soon found themselves as isolated and apparently cut off from life as they'd been minutes earlier.

That night they slept in the back of the car: watched over by vultures, and too tired to think of making love.

On the third day the trail seemed less tricky.

'We're getting closer,' Vanna declared.

'Sure, but to what?' Guido joked unsubtly.

Since their conversation the day before yesterday something had been intriguing him. He broached the subject again: 'If I recall your theory rightly,' he said, 'every metre bringing you nearer your father distances you from your mother. You're so close to her that that must hurt you . . . . '

'As you've seen in the desert,' Vanna answered, 'distance doesn't invariably blur images, often it brings them into better focus. As you know, too sharp a photo doesn't always make a good picture.'

'Am I to understand that seen from here, Mama Iñez doesn't seem so appealing to you?'

'A conversation with Nesrin the day he hired me, when you'd arrived in Cairo, gave me more insight than I'd ever had into the nature of my relationship with my parents: I admire them too much really to know them.'

'Did Nesrin make you realize that?'

'No. I understood it while listening to myself talking to him about them,' Vanna recollected.

'So you think that to know someone really well one mustn't love them too much?' Guido inquired.

'Not necessarily. That depends on what sort of love is meant. The love we have for our parents is bound up with our most primitive instincts: those of our common or subliminal memory, as the specialist has it.'

'I certainly wouldn't call it that,' Guido said reprovingly. 'But you aren't a specialist.'

'Not in pop biology, that's for sure.'

'Political biology, perhaps?'

'That wouldn't be such a bad idea. But what exactly do you dislike about your mother, since seeing her more objectively?'

'The snobbery and jargon of her profession.'

'It's in keeping with her science,' Guido said.

'The history of art isn't a science but a liturgy. A religion with priests but no believers. Its mumbo-jumbo doesn't enlighten, it stupefies. It's designed to hide the utter ignorance of its following. That's because in reality there is nothing to know or understand: all everyone has to do is sample it, listen, look.'

'And isn't your own profession, archaeology, a cult too?'

'For some people, yes, but not for me.'

'To you it's a game,' Guido teased her. 'But whether you like it or not, you belong to an elite, and an elite only knows how to play its own games. To the elite art like everything else is a sort of club, a club where occasionally one talks business. The artists are serving behind the bar.'

'Mafias proliferate, yet it's possible to remain outside them. All the same, it's true that even integrity can be a pose.'

'Everything is a pose,' Guido maintained. 'Everything

within society is a class pose. There are fashions in archaeology and art history, just as in haute couture. Or anything. And one only holds to the same aesthetic belief or the same disbelief in as far as one is rich or poor.'

'I don't show off a broken jar in the same way as one launches a miniskirt,' Vanna said animatedly. 'I make no choices for others. I don't claim to put myself in their shoes.'

'Education means teaching others to see,' Guido said. 'To see in a particular way, that is. Hence, partially.'

'But who told you I wanted to educate anybody?' Vanna exclaimed. 'The moment my mother thought she had to teach, I proved her wrong. Every pedagogue, even if only in aesthetics, tends towards absolutism. And thus to lies. For knowledge can only be relative.'

'Good and bad taste are not perceptions of the real. They are not part of knowledge. They do not reach us via a learning process in personal detachment. Nor are they imaginative exercises or discoveries. They are decisions taken for us by others. You won't change all that.'

'Yes I will, by not choosing.'

'Like it or not, you do choose. You're simply unaware of it, that's all. You select your broken jars in all good faith, just as you pick out the best-looking guys to fuck when your digs happen to take place at Adly's steam-room.'

'There Maika beat me to it, I grant you,' said Vanna.

'She? Because she prefers the upper crust to somewhat plainer fare? Don't make me laugh! There's no justice. Resign yourself to that.'

Vanna angrily shook the sand from her hair, proclaiming: 'I'm not resigned to what doesn't make sense. Everything unjust is insignificant.'

The Land Rover bumped over a ridge of sand the other side of which lay a garden of green. The cry of buzzards

130

heralded the strangers' arrival. A few steps from them, between the aloes, a young girl clad in white linen was walking along with a bundle balanced on her head. Her narrow face with its delicate nose, her skin darker than that of the Delta dwellers, and the large almond eyes, were stunning in their beauty.

To annoy Vanna, Guido addressed to the young girl the Castilian compliment that sprang to mind: *'Vaya mujer! Viva tu madre!'*

The girl certainly did not understand the words, but their implication was clear enough for her to respond with an uncomplicated peal of laughter. Guido read into this the moral which suited him: '*She* doesn't renounce her ancestry,' he observed.

'Each of us must live out his schizophrenia to the bitter end,' Vanna commented.

'Who seems crazier to you, that girl or yourself?'

'I am, because I want to be different from my mother. And she is, because she wants to resemble hers.'

'Your Iñez, however, didn't seem as though she conformed much to any norm.'

'To reject the customs and habits of one tribe in order to embrace those of another doesn't constitute a progress towards freedom,' Vanna said. 'Which is the more independent, the woman who shows her legs or the one who exposes her breasts? The woman who loves girls or the one who likes men? The one who swears by Aalto or the one who worships Gaudi?'

'Shouldn't one have preferences in anything, then?'

'Guido, what are you saying? You'll end up talking like me. If I dislike choosing, isn't that because I don't want to exclude anything? Not to deprive myself in advance, nor set myself moral limitations? How should I distinguish good from bad in this primitive cauldron of a world, or among those elements within myself? I'm neither witch nor prophetess. It's not always possible to stir up the brew and discern true and false. First I want to taste what's cooking. Sample it, revive myself.'

'Look at all this!' Guido shouted, suddenly overcome with schoolboyish enthusiasm. 'Poppies and daisies! And over there, poplars! An apricot grove! And figs and dates everywhere, of course. And so many olive trees we might be at Delphi! Yes, this is a country of oracles all right. Not surprising that Alexander the Great came here to consult the authority of his time.'

Vanna couldn't desist from qualifying:

'That was a political gesture. By acknowledging himself to be a son of Amon he wanted to please the Egyptians, but only to conquer them the easier. An act of piety prompted by the desire for power shouldn't move you so much Guido, not you, who always extol the emotions.'

'Everything in this world boils down to power. You obey it. What's more annoying is when one yields like your ancestors did to the Greeks – without realizing.'

Guido began quoting, as if talking to himself: ' *It wasn't an island but a wild beast sprawling on the sea . . . when you find freedom again, my lips will once more learn how to smile.* A poet's function is to rise up against power and make those who submit to it ashamed of their submission. But it's in vain. Kazantzakis wasn't afraid, yet nor did he hope.'

Vanna continued as if she hadn't heard Guido's interruption:

'This siren sister was actually a Siamese twin. A female body inside his own, from which he was never parted.'

'I like your way of remaking creation,' Guido said appreciatively. 'You'll end up converting me.'

Vanna still seemed not to hear, going on:

'Maybe you came to look for *her* at Siwah? That Siamese twin sister inside yourself?'

'Are we here?' inquired Guido.

'No,' said Vanna, looking at the white-hot sky without saying a word further.

They passed another cluster of palm trees and more rose-beds before Guido asked Vanna calmly: 'So this oasis isn't the one we were heading for?'

'The one we *are* heading for,' Vanna corrected him, 'we're still heading for. This is just one of its outposts. There's more than twelve of the olden leagues before we reach Sekhet-am.'

'What's that?'

'I'm using the ancient Egyptian name for Siwah: it simply means country of palms.'

'Where in fact are we?'

'At Djebel Muta,' Vanna replied. 'We must come back here to see the Ptolemaic and Roman tombs, likewise those east of Aghormi and the Ksar Roumi temple.'

'Christian or Roman fort?'

'You didn't tell me you knew Arabic!' Vanna said. 'Another secret!'

'Don't get any ideas, now! I only know what I picked up in the adventure stories of my childhood: *ksours* always featured in last-ditch stands, while a *Roumi* is someone, crusader or not, whom the faithful happily put to the scimitar. Let's hope they've lost the habit.'

'Who knows?' Vanna mused. 'Maybe you need a Caesarian to bring you fully into the world.'

'To whom are you referring, Vanna? Me or my Siamese twin sister?'

'You understand me so well, Guido! We're made to travel together.'

'Stop!'

'What?'

'Look!'

By the side of the track a somewhat androgynous deity kept watch from her sulphur-coloured sandstone niche. They descended to touch the hand worn smooth and warm

133

from twenty centuries of such contact. Vanna slowly deciphered the Greek inscription on the plinth: *Ye who come here seeking Amon, know that I am this God's mind.*

'My compliments,' Guido retorted. 'Well, sir or madam, lead us into your brain.'

'Leave that bit of stone to its memories.' Vanna said. 'We'll find our way on our own. Anyhow, we've already found it: no need to ask where the oasis of Siwah is any more, as we're right there.'

Sheep were trotting along beside them, A shepherd followed at a distance. Vanna hailed him but the man gazed indifferently at her and made no reply.

'First contact, first failure,' Guido observed.

'My voices betrayed me,' Vanna commented. 'I get the impression that not everyone in this region cottons on to Arabic. We'll have to try something else.'

Guido looked up at the arching palms overhead with a sudden warmth. Clearly he hadn't expected to feel so at ease in this place.

The first car passed, a rather aged American sedan with its windshield wipers missing. Moments later a second vehicle followed, in the same condition.

A group of peasants were walking along the track. They all had short black or grizzled beards which rèminded Guido of the ones Nikos and Nesrin sported. Some of them wore European clothes, others the traditional white handwoven robes with ankle-bracelets which Vanna raved about.

The travellers halted again to take a look at various tiny shrines along the dried mud walls. Scrawny dogs and long-legged cats came and sniffed at them. In clumps of trees at whose feet were hoses no one saw fit to turn off, they recognized hoopoes, kingfishers, quite sociable owls and falcons. They skirted ponds in which heron and ibis took up sculptural poses; fields of clover Vanna thought suspect, for these were the favourite terrain of snakes; maize plantations through which small donkeys freely wandered.

'No one here seems too worried about economizing or waste,' Guido said loudly.

'The wind is cool, as you can feel,' Vanna said. 'Cool and good. In this country, that means wealth. So who'd think of hoarding the wind?'

Suddenly they were facing twin hills, or rather rocks, which bulged from the luxuriant mass of palm trees like a dromedary's humps. In the cooler evening air appearing through a trick of perspective slightly larger, a sort of sandy-coloured fortress squatted between the twin mounds.

'Siwah-el-Kabir,' said Vanna.

'Hat-en-Shau,' Guido murmured, his voice betraying emotion despite himself.

'You're happy,' said Vanna, smiling at him. 'I'm pleased.'

They advanced towards the ancient wall. There was a control post beside the town gate.

'Our permits are going to be some use after all,' said Guido.

Vanna held out the documents to the officer, who'd seen the new arrivals from a long way off. He sauntered across to the car, finally, gave its occupants an easy-going glance and without so much as looking at the mass of papers proffered to him, waved them on.

'After all that!' Guido exclaimed. 'As easy as a Swiss frontier! If only we'd known, Nesrin Adly could have gone on his nude romp in the steam bath all on his lonesome.'

The streets were little more than alleys. Narrow and irregular, they would turn sharp right or left, without

135

rhyme or reason. The Land- Rover could hardly get through them.

Vanna indicated an arch across the street, upon which there was an ancient, solid single-storey house.

'Ponte del Rialto,' Guido recalled. 'Or the Ponte Vecchio at Florence.'

'Or Rome, Via Giulia,' Vanna added gently.

This architectural feature was repeated, and Guido remarked that it was far older than anything of similar style to be found in Italy. And more impressive, being higher and narrower.

'I like it,'Vanna confided. 'It's lovely.'

'What happened to your principles?' said Guido. 'I seem to remember your condemning aesthetic judgements as religiose and tyrannical.'

She simply laughed, pointing out minarets, sky-blue and gold domes, surbased arches and trefoil or decorated Gothic arcatures adorned with scrolls and knot-work, floral or geometric motifs, and patterned with strange characters picked out in wood and ivory which the sunset bathed in its warm glow.

'If as a little girl I could reach climax in a Christian church why should a Moslem shrine scare me off today? Or a temple of Amon?'

'This is a big town,' Guido said in astonishment. 'I was expecting a tiny little hole.'

In reality Siwah was only an extended village, casually sprawled upon its twin eminences and spilling over on to the hillside. Life there seemed to go on uncomplicatedly. The crowds were thick, not unsual in Egypt, and the strangers passing in their dust-caked vehicle aroused scarcely a token curiosity. The children did not even block their path or clamber over the Land Rover's bodywork. Small carts backed out of their way and into corners to let them pass. When animals stood obstinately in front of the car's bonnet their owner or a self-appointed guardian would waste no time hauling them aside. Rubbish from fruit and vegetable stalls was thrown into a stinking gutter set into the centre of the alley. Its effluvia mingled with the odour of pastries and sweet tea coming from the tiny cafes.

Nothing here, thought Guido, that you couldn't find anywhere else. The lamb some Bedouins were roasting over a brazier upon the pavement, that was a bit more exotic. But even though they were archaic boneshakers, the bicycles bumping into cows and mules, the old trucks shoving donkeys out of the way with their bumpers did not, any more than the pedestrians waiting at intersections, evoke a culture miraculously preserved in its primitive form and untouched by cross-breeding or modernization.

The same uninspiring second-hand impression greeted the travellers when they came face to face with a Victorian-style building whose two threadbare turrets flanked a small pillared façade at the top of a pretentious flight of *faux-marbre* steps: a folly carefully scaled down to a low budget and whose anonymous ugliness in the middle of this agricultural village filled one with dismay.

Gilt lettering informed the onlooker – in English – that this was Government House. Apparently no one had thought to replace this inscription with its Arabic equivalent, nor even to provide a translation.

'I'd have assumed Egyptian nationalism was more sensitive,' Guido remarked. Seemingly interested by this anomaly, he suggested an explanation: 'Maybe no one gives a damn about it, here.'

'Maybe,' said Vanna absently.

She was thinking that her father was sitting somewhere inside that awful building. Why go and hide there?

'Do you want to go and ring the bell?' said Guido.

'In this state?' she said at once.

She spread out her arms, looked down at her sandy

khaki slacks, and plucked at her sweat-soaked, creased shirt with distaste.

'You're really quite conventional, aren't you?' he teased.

She didn't answer, and they went on. There was only one main street in Siwah, which they knew led to the hotel. They weren't expecting anything too marvellous there, either. However, what they saw at the end of the road took their breath away. It was a sort of spa casino in late-Victorian colonial style, its plaster still white, and embellished with baroque gables, yet modestly proportioned and on just one floor, amid terraced gardens where geranium and chrysanthemum flowered between neatly-spaced fountains.

Was this then, the end of the trail? They alighted from their old vehicle, almost with shame, aware that they'd have been less out of place getting out of a tilbury and clad in lawn and serge.

Casting a glance at their filthy clothes they made half-hearted apologetic gestures for the benefit of the inscrutable flunkeys who had come for their luggage. Vanna felt momentarily embarrassed when they removed the cooker, sleeping bags and all the other camping paraphernalia she had packed. And what impression would all this ironmongery – picks, shovels and so forth – make in this rest-home for retired civil servants?

Five or six veteran limousines imported many years ago from America or Germany were parked alongside. One of them bore Saudi-Arabian plates as well as diplomatic ones.

'I'm sure I'll meet my good friend Zannipolo Gatto again here, sporting all his decorations,' Guido laughed. 'The place seems so popular.'

'Not with the Knights of Malta or the Holy Sepulchre,' Vanna returned. 'You can expect to be the only representative of Christianity in this castle.'

Guido shrugged.

'Rubbish!' he said. 'Watering places don't choose their customers. They come here as if to Montecatini. The Ministry buffoons have really conned us: the bit about permits is the hoax of the century.'

'Don't trust to appearances too much,' said Vanna. 'An oasis is still the desert, and this desert stretches from Persia to Atlantis. Perhaps that Mercedes in widow's weeds is just one more mirage.'

A bellboy arrived, his green and white uniform somewhat threadbare, and asked in very correct English: 'Would you like me to garage your car, sir?'

'Indeed I would,' said Guido. 'Make sure you give it a wash.'

'The keys please.'

Guido hestitated for a split second, then felt ashamed of his suspiciousness, and having curtly surrendered his keys, followed Vanna into Reception. As luck would have it, the foyer was decidedly more dusty than the outside might have led one to believe.

'Your rooms are ready. Kindly fill in these forms,' the receptionist said. 'In which room would Madame like her luggage?'

Guido turned to Vanna and said to her in French: 'Maybe we could dump all the stuff in one and share the other?'

'No!' she said sharply. 'I didn't come all this way to play Mr and Mrs.'

He was surprised by her tone and looked at her a little sadly.

'I didn't mean to offend you,' he began, 'just . . . .'

'Come on,' she interrupted him, 'I can't wait to have a bath.'

'We have running water all round the clock,' the receptionist boasted. He had switched from perfect English to immaculate French, doubtless hoping to please. Guido scowled, annoyed that their little argument had had such a witness.

'*Ci mandi una bottiglia di malt whisky, con due bicchieri ed un secchiello di ghiaccio,*' he requested, so as to confuse his adversary.

'*Certo, signore, subito!*' came the man's reply.

Guido waited until he was half-way up the staircase to mutter:

'*Vaffanculo!*'

The young man carrying his bag, right beside him, flashed doe eyes and a charm-laden smile at him.

'He thought your swearing was a sexual proposition,' Vanna teased, for by now she knew that much Italian at least. 'So why don't you do something about it, straight away? 'When in Siwah . . . .'

Guido flopped into the embroidered armchair in that enormous crystal-chandeliered room. The tips of his fingers and thumbs met in an academic (or vaginal) lozenge shape as he intoned in his best lecturer's voice:

'Among the *Sipunculus Nudus,* of the Sipunculid genus of marine worms, sometimes wrongly classed with the priapulid *Sipunculides* – since the union of genital and excretory apparata is a special feature of the deep-sea Priapulida, whose commonest species *Priapulus Caudatus* was recently discovered – the anus is placed next to the mouth. However, we have no indication as to how this arrangement has in any way encouraged the development of aquatic pederasty.'

2

Goddess Of Stone, God Of Dust

Inert and rigid as a mummy, Guido lay flat on his back, shoulders and nape sunk deep into the bed's soft pillow. He appeared to be sleeping, but his brain was functioning with speed and alertness and the precision of an electronic mechanism. He was examining, sifting and classifying the aural and visual information he had stored since crossing the oasis and the town.

The majority of the material relating to vegetation and architecture, after being studied and compared, was summarily rejected – unlike everything to do with the appearance and behaviour of living creatures, whether animal or human, which, by contrast, was carefully and clearly registered in his memory with nothing essential omitted.

Had anyone just then been able to draw upon that memory bank he or she would probably have marvelled at, or been awed by, the near-documentary precision with which Guido's senses, in just a few hours, had collected and filed an incredible variety of different data. The shepherd, the peasant, the shopkeepers, small boys, muleteers, truck-drivers, nomads, traffic police, hotel staff, chefs, waiters, diners, and all the curious idlers who had passed in front of the traveller's eyes, were here inventoried and ranged in assorted pigeon-holes by headings under which Vanna – who had also seen the same procession at the same time as Guido and with what she imagined was a similar vision – would have been astonished to rediscover them.

This motionless activity continued late into the night. The traveller, with eyes shut, gave no more indication of effort or fatigue than a machine would have done. The mental concentration he needed to sustain isolated him from his surroundings as surely as if he had stopped his ears with wax plugs.

So he did not hear the sounds which for a long time kept Vanna awake in the adjoining room: old ceilings cracking, doors banging, keys rattling, footsteps echoing, snatches of conversation in the corridors, assorted street-noises, insects humming, sleepers snoring, pacings up and down, sighs of orgasm, annoyance or unhappiness, the scuffle of rats. Though exhausted by the trip, she found herself far less comfortable on the hotel bed than she had been upon the hard desert sand.

Besides, her insomnia was the result of anxiety rather than of these external annoyances – an anxiety in which her father and her lover either alternately or simultaneously featured.

How would Selim react to Vanna's unexpected appearance? What would she do if he threw her out of his office as unceremoniously as he had rejected her from his life twenty-five years earlier? Perhaps he would be outraged that she had come to pester and disturb him even in this hide-out? He might consider such an intrusion indiscreet, hateful, presumptuous. And after all, she told herself, he could be right. The thought in no way reassured her.

As for Guido, how would he behave now that he had arrived here, where he'd wanted to go? Wouldn't he deem Vanna's mission accomplished? But whose fault was that? He didn't really need her: their relationship was only a convenient game. Would the game continue or would Guido move without warning to more serious matters?

What in fact were these serious matters? Vanna had

until now prided herself on not wanting to know. She had asked no questions of Nesrin nor of Guido himself.

She wasn't stupid enough to give credence to the absurd theory of an espionage operation. Real secret agents don't reveal themselves to be so intelligent even when they intend only some industrial espionage, illegal prospecting, or the tracing of suspected information leaks.

Through pure intuition rather than from any basis of concrete fact or special clues, she had certainly guessed that her companion was working for an oil company. But in what capacity? Detecting a deposit in a country like Egypt isn't entrusted to only one man, still less to an amateur. And it was quite obvious that where drilling and boring were concerned Guido wasn't much better informed than herself!

Even if he'd only come to reconnoitre, ahead of the true search party, in order to make contacts and test out the terrain, literally or figuratively, he would still have needed – if not instruments – maps, and basic documentation, or at the very least a list of addresses or acquaintances in the region. Now Vanna was positive, having herself packed her companion's luggage in Cairo – and God knew that baggage was lightweight enough! – that he possessed no technical apparatus at all. What Guido had confided and asked had also convinced her that he was keeping no professional secrets either in the capital or the Siwah area.

What unusual purpose then, could such a risky and unexpected way of going about things serve? Vanna could find no logical answer to this question.

She wound up wondering whether Guido wasn't after all simply what he said he was, a well paid holidaying bureaucrat who wanted to indulge some pretentious intellectual hobbyhorse: studying the history and customs of a people neither too obscure nor too savage, and from

143

whom, ultimately, there wasn't much of interest to learn.

Why couldn't he have set his sights on some bush tribe and had the guts to sleep in a tent? The most primitive discomfort would have pleased Vanna more than this stinking, smart-Alecking hotel! Just then somebody began knocking discreetly at her door in a series of faint taps.

After her initial reaction of exasperation, she smiled: Guido, of course! He had got over his resentment of being excluded from Vanna's bed and had come to set things to rights.

She was touched by that. Leaping out of bed, she went to open the connecting door to their rooms. But his room was deep in darkness. She heard the regular breathing of its occupant, who was not even stirring in his huge bed. She had no doubt that he was sleeping dreamless and undisturbed.

Disconcerted and disillusioned, she closed the shuttered door noiselessly and returned to her own room. The tapping began again. She realized now that it came from the door opening on to the corridor.

'Who's there?' she inquired, first in English, then Arabic.

There was no answer. After a few minutes the knocking started again. She was scared and thought of going to wake Guido, but her pride wouldn't let her. So she stayed sitting where she was, in bed, her arms around her drawn-up knees, and her eyes fixed upon the door. The taps continued to be audible at irregular intervals.

She reflected that if someone broke in and found her like that, naked, she would be more exposed than if she hid under the sheets. Yet she still did not move. Should she put something on? But what? She had no pyjamas or nightdress, and it seemed ridiculous to get dressed at that hour, as if going out.

Anyhow, she reasoned, the unknown would-be intruder

certainly didn't want to kill or steal: he wouldn't have made such a noise in the first place. He wanted to enjoy Vanna's body, that was all. No need to kick up such a fuss about it! The young woman's anxiety at once vanished as soon as she had decided to let herself be raped.

She fell asleep before she could muster enough energy to go and open the door.

Guido woke at seven, had a Turkish coffee sent up, and without wasting time or leaving Vanna any message, went into the town on foot.

He returned at noon. The receptionist – not the man of the previous evening and whose command of languages Guido did not this time test – informed him that Madame had just gone out. No, she had not said where she was going nor when she would return.

'If I'd known, I'd have lunched in an Arab bistro,' Guido complained, sitting down alone at table in the mock-Regency dining-room. He skimmed the menu peevishly, when a shadow fell across it. Guido looked up to see a not very tall man of perhaps forty, with a tendency both to plumpness and baldness, clean-shaven and with a pale brown complexion and a dimpled chin. He wore a freshly pressed silk suit, a mauve club tie with diagonal black and orange stripes, well-polished shoes, and carried in his manicured, silver-braceleted hand a thin cane with a tortoiseshell handle. He was staring at Guido, smiling shyly.

'Haven't I had the pleasure of meeting you in Cairo recently?' he asked, putting no more expression into this conventional formula than necessary.

The tone of his voice was sympathetic, courteous without obsequiousness. He spoke English with what might have been an Italian accent. Guido's look showing no recognition whatever, the stranger immediately confessed his embarrassment.

145

'I must have been mistaken. I do̅ apologize most sincerely.'

He bowed slightly. His short torso half turned, prior to making a decorous retreat, but Guido waved a magnanimous hand and stopped him in his tracks.

'Allow me to introduce myself,' the Egyptian continued. 'My name is Mehdi Yasserit. I am a teacher, currently employed in an administrative capacity by a Ministry.'

'Ah!' said Guido as if delighted to hear this. 'And are you here in an offical capacity?'

'Not at all! On holiday. As you yourself are, I take it, Mr – '

'Andreotti. Guido Andreotti. Engineer. But I occasionally go in for studying the history of civilizations – something of a hobby.'

'Time passes more quickly when one's interested in time past,' the holidaymaker – who for his part seemed in no hurry at all – declared.

'Why don't you sit down? Let's have lunch together.'

'I don't like to impose. Maybe you're expecting someone?'

'No, no one. Somebody's let me down, in order to rediscover her own past,' Guido said.

'Well then, I accept with pleasure.'

The newcomer sat down. They ordered identical meals and began eating. Mehdi Yasserit finally asked the first question:

'Have you been here long?'

'At Siwah? Since last night. And you?'

'Just arrived.'

'By road?'

'Oh no! Of course not. By air.' Yasserit seemed dismayed. 'There are weekly flights from Cairo out here. Did you know that?'

'No. I thought no one ever came here.'

'That's true,' Mehdi Yasserit said. 'I was the only one on board. As a passenger, I mean.'

He smiled at his own little joke.

'Is this your first visit to Siwah?' Guido asked.

'Of course not!' the man smiled again. 'I come here nearly every year.'

'Really? The place must appeal to you. What do you see in it?'

A further outburst of mirth.

'Nothing special, I grant you. But I find the climate agreeable and it does me good, I know of no other place more restful than Siwah. The salary one gets in Egypt doesn't, alas, allow one to travel too far afield,' he concluded somewhat apologetically.

'But you got to Italy, anyhow, I trust?' Guido asked.

'Yes. I don't speak your language well, though. Do you mind if I make you go on talking in English?'

'Not a bit. What do you do when you go to Italy? Rest up?' Guido said flippantly.

'Alas no! I've only ever been there on business. My brief consists of looking into the opportunities for study abroad offered to our young people: obtaining grants for them, that sort of thing. Unfortunately most of the time my superiors consider I can do this all too well by correspondence, without leaving Cairo. So I'm condemned to being largely deskbound – when I'd accepted the job because I thought it would give me plenty of scope for foreign travel!'

'There is a time for all things under the sun,' said Guido, slyly recalling Vanna's favourite quotation. 'A time for activity and for inactivity. Anyway, do you at least send many Siwah students abroad?'

Yasserit smiled again.

'The Egyptian intelligentsia isn't recruited here, you know!'

'No? Why not?' said Guido.

147

'That's not to imply that the Siwahs are less intellectually gifted than anyone else. Simply that they're not too concerned with what's going on elsewhere.'

'Even in Cairo?'

'Even there, to tell the truth.'

'To what do you attribute this indifference?'

'I don't know. To the good life, maybe. Here they have everything they need. This oasis is a fortunate region.'

'That's not the impression I get,' Guido contradicted him curtly. 'Even if so far I've only had a brief look in the streets and at all those shacks, it seems to me that your paradise isn't as perfect as you make out. There are just as many sick, crippled and blind here as in Cairo, just as many dirty, undernourished and rickety children.'

The other man didn't seem convinced, remarking:

'The soil is amazingly fertile, however. Aren't you struck by the abundance and variety of fruit and vegetables it produces? The cattle grazing on it? I'm staggered that you could have encountered half-starved children.'

'My dear sir, this oasis is by no means the only place in the world where the soil is rich and the inhabitants poor. Anyway, who owns the soil? I wouldn't mind betting that it belonged to a small monopoly of landowners. Naturally I didn't include *them* among the undernourished. I'm not even sure they'd be found here among the Siwahs. I can visualize them cooling off their paunches inside air-conditioned villas by the Nile.'

'Since you're interested in this problem, you must surely realize how greatly the necessity for agrarian reform weighs upon our government.'

'Far more than it weighs upon me personally, you can rest assured of that,' Guido said brusquely. 'What I was saying to you was only nit-picking on my part. If the Siwah are happy to let themselves be exploited, and get their kicks from feeding up landowners and bureaucrats, who am I to disillusion them? To each his own!'

The smiling Mehdi appeared a little put out.

'One must try not to worry too much. Life's too short,' he opined, greedily finishing off the plate of sugary sweetmeats they had been served after their tasteless *poulet au riz*. 'You and I are free to forget our professional cares and enjoy our vacations. And our hobbies!'

'I'm not sure my firm would send me out here again,' Guido said. 'I work for an oil company, you see.'

'Really!' Mehdi exclaimed. 'In that case I'm not surprised that the history of other civilizations is your pet subject.'

'I don't see the connection there.'

'Petroleum put paid to one civilization and has founded another,' Mehdi explained. 'It plays, where civilization's concerned, the role traditionally assigned to Providence: sometimes a blessing, sometimes a curse, yet always a perplexity. That's why it's held in reverence everywhere. Men prefer to have gods they can hate when human affairs go badly. Religion is a continuation of this war by other means.'

'You talk well,' Guido said. 'What do you teach when you're not administrating? Literature? Mass psychology? Metaphysics?'

'Logic,' said Mehdi.

'Well, well!'

Guido turned suddenly reflective. Mehdi let a moment or two pass before resuming the conversation.

'It'd be better if the secret of your own background didn't get out,' he said jokingly. 'Imagine the Siwahs' excitement if word got round that maybe there was oil under their old rock!'

'What harm would that do?' Guido said distantly. 'Are you scared they might blaspheme?'

'Is it charitable to give the poor false hopes?'

'What would you say if the Siwahs just didn't give a damn?'

Mehdi frowned sceptically, giving the impression also that he considered their last exchange no more than a good-humoured exercise in banter.

'Cigar?' he suggested.

'No thanks. I'm going back into town.'

'Won't you have a siesta?' Mehdi said, shocked.

'I sleep so little,' said Guido.

They parted company after an extended bout of handshaking.

'That fool's shown up just at the right moment,' the Italian told himself while trotting down the front stairs, 'I'll get him off his arse – and how!'

He plunged into a labyrinth of alleyways he had not explored earlier that morning. These streets were less thronged probably because of the time of day, although the heat was quite bearable.

He strolled around like a complacent tourist, wandering by all the stalls which gave him opportunities for bargaining. He picked up every worthless trifle that caught his eye, evincing as much interest as if it had been some museum piece. He embarked upon endless discussions with the merchants in the bazaar, who, to a far greater degree than expected, showed themselves skilled in pidgin-English or capable of jabbering fragments of French, Italian and even German.

Vanna, had she been there, would probably have had difficulty recognising her habitual companion – the snobbish idler – in this tireless, sociable stroller, so debonair and jovial, easy-going and evidently well-liked. Apparently all Guido had to do in order for the most repulsive tea-sellers to tell him their life-stories was crack one or two broad and preferably suggestive jokes.

His newfound conversation partners would also show hitherto unwonted enthusiasm when he suggested photographing them and their brood. But he didn't expend too much time or energy on exposures and focusing: doubtless trusting implicitly in the mechanism of the Olympus he had borrowed from Vanna.

After releasing the shutter for the fiftieth time that afternoon, he allowed himself a giggle which was nonetheless a little arrogant. He said to himself: 'I'd like to see the faces on those cops when they open up this contraption while I'm not around. Copying the photos I've taken is going to give them a headache!'

He hadn't even bothered to load the camera with any film.

Anyone who took it upon themselves to search through his possessions in his hotel room would get much the same surprise. Not only would they not find a tape-recorder or any other gadget which scientists – not to mention seekers of the exotic or putative special agents – usually carry, but they'd also wonder why this self-styled researcher had not brought along any sort of handwritten or printed document; no maps, guidebooks or tourist brochures; no diary, no dictionary, not even a novel .... How did he take notes? He had not a single notebook, pen, pencil or scrap of paper!

All they'd be able to lay their hands on when rifling his cases would be brand-new Gucci shirts, belts and scarves, trousers with the Valentino label, Battistoni shoes and silk briefs from Marina Lante della Rovere.

'Funny fucking spy we got here!' (Guido mimicked the investigators he could imagine.) 'Some illiterate sod with not even any equipment. Obviously those Wops don't hire their James Bonds for their brain-power!'

'Well lads, what do you expect?' he sighed. 'Times is hard. Even oil revenues ain't what they used to be.'

Amiably he ruffled the auburn mop of a street-urchin who was tugging at his trouser leg.

151

'And where do you want to take me, *piccino*?' he asked.

But the kid seemed to know no other language than that of smiles of invitation.

'Don't you mind getting arrested?' Guido said, astonished.

He followed the child, who charged on blithely, holding his hand. They reached a portico of old openwork wood, adorned with arabesques and flanked by tubs of white jasmine. This gateway led to a small room furnished with blue pottery, big round or octagonal trays of beaten copper and camel-saddles in lieu of seats.

The small child went through this room without stopping, then into a patio decorated with a stone-lobed mosaic basin, whose fountains freshened the dry air. Fruit trees, ornamental shrubs and rose arbours surrounded it. In a yard, tobacco leaves were drying in the sun.

There was a covered arcade on each side of this indoor garden, alternate black and white flagstones in each arch – or perhaps they were just very dark green, made of olivine. The columns with beautifully shaped, delicate and almost mannered shafts had been fashioned either from a scarlet porphyry or a clouded conchitic marble, which crumbled to the touch, and whose final disintegration could be measured in a matter of a few years. Yet this erosion, rather than the assurance of the ophite and obsidian capitals, contrived to give to the ensemble a mild and graceful quality like that of the Saracen palaces of Granada or the Franciscan cloister of Assissi.

The visitors traversed this secular ambulatory and entered a room the size of the first, but whose floor was carpeted and strewn with brocaded cushions and leather pouffes. A large red and green stucco-framed mirror disfigured one wall. Another wall boasted two very small ogive windows, between which was a whole array of jet and silver weapons and antique swords. The daylight their coloured glass admitted struggled fitfully with the meagre illumination of the strongly-scented oil lamps.

A draughtsboard with its pieces rested on a mother-of-pearl encrusted pedestal table. Guido also noticed great bronze vases, blue carafes and glasses, frayed silk shawls scattered around, and facing him in a dark corner, a life-size stone sculpture of a naked girl.

Her plaited hair formed a sort of helmet covering her ears and part of her cheeks and nape, but leaving her sloping shoulders bare. The delicate features, straight nose, slanting eyes, high cheekbones and half-smile playing about her fascinating lips, immediately revealed to Guido the legendary being's identity: only Karmem, Amon's immortal wife, could ever have been so beautiful. Guido had only once seen the superb effigy in gold-inlaid bronze, dating from the Libyan period and on show in the Louvre, but he had not forgotten it.

The torso he remembered was clothed not with draperies but precious metals. Far more impressive than all that richness, were this statue's tiny stone breasts, naked as real flesh. Her hard nipples seemed to have just been stroked, while Guido sensed that centuries of caresses had smoothed that flat, compliant stomach. To his amazement, however, a penis sprouted unmistakably from the lovingly detailed vulva. It was not an enlarged clitoris but a genuine male sex lacking only – who knew why? – the testicles. Though not erect, its length was such, even detumescent, as to arouse latent desires.

A tall, thin old man in a turban entered the room. His black face was creased with deep wrinkles; his green eyes were watery; his bearing dignified and weary. He wore a close-fitting ankle-length damask robe. He offered Guido some *raki* and the stem of a *chibouk*. Then in a barely audible voice he asked whether by the grace of God the visitor spoke French.

At Guido's nod of acquiescence, the African (doubtless

of decayed imperial lineage) asked him how he was fixed.

'Fixed for what?' Guido wondered.

But he made sure it wasn't aloud. He confined himself to a facial expression implying polite uncertainty.

His host gestured towards his pocket. Guido produced his wallet and showed him its contents. The old fellow took the wad of notes, counted it several times extracting just under half of it and replacing the rest. He returned it to the stranger, who thanked him. The master of the house then bowed elegantly and left Guido and his little guide.

'What do you think he'll offer me, at that price?' the Italian gaily asked the boy. 'Do you reckon I can carry off the goddess?'

As nothing happened during the next ten minutes, Guido began to nurture a suspicion which jolted him from the torpor into which he had sunk: 'Hey,' he said to his companion, 'I hope the old fogey wasn't selling *you*!'

The tapestry concealing a door set in another wall was pushed aside and two young men appeared, both barefoot, and both wearing spotless long white linen tunics. Chain necklaces encircled their necks and their brows were adorned with fresh flowers. Guido, examining their outfits, decided they were like those of youths about to participate in the Panathenea.

How old were they? Fifteen or sixteen, maybe younger. How could one be sure, when even their sex seemed indeterminate? Their hair was curly, their skin almost white, their teeth clean and dazzling, their hands delicate. Heavy kohl-emphasised eyelids and lashes hooded their great lustrous brown eyes.

One of them sat down on a cushion, displaying silver anklets. The other poured the contents of a carafe into a glass and offered the drink to Guido: it had a darkish golden colour.

Guido let the liquid touch his lips before returning it

154

with a gourmet's headshake. The slightly bitter flavour of almond he distinguished amid the wine and honey didn't fool him: he guessed it was some little-known aphrodisiac, not too wonderful at that. As he gave back his glass to the Ganymede he indicated that the latter should himself drink.

The ephebe smiled, calmly swallowing half the mixture, then took the rest over to his acolyte, who drained it without batting an eyelid.

'Well, now things might get moving,' Guido commented.

His companions were not, however, as talkative or multilingual as their protector. They therefore confined themselves to winks and nods, grimaces and coy licking of their red lips, wriggling their hips and waving hands winsomely.

'It's enough to give a corpse a hard-on,' Guido said.

But he himself remained unaffected. When these desert sodomites tried to undress him, he made it clear firmly but pleasantly that it was up to them to provide the show, not to him to participate in it.

They didn't need asking twice. The next minute they were locked in a wild embrace, kissing each other's mouths with such fervour that Guido had to conclude that his invitation had cured them of a complex long-suppressed. Gradually their pepla became hitched up around their waists.

Guido regretted not having explored the beautiful labia of Karmem. Anyhow, whether or not it was the effect of the potion, the erect pricks now visible were no phoneys.

'*Mamma mia!*' he marvelled. '*Que cazzi di monstra!*'

He consulted the little kid, who had not let go of his hand, and was not missing a moment of the show.

'You're obviously well-educated – do you think they borrowed those from the museum?'

But the museum pieces were proved beyond doubt to be natural rather than artificial when they engaged in the fray. First the participants indulged in separate manustupration, with a zeal Guido considered excessive.

'*Calma, ragazzi, calma!*' he admonished them. 'Or you'll do yourselves an injury.'

But the adolescents were made of sterner stuff. When sufficiently self-stimulated they mutually masturbated – hands and mouths were employed simultaneously and without a moment's pause. After a good ten minutes' worth of this posture, Guido began getting bored.

'This tired old soixante-neuf's lasted long enough. Let's move on to the next trick,' he intervened.

Probably guessing the tenor of his complaint from long-practised artistic intuition, the two actors at once changed position. One knelt on all fours, his buttocks spread and trembling.

'Very sweet,' Guido adjudged. 'For two pins, I'd almost bugger you myself.'

The other youth it was, however, who put the project into practice, having first lubricated his comrade's arse with saliva. His gigantic prick buried itself into the proffered aperture as if it had been a soft rubber glove or an open door.

'Practice is everything!' Guido exulted. 'Nothing's impossible – just that organs rust from lack of exercise. Of course, I'm referring to the world in general – here we're right in the thick of vulgar particularity.'

Such a long speech couldn't fail to impress his urchin guide, who acknowledged it with an adoring laugh which quite won Guido over.

'If I'd conceived you myself,' he averred, 'I couldn't have done better. But probably we wouldn't have understood each other so well.'

In the meantime, the active one was buggering his

passive partner with the same reckless savagery with which he had previously masturbated.

'These kids are crazy!' the Italian said in alarm. 'Take it easy, for fuck's sake!'

The musicians did not slow down the rhythm of their duet, so Guido undertook the role of conductor: 'Watch it! First a nice *decrescendo*. Fine. Now let's go back to the beginning. There, like that. *Legato*. Excellent! Let's start with an *andante*, preferably *cantabile*. Right! Did you hear what I said? *Andantino*, I said. Good, carry on, but *moderato*. With feeling, that's it, yes: *adagio*. Keep going, *lento, maestoso, dolce*. Nice deep bass, soft and deep, soulfully now. *Piano, pianissimo* even . . . . '

He sense that the piece was nearing its end.

'I'm the conductor, I have to direct them,' he explained to his coadjutor, accelerating the rhythm. 'Come on then, *presto*. *Forte*. Come on darlings *con moto*! And for the coda, before the final *staccato, allegro ma non troppo, a scherzo brillante, brillantissimo*!'

The artist ejaculated with the cry of a slaughtered mule. For a moment he remained inert, skewered to his partner. Then the latter shook himself, heaving him off his buttocks.

The roles were promptly reversed: the youth who had just come adopted the posture which the other, who was still erect, had just abandoned. The new penetration took place as easily and with as much agility as the original one. This second bout displayed the same endurance and verve. The style, however, was even more sensual: it was clear that the sodomist really enjoyed sex. That much was obvious from his face and the hissing noise he was making. His colleague, no doubt quite emotionally drained from having come so copiously moments earlier, contented himself with a frozen smile.

Solicitous to revive him, Guido motioned to him that perhaps a direct swig from that fountain soon to spurt forth, might give him renewed impetus. The boy didn't understand and, probably thinking that the spectator wished to join in (and in this particular fashion), opened his mouth wide and stayed thus, eyes closed and saliva dribbling gradually from his lips, while the other – whom Guido's interruption hadn't enlightened either – persevered to perform a spectacular finale.

'*Bravo ragazzo!*' Guido congratulated him. 'Well played.'

The instrumentalist had now put his flute away, almost as imperturbably as at the start of the interpretation. After coolly accepting a generous tip the two young men rearranged their womens' clothes and gracefully bowed out.

'Did you enjoy that?' Guido asked the kid as they crossed the flower-strewn room. 'When are you going to start doing it yourself? You already look quite knowing to me.'

The little brat clung on to Guido's legs with apparently genuine affection.

'As for me, old chap, I'm past it, unfortunately. I didn't learn early enough. If you don't start young enough, you never really get the hang of it later. Believe me, you're listening to an expert.'

A melancholy Guido ruffled the brown curls of the child now watching him excitedly. He concluded: 'That's why I advise you not to wait too long before you do learn. High time you got going, little mouse. Otherwise you'll become a stupid bastard like everyone else.'

'Did you see your father?' he asked Vanna when he saw her at dinner time. 'What happened?'

She made a vague gesture whose significance was impossible to interpret.

'Oh, it was OK,' she replied. 'What happened to you?'

'I didn't see many women about. And the little I did see of those who ventured outside was squeezed into those nasal masks unsuited to optical liaisons.'

'You should have explained to them that g-strings give you hay fever.'

'Women's Lib doesn't seem to be getting very far in your hidden paradise,' Guido observed.

'No more than anywhere else in the world.'

'So where's the well-known sexual freedom of the Siwahs?'

'In the only two areas which have previously been forbidden almost everywhere – homosexuality and incest.'

'And what about the other areas?'

'There Koranic Law prevails,' Vanna said.

Guido interrupted their conversation to signal to Mehdi Yasserit that he should join them.

'Who's he?' said Vanna, surprised.

'An epistemologist,' said Guido.

'Well really, you can see it all here, at Siwah!' she smiled.

After making the introductions and inviting the guest to sit down (he didn't need asking twice) Guido said to him: 'What do you think? My friend maintains that in this oasis Muslim Orthodoxy generally holds sway. I'd thought myself that it was distinguished from the rest of Egypt by a moral and personal emancipation of which modern nations ought to be envious.'

'Here's a quotation,' said Mehdi. "Every innovation without a religious basis is an aberration which must be resisted and suppressed by every means possible. The unchangeable freshness of the Revelation can timelessly embrace and include all new facts". End of quotation. Wherever such convictions predominate, there can be no alternative to *Chariah,* the Islamic Law.'

'Do you agree with that?' Guido asked.

'Not at all. The sentiments are those of my late colleague, Professor Hassan El Banna of Ismailia, who in 1929 founded the Muslim Brotherhood.'

'Do you belong to the movement?'

'Good God no!' exclaimed the Egyptian.

'Then why do you quote its tenets?'

'So you'd be aware of the inner contradictions of an Egypt which must, willy-nilly, become a contemporary nation.'

'But Siwah wants to remain timeless!' Vanna affirmed.

'I don't know what Siwah wants, if indeed it wants anything!' Mehdi sighed. 'I just wonder how some people decided what's best for a small minority.'

Vanna looked annoyed.

'Maybe you haven't too high an opinion of what women think?'

'On that subject,' Guido cut in, 'I was surprised (at first sight, that is) to find that here women don't seem to enjoy any higher status than they do elsewhere in Egypt.'

'How should they gain that?' said Mehdi. 'With the help of Amon? Do you think that our Antiquity held mothers, sisters, wives and daughters in any more esteem than Islam does now?'

'Certain traditions would have us believe it.'

'How do you distinguish tradition from legend?' retorted the logician.

'Why should the people of Siwah show such a curious devotion to an otherwise forgotten cult,' Guido argued, 'unless the past didn't seem to them better than the present?'

'A mere cultural flirtation. To be different from their fellow-countrymen.'

'And why do they care so much about this sort of differentiation?' the Italian persevered.

'It's a common obsession.'

'Not so common as its opposite: everyone wanting to belong and be like everyone else.'

'Not everyone. There are rebels everywhere.'

'The Siwahs don't rebel. They're happy to think – or believe – themselves different,' Guido maintained.

'In your country too,' said Mehdi, 'people go along with illusory ideologies or obscurantist sects out of boredom with society.'

'Yes, but the Siwahs have behaved like drop-outs for two thousand years: it's this ongoing mental escapism that's intriguing.'

'Do you find it disquieting?' Mehdi enquired.

'Quite the contrary!' Guido declared. 'I think it's reassuring. Weren't we saying that the Siwahs never revolt?'

Mehdi finished his roast lamb in silence.

'I'm not sure your gods interest me,' Guido said, when Vanna suggested next morning taking him to Amon's temple.

'If you don't take a look at the gods, you won't be able to see men plain.'

'I keep my eyes open as best I can. Is it my fault if I don't see double?'

'No one is barred from make-believe,' Vanna said.

'I know myths and rituals exist. Is that reason enough for me to believe in ghosts?'

'Yet those who do are your fellow-men,' Vanna reminded him. 'Religion wouldn't exist if there were no unhappiness.'

Guido was silent for a moment, then said: 'Criticism of religion still remains the precondition for all criticism.'

'I'm goind to surprise you now,' said Vanna. 'The furthest-out thought doesn't scare me, because I know that the origin of all things is matter alone.'

'Which proposition do you prefer?' Guido asked. 'That

resemblances are the differences of which one is unaware, or, that differences are unconscious resemblances?'

'Neither. They're both true.'

Aghormi is at most two miles from Siwah-el-Kabir. Once it boasted colonnades, a forum, temples, a courthouse, houses with patios, paved streets. Today all that is left of the walls of ancient Ammonium, Amon's city, is mostly dust.

At Oumm Beda there's scarcely a trace of what was once a temple dating from the fourth century BC, but Amon's sanctuary is a few feet from it.

Had the visitors expected (which they did not) a monument rivalling in grandeur and splendour those of Karnak, where Amon was also worshipped, they'd have been very disappointed.

A hotchpotch of previous restorations and recent reconstruction work have disfigured the site as much as age, demolitions and neglect. Vanna and Guido searched in vain for the pathway with the ram-headed sphinx which should have led them to the enclosure made of local brick. The latter had in any case been reinforced with cement, which itself had crumbled. What remained of the pylon, surrounded by slabs of masonry shaped like smaller, truncated pyramids was not flanked by any colossal statue. Depicted everywhere upon it were faded, painted representations of mythology: bulls, cows, oryx, horses, dogs, trees and – usually in profile – potentates with *pschents* on their heads, holding in one hand a figleaf shaped spear and in the other, by its handle, the *ankh* of immortality. But the hieroglyphics, hieratic symbols and more recent demotic inscriptions which had been carved round them had mostly been obliterated or rendered illegible by vandals' graffiti.

Such columns of the hypostyle as were still standing were no more impressive than those of Government

House at Siwah. In the empty sanctuary, artificial flowers (in a region so florid!), faded pennants and some shoddy decorations were the sole offerings upon the altar.

The *naos* was closed, but Vanna knew there was only a cracked statue inside. The original likeness of the God had long since been placed in safe keeping, somewhere overseas .... In an adjoining room the only authentic thing was the portable float upon which the divinity stood when on display, taking the air.

Which was what Guido and Vanna did too: outside, they could imagine more easily the pleasant vista the idol must have faced. Silver-leaved olive trees would have been growing there. Mulberry trees, in those days, would have been full of birds. For generations orange groves blossomed.

But nature alone seemed to remember the god. Men and wealth had long ago been given over to other masters.

'The days of Amon's opulence are well and truly over,' said Vanna. 'Did you know his possessions exceeded those of Pharaoh himself? Acres of land, flocks, vineyards, quarries, mines. Maybe having oil would be some consolation to him.'

'Of course, if he's enough of an Arab.'

'Amon is a modern god,' she reminded him. 'He only goes back about two thousand years before Christ. Compared to the six or seven thousand years of Horus, Neter Nefer, the handsome god of youth.'

'That's probably why Hatshepsout liked him so much,' Guido recalled indulgently.

'It's largely thanks to her that he became king of the gods,' Vanna said.

'So she wasn't such a slut as you make out!'

'Yet your Romans did all they could to kill my Amon and his religion. But that hasn't prevented its survival, as you see.'

'I don't see anything at all. Where are the faithful?'

'An Egyptian temple isn't intended for a public,' Vanna informed him. 'Except for the externals, and a few specific ceremonies. Its daily functions are the preserve of the clergy. The priests' job is to make sure the god is happy: flattered by the pleasant chanting, well looked after, clad, washed, perfumed and, of course, protected from sickness and change.'

'To sum up, the gods are like us: though wanting for nothing, they ended up by dying.'

'There are no more priests here than believers,' Guido pursued. 'Would that explain why your Amon has retained a sort of life?'

'Perhaps it's just not the time for worship. The important thing, for Egyptian priests as for others, I guess, has always been to carry out the rituals punctually. Here, though, in order to be sure of being precisely on time, they had people whose special task it was to watch the stars and thence calculate their mathematical piety. Today they're called horologists.'

'We're definitely indebted to them for the valuable institution of the horoscope.'

'Not to the ones from my country,' Vanna corrected him. 'Egyptian civilization didn't hold with astrology. At least not until that superstition was forced upon it by the Greco-Roman conquest. So once again, I'm right in holding you responsible for cretinizing my ancestry.'

'Don't let's exaggerate,' Gudio said. 'Your ancestors hadn't time to consult the stars because they were too busy interpreting dreams. It was they, not the Romans, who enriched the world's cultural heritage with the first key to dreams. We're quits.'

'What I like about them is the significance they attached to names. Everyone *was* what his name meant.'

'What would they think of me if they saw that I let a woman guide me?' Guido joked.

'They'd be magnanimous enough to think that you want

164

to follow me on the path to the two virtues they valued above all others: justice and righteousness.'

'Aren't you, with hindsight, rating them rather too highly?' Guido said doubtfully.

'Then read *The Book of the Dead* and think about the section on *Judgement of the Heart.* When the king was presented by Anubis before the tribunal of the after-world, presided over by Osiris, assisted by Isis, Nephitys, Râ and forty-two assessors, his heart was placed on a pair of scales. Who stood on the scale – who but my dear Maât, representing Justice and Truth?'

Guido smiled conspiratorially at her. She went on, glassy-eyed, as if visualizing the scene as a memory: 'The ibis-headed god Thoth was in charge of the scales. If the scales tilted towards evil, a hybrid monster, the Great Devourer, would rip the lying King to pieces.'

'Why lying?' Guido wondered.

'Because he had previously sworn the "declaration of innocence" which goes like this:

> I have committed no iniquity against men.
> I have wrought no evil.
> I have not raised my hand against the lowly.
> I have deprived none of food.
> I have made none weep.
> I have not killed.'

Moved by the tone of Vanna's voice, Guido looked at her. The young woman's eyes were filled with tears.

3

Taha And Ilytis

A message from Mehdi Yasserit awaited Guido and Vanna at their hotel. The vacationing teacher had invited them to tea at the home of a local resident whom he knew from an earlier stay. A taxi would collect and drive them to his house.

They were amazed to see many guests there, formally dressed: they'd been expecting a smaller, informal affair. Mehdi Yasserit came over to enlighten them: 'I wanted to surprise you. Today my friend's son is getting married. I thought you'd like to come, but if I'd told you about it in advance you might have been embarrassed or reluctant to do so.'

Such tact was disarming. Guido wanted to know, however, why many of the guests looked more European than African. Mehdi seemed at a loss for words and it was Vanna who replied: 'For the same reasons that I'm of mixed blood. The only way the Siwahs differ from myself is that they didn't need to look for the white half of their origins: that part was right here, without being imported or invited. Persian warriors, Greek heroes, Macedonian troopers, Roman legionaries, French crusaders, Napoleon's Old Guardsmen, Hitler's soldiers, worked away, come what may, to create a new race. Did you know that the oasis of Siwah was a refuelling base for the Afrika Korps during the last war?'

'Refuelling? Of course!' Guido said delightedly. 'But

there was no oracle left to warn Rommel of his impending defeat.'

'Anyone can predict a conqueror's end just as certainly as a soothsayer,' Vanna moralized.

'I'm just as ill-qualified in one capacity as the other,' said Guido, whose good humour was well and truly in evidence. 'My freaky brain is as incapable of conquest as it is of divination. So the future doesn't worry me.'

Various strangers who had been shamelessly eavesdropping, clearly and jovially approved. Nobody seemed particularly interested in the ceremony being prepared. The huge garden round which everyone aimlessly circulated brought to mind many another garden party: the gaudy outfits of some of the guests were more appropriate to the Borromean Islands than Egypt. Amid multi-coloured plants and trees, almonds in blossom, miniature palms, giant cacti, bougainvillaea and oleander, whose profusion seemed slightly too calculated, Guido didn't feel quite so disorientated. He had to remind himself that he wasn't back home.

'I haven't the least idea of what Moslem marriage rituals are like,' he murmured.

'Well, at last you'll have the chance to learn,' Vanna joked.

'Only up to a point,' Mehdi cut in. 'Our friends are good Moslems of course, as we all are. But there are some influential organizations hereabouts which still adhere to customs that predate Islam. Our conversation yesterday Mr Andreotti, led me to think that you'd be interested in taking a look at some of these curiosities. That's why I saw fit to get you invited here today.'

'Dear Mehdi, how sweet of you,' said Guido.

The teacher didn't know what to make of such unexpected familiarity. He himself remained extremely formal.

'Look, here's our host,' he said. 'Do you want me to introduce you?'

'Of course!' Guido confirmed.

They made their way towards a group of men in djellabas of white or blue and often richly embroidered in silver and gold, who were engaged in the serious business of choosing from the sweetmeats arrayed on a long table. The youngest of them offered the two men glasses of a thick steaming tea, before Mehdi had a chance to say anything. A scent of sugary mint rose from the liquid.

Yasserit introduced everyone and thus Guido learned that the man who had given them the tea was their host and that his name was Khaled Ayaddin.

His lips were thick and his nose hooked, but his skin was pale. Streaks of clay heightened this pallor, serving as a kind of facial make-up.

'These are emblems of my status today,' he explained. 'Here a father who is marrying off his son plays a more important role than the bridegroom himself.'

He burst out laughing, hoisting folds of his impressive woollen burnous across his shoulders for comfort. Guido expressed surprise that he who was so young could have a son of marriageable age. Once again their host laughed freely.

'I have five children,' he said. 'Taha, the one getting married today, is the eldest. He's twenty one. The youngest was born last year.'

Guido was about to ask him where their mother was, but he realised in time that no women were to be seen and that Vanna too, when he looked around for her, had disappeared. But on reflection the stranger reckoned he could enquire about the reason for this collective absence without seeming rude.

'They're all busy preparing the bride,' explained Khaled, nonchalant and imperturbable as ever. 'It's quite a business! You'll realize why when you see her.'

'What about the bridegroom?'

'He's with his friends, having a last drink.'

'Just like we do,' Guido said. 'You have a stag-party till the last minute.'

'After which, farewell to freedom!' joked Khaled.

'For women especially, eh?' Guido remarked.

The host was obviously amused.

'I haven't travelled much,' he said, 'but I know we're really all alike, Siwahs or Christians. We have rules, but who sticks to those?'

'In our country we can bend them,' Guido told him. 'Once adultery meant prison, if not the stake. Now it's taken to be an obligatory corollary of marriage.'

'For both sexes?'

'Practically speaking, yes. Isn't it here?'

'Here, being unfaithful to one's husband with another man, or one's wife with another woman, is always frowned upon. But no wife objects to her husband making love with boys. And what husband would dream of forbidding his wife to have sex with other women?'

'Don't such relationships cause people pain?'

'That'd be the limit!' Khaled laughed. 'Were they invented for that?'

'So there's no jealousy?'

'No one's ever jealous here. Only preferences exist.'

'What do people think about love, then?' Guido said.

'What we hear in songs and from public storytellers. For the literate, whatever ideas they glean from novels. Also, for some time there's been a cinema in town. So love has come to mean, for the majority of us, what we see at the movies.'

Guido let things simmer for a while before taking up the conversation again.

'And politics?'

'Politics?' Khaled repeated, flabbergasted.

'Yes. How do you view politics?'

'Not at all,' said the Siwah, laughing again. 'Who bothers?'

'There's a government in Cairo and a governor at Siwah,' Guido reminded him.

'So?'

'You have to take them into consideration.'

'Why?'

It was Guido's turn to smile.

'Oh, I don't know. To ask a favour or get a law passed, for instance. To obey or disobey them, accept or refuse them. Anyhow to know their wishes, limits and capacities.'

His host slapped him on the back almost hard enough to fracture a clavicle.

'Strangers' jokes aren't always very easy to understand,' he admitted. 'But that one really is quite excellent!'

A large black Austin, at least fifteen years old, pulled up outside the garden gateway. The chauffeur got out casually to open the rear door.

A man in a white linen suit alighted with the cautious air of someone with rheumatic problems. He was above average height and very thin, almost emaciated. His face was lined with deep furrows. He had close-cropped greying hair and aquiline, dark-eyed features that betrayed his Arab blood. Standing fully erect he gave the impression of a haughty, even imperious, nature.

He gazed coldly at the assembled company, no doubt looking for Khaled. When he had spotted him he walked over unhurriedly to shake his hand. Taha's father shook hands without displaying any special deference. The other guests did not give the newcomer a second glance.

Guido still suspected that the latter was someone of importance. He sought out Mehdi for information about him, but Yasserit had momentarily disappeared into the

170

crowd. So Guido buttonholed a young man to whom he had talked earlier, remembering that he understood English.

'Who's that gentleman?' he asked.

The young man took a look, hesitated a moment, then decided: 'Ah yes, I think that's the governor.'

'The governor of Siwah?'

'Of course!'

'Why isn't anyone bothering with him?'

The young man stared at Guido in amazement.

'Do you think he needs something?' he said anxiously.

'That's not what I meant. Almost everywhere else in the world somebody in his position, of his rank, would be surrounded by people. People would be honoured and eager to speak to him. They'd take advantage of catching him in person in order to make some request or ask a favour – that sort of thing.'

'Really?' said the man, looking at Guido as if he were crazy.

The Italian was not a whit disconcerted.

'Isn't he respected?' he pursued.

'Why shouldn't he be?' the man protested. 'He's certainly respectable.'

'He's not feared, anyway.'

'Should he be?' the other said, astonished.

'If only for the power he embodies,' Guido said.

The young man had obviously started to get bored, so Guido let him go.

The governor slowly circulated from group to group, shaking hands or exchanging a few words here and there. Most of the time no one went out of their way to greet him nor to interrupt a conversation when he approached.

On the face of it, the man himself did not consider such indifference a breach of protocol. His own attitude showed that he was used to such behaviour, and that for his part he deemed it quite normal.

Guido watched him closely, resisting the impulse to go and hail the official. 'All in good time,' he told himself. 'Let's not rush.'

He tugged Mehdi's sleeve when he found him again. Yasserit might, if not pushed or badgered . . . .'

'Hello friend,' Guido said. 'Do you think you're here just to eat crystallised figs?'

As usual the Egyptian was undismayed.

'I do hope not!' he exclaimed. 'When the ceremony gets under way I expect they'll serve us a proper meal. Aubergine pâté, *mouloukhiah,* rabbit, spiced rice, locusts, lamb *au kourkoum,* chicken, candied quails, dune shrimp curry, fricasseed hearts, cactus fruit stuffed with fresh mint, agave shoots *vinaigrette,* rose pancakes, eglantine jelly . . . .'

'Pomegranates in ammonia, and acetylene tart,' Guido concluded. 'The best the country can offer, eh? One shouldn't dwell on its food shortage, right?'

'What can I tell you?' Mehdi sighed. 'You already know almost everything. And as you see, this place holds no mysteries.'

'I'm not interested in mysteries,' said Guido. 'Nor in what people think. I'd like to understand *how* they think.'

'Do as I do. Observe how our friends behave and draw your own conclusions from that. Wait a minute! I think you're going to get first-hand experience.'

There was a commotion somewhere in the house, punctuated with cackles and cries of laughter.

'You'll soon have the opportunity of seeing married-couples-to-be and how they become married,' Mehdi announced.

'Almost everywhere else it's the bride's parents who

172

throw parties of this sort,' Guido remarked. 'How is it that the custom's different here?'

But his question was lost in the pandemonium which broke out amid the crowd.

At the same time a group of women came out of the house, in what Guido guessed was a sympathetic panic. Vanna was among the first, easily distinguishable by the simplicity of her dress. Everyone else was decked out as if going to a dance: lots of pink, blue, yellow, and grey muslin, and far too many sashes and trinkets. None of them, young or old, hid their faces behind the Islamic veil.

The number of old women set him thinking about younger ones. And looking at the ugly ones made him think of the beauties. After a quick inspection Guido honestly didn't see a single one there he could fancy. You could see why, he told himself, the Siwahs were homosexual!

He wanted to tax the indispensible Mehdi with this, but the latter seemed so genuinely delighted by what he saw that Guido couldn't bring himself to spoil his pleasure. The buzz of excitement turned to clamour. At the same time an orchestra situated in a honeysuckle arbour and hitherto inaudible, burst into a cloying melody. Guido tried to make out which of the half-dozen bandsmen was responsible for the most plaintive tones he was hearing, but he couldn't easily see. It seemed to be a mixture of flutes, stringed instruments like violins, and xylophones accompanied by small bells and cymbals.

He had no more luck even when standing on tiptoe and trying to get a glimpse of the heroine of the festival. Her companions surrounded her in an impenetrable circle. He then tried to rejoin Vanna, a task only accomplished by much shoving and some trampling upon feet. She seemed glad to see him again.

'What were you doing in the gynaeceum?' he said curtly. 'None of these houris is worth your attention.'

She smiled enigmatically, claiming without too much conviction:

'The little one isn't at all bad, wait and see.'

'Which little one?'

'The bride. She's only fifteen.'

Vanna craned her neck to catch a glimpse of the bride. The latter only emerged from the swarm of her attendants when pulled aloft on to a small dais in the middle of the garden, strewn with garlands of flowers. The musicians at once played even more poignantly. Guido resorted to further unembarrassed shoving in order to work his way to the front row, hauling Vanna along in his wake. The young girl was, he had to agree, very pretty, and her dress still more so. At the same time he understood why the two dudes who had regaled him the other night with their sodomistic prowess had been wearing robes that suited them so well: they were wedding-dresses!

'Does everyone in Egypt wear those for weddings?'

'No,' Vanna told him. 'It's the style here at Siwah.'

'The ancient style?'

'You guessed it.'

But as they soon discovered, the fine sleeveless pleated white tunic which covered the young girl's body from her shoulders down to her feet was actually only an undergarment. The bridesmaids began solemnly completing the outfit, publicly adorning her with a variety of ornaments which they took, piece by piece, from trays held by other assistants. There was something resembling a chasuble of gold thread, and a sort of crisscross strap which was fastened just beneath the bride's breasts, forcing them upward so that their outlines and erect little nipples were clearly visible.

Guido made clandestine amends for the coolness he had earlier shown. The swelling he felt in his loins belied the blasé expression with which he hypocritically persisted while looking up at the rostrum. Vanna wasn't fooled. Her fingers surreptitiously confirmed the phenomenon and her sly glance of complicity and approval quite won Guido over to the bride's cause.

The latter was just then spreading out her arms to allow her companions to fasten a belt around her waist. This belt was in the shape of a gold and enamel serpent, whose triangular head pointed down to, and covered, her pubis.

Guido's sex stirred at this juxtaposition.

Then the women set in place a huge necklace of engraved gold bands loosely linked. This amazing piece of jewellery was so large that its smallest circlet went round the young girl's neck while its widest and lowest one reached the tips of her breasts, falling over her shoulders and halfway down her bare arms.

The initial preparations completed, the bride's attendants set about arranging her black hair. They separated unequal locks, then plaited it with a dexterity which drew Guido's admiration. However, they still took a good half-hour to transform that once long and wild mane into such neat, well-trained braids that it resembled a great circular helmet.

Now it was beyond doubt: the image of the goddess, which Guido had so admired in the boys' brothel had just been recreated step by step right in front of his eyes.

The nubile girl was now as immobile and seemed scarcely more alive than her stone model. She too had become a work of art, even if her small face couldn't compete with the superhuman ideal incarnated by the wife of Amon, and if her body did not (as the realistic and resigned Guido assumed) match the monoecious perfection of a hermaphrodite sculpted by man.

As her preparation progressed, silence deepened among the assembled guests. The attention of those staring intently at this metamorphosis, together with a hypnotic sort of hymn music – nearer a requiem than a wedding-march – grew more and more absorbed, to the point of a quasi-religious contemplation. When the idol of flesh and gems was ready, there was complete stillness for a moment or two, but the crowd's state of almost mystical reverence and the homage it paid to its recreated goddess was so compulsive that Guido himself found the time passed quickly.

Vanna seemed the only one unaffected by the collective trance. Her hand continued linking Guido to the deified bride – a hand as supple as that delectable vulva hidden under its folds of material, firm as the stony phallus of the statue Guido liked so much.

When, thanks to this friendly hand, he melted for an infinite instant inside the mortal body of the young girl and had come within the timeless duality of her immortal sex, the sky suddenly changed. It was the evening sun, setting behind the rocky heights of Hat-en-Shau, transmuting the colours of the gold with which the subject of the ritual was adorned.

The cymbals sounded; then a loud, crisp trumpet-blast, following which the entire assembly shook off the spell which had struck it dumb. There was a deafening shout from everyone, succeeded by a series of responses in unison, as if issuing from a single speaker.

'What are they saying?' murmured Guido, who was slowly recovering his senses.

'First they shouted the bride's name,' Vanna explained. 'Ilytis! Ilytis! Now they're chanting a propitiation stanza.'

'In Arabic?'

'No, a language I don't understand.'

'Probably the Siwah dialect.'

'Not that either. Words far more ancient.'

'Pity no one can translate for us,' said Guido, looking

around to see if there was anyone on hand to perform this service.

'Someone told me earlier, roughly what it was about,' Vanna assured him. 'I'd already picked out stylistic similarities to certain Pharaonic odes.'

'Tell me.'

But at that moment the incantation ceased as abruptly as it had begun. Delighted smiles at once replaced sacramental din. Upon the dais it seemed the goddess herself had also come down to earth. She exchanged sly smiles with her entourage, giggling quite openly and behaving like any schoolgirl who has just played a good trick on the adults.

'Is that it? Is she married?' said Guido.

'You're crazy!' Vanna exclaimed. 'The bridegroom hasn't appeared yet.'

'As things go at present,' he remarked, 'I wouldn't find a marriage without a groom immoral. To whom was the communal oration addressed, though? A hidden divinity?'

'No, to a current one. The last virgin.'

'Ah, I see. With every marriage a little of the world's virginity dies. Hence the mourning of the flutes.'

Guido added reflectively: 'Are you sure, however, that the divine must be virginal?'

'What can reality do?' remonstrated Vanna.

'True,' he acknowledged. 'If marriage were an exercise in objectivity, the human race would have died out long ago.'

'In this ceremony the faithful are definitely not positivists, yet their sacred chants are damn well believed!' Vanna quipped.

'How do you mean?'

'According to what Ilytis's attendants, the older women, told me, the invocation you just heard contained this sort of thing:

177

'Two doors has your castle:
Be not shy, open the front,
Admit your husband to your cunt.
As for the back door, this love-filled night
Play brother to your husband quite,
And open wide your arsehole.'

'How very contemporary the Siwahs are!' said Guido.

'That text dates back five thousand years,' Vanna informed him.

'What about eating something?' one of the men beside them suggested.

'Good idea!' Guido agreed. 'And let's have a drink.'

He was worried he had committed a sacrilege: drinking tea isn't exactly the same as having a drink. But he was rapidly put at ease: beer began to circulate, and they were also passing round a strong sweet *vin rosé* which wasn't as bad as it seemed at the first sip.

'What's the virgin doing, all this time?' Guido inquired.

The stranger, who seemed to have taken them under his wing, told him:

'She's swapping dirty jokes with her friends.'

'How about the groom?'

'He's getting rid of his hangover,' the guest revealed. 'He's got to have time to make himself presentable.'

No doubt the man was a straight-faced humourist of some considerable skill, for this interval lasted until nightfall.

When the young man was finally pronounced fit and sober, the state of most of the guests was scarcely better than his own. Mehdi Yasserit for one, was reeling around like a collapsing camel.

'If this shindig goes on much longer,' he declared, 'it'll be too dark to see if the sheet is stained with blood or wine.

It's all one of that bugger Ayaddin's tricks to hide the fact that his kid's been fucking like a rabbit for all of her twelve years.'

'You're a bit confused, old man!' Guido teased him. 'It's not Ayaddin's daughter who's getting married but his son.'

Mehdi made a would-be magisterial gesture, as if clarifying some abstruse hypothesis, then he slumped against his friend, out on his feet. Guido carefully deposited him in a clump of azaleas and thorn-bushes and yet again went off to search for Vanna. He was again stopped in his tracks by a new explosion of brass and percussion which heralded a general hubbub of satisfaction.

'Is this the big moment?' Guido asked. But his neighbour's mouth was too full of *loukoum* to answer.

The bustling crowd thrust the stranger towards the podium where the bride seemed to have fainted. The fuss made by her attendants, the noise, exhaustion, the weight of the ornaments she was wearing and of the cakes she had gorged had taken their toll of her strength.

She only paid token and enfeebled attention to the new rituals whose focus she was. First she was made to sit on a stool so high that she seemed as tall seated as she was when standing. Then a head-dress like a flattened cone was perched upon her braided hair, making her taller still, and this was secured by long pins tipped with enamel. A jasmine wreath whose heady odour reached Guido was put over her neck; then a second, of frangipani blossom; a third, of gardenias; a fourth, of hibiscus; and finally a fifth, of mauve and yellow orchids. The lower half of her face disappeared altogether in this mass of blossom.

'She's going to die of suffocation without having known love!' Guido lamented.

No one, however, appeared to be interested in the unfortunate's life-expectancy. They continued piling upon her the heaviest and most cumbersome accessories. A large bronze tray was placed across her knees and clay and glass animals in turn set out thereon: an owl, a lion, a goat, snakes, scorpions, a cat, a dog, a camel, a seahorse, beetles, rats; then fruits, leaves, feathers, clods of earth; a writing-case; loaves of bread, cloves of garlic, a dish of seedlings, a cruse of oil and a jug of water.

On top of the serpent encircling her waist they wrapped several yards of thick hempen rope which accentuated her waistline even more and looked as if sooner or later it might asphyxiate her.

On her shoulders they balanced a sort of heavy wood yoke at whose ends hung brass cups – one filled with seeds, one full of lambswool.

In one hand she held a sceptre made of rushes, in the other an iron chain. Round her ankles were, respectively, bracelets of silver and wood. Her bare feet were smeared with mud.

Upon her cone-headdress had been fixed a large, live bird, secured by its claws – a black bird of prey with a metallic beak, which was spreading its magnificent wings and trying to fly away.

Then Khaled Ayaddin moved forward. He held an ivory-handled curved dagger in his right hand. He brandished the weapon above his head like a Moorish horseman whirling his scimitar, then brought it down. The steel tip just missed the young girl's chest, cutting below the gold ornaments, cleanly into the swathes of material she was wearing.

The bare skin of Ilytis flashed in the ochre light from the lamps. Her firm tiny breasts remained sandwiched between the twin restraints of necklace and belt. Their pointed nipples were so red and appetizing that Guido thought the eagle could not help devouring them.

The trumpets sounded again and the groom appeared.

He was clad in a plain, tight red robe covering his

shoulders like a toga, and was carried aloft on a wooden platform surrounded by wrought-iron work. The bearers, youths of his own age, wearing blue tunics, set him down smartly at Ilytis's feet.

The crowd yelled: 'Taha! Taha!'

Then there was an incomprehensible exhortation whose sense was, Guido could guess, a bawdy one.

The young Siwah bent down and wiped the mud off his bride's feet with his hands. He snapped the wooden anklet between his fingers and stretched the silver one until it broke. He then took the loaded tray and placed it on the dais floor beside Ilytis. He unhitched the heavy yoke weighing her down, and unwound the long rope around her wrist, also undoing the gold snake-belt. He tore off the garlands of flowers, unhooked the splendid necklace, unbuttoned her waistcoat, and then divested her of the sparkling-threaded chasuble with its dazzling reflections.

She climbed down from the high stool, standing straight and dignified before him, clad only in her ripped white tunic, her breast bared. The huge dark eagle slowly beat his wings above his inscrutable head.

Taha gripped the edges of the torn material with both hands and in one swift motion ripped the dress apart, down to the stomach, the sex, and finally the feet of his bride.

.She gave him her reed sceptre and chain. Then, quite naked, she reached up and her fingers fiddled with her headdress.

The bird of prey, suddenly released, flew off with a wild cry that everyone there, men and women, mimicked, amplifying and echoing it a hundred times over.

All the lights went out and silence fell.

When one by one the lamps were lit again, the couple had gone.

An exhausted Guido, together with a soberer Mehdi, the cool Vanna and Khaled (now very relaxed), were seated in a circle on the grass drinking lemonade, each thinking about the ritual in which they had just participated.

An aquiline profile hung above them momentarily.

'The eagle?' murmured Guido sleepily.

'Do you know my friend Andreotti, the engineer?' said Khaled. Then he turned to Guido, indicating the silhouette: 'Selim El Fattah.'

Taken by surprise, Guido had to make as much effort to get up as he had done while struggling to stay awake. His amazement grew when he saw before him the tall emaciated man with the economical gestures whom he had been told was the governor. Guido recalled how no one had been afraid of him, and smiled.

'*Ciao,*' he said.

Selim acknowledged him with a nod.

Guido glanced at Vanna. Her eyes on her father didn't reveal anything Guido could distinguish. The administrator went over to her, patted her cheek and said to Khaled Ayaddin: 'When I too marry my daughter, it will be with the same rite used today.' He leaned forward, adding: 'Isn't that right, Vanessa?'

Before Vanna had time to reply he had straightened up, giving the group an expansive wave that was almost a benediction: 'Goodnight my friends.'

With which he calmly walked over towards his car.

When they were alone again at their hotel, Guido wanted to say something about her father which Vanna wouldn't mind hearing, without her taking it amiss.

'Your father talked of marrying his daughter, as though Khaled had just married his. That's the second person today I've heard make that mistake.'

'It's no mistake,' she said.

'What?' said Guido. 'Isn't Taha Khaled's son or not?'

Vanna explained coolly:

'Taha and Ilytis are both Khaled's children. Ilytis is Taha's sister.'

4

Abandonment Of The Barbarians?

Throughout the following month Guido indulged in bewildering activity. He would get up early and be on the move, crossing the town – without, apparently, any predetermined plan, as if he had decided quite arbitrarily to turn right or left. In fact he never explored the same area twice, nor did he re-enter a house already visited or speak to the same people.

The first week he succeeded in dragging Vanna along with him as interpreter, but she soon asked to be excused this chore. His endless and baffling social calls really began to annoy her. She maintained she had been born to dig the soil not to pick brains and ferret through hovels.

Guido briskly replaced her with Mehdi Yasserit, who seemed only too eager to be at his disposal and had plenty of time available, what was more. His holidays must have been extended indefinitely or else his superiors were extraordinarily accommodating, for he never breathed a word about having to negotiate the dusty floors of his Ministry once again. The teacher's devotion to his newfound friend in no way prevented the latter from displaying the most obvious ingratitude and treating him at every turn like an overfed pen-pusher, an introverted provincial and a well-meaning but out-of-touch representative of the Platonist Fifth Column.

Actually his aid wasn't really vital to Guido. With the three dozen or so phrases in the local dialect which he'd soon picked up, Guido would very likely have got by quite well on his own. Whether he had some special talent for winning them over, or whether the locals had never actually been suspicious or unfriendly in the first place, the welcome Guido had initially received since his arrival there was everywhere repeated.

He soon gave up lugging around the camera which he'd originally relied on to help him make contacts. He didn't need to play the tourist in order to be invited into family homes: the most surly old man would start laughing when he appeared and the scabbiest kid would hurl itself against him.

Anyway he was far more interested in children than old men and in men rather than women.

Sometimes, to make quite sure of things, he would subject the children to simple tests. If they were two-year-olds, they would invariably choose the narrow glass into which they'd seen Guido pour the biggest pile of sweets, rather than the large glass into which he had poured the smaller pile. The four-year-olds like idiots would go for the larger glass. In this they were no different from any child the world over: during the intervening two years they had lost the use of several million neurons.

The adults and the elderly had lost far more than that. Yet they had enough left to give Guido information – at incredible length and with unbelievable frankness – about their wives, their houses, family life, secret desires, enjoyments, sexual proclivities, their particular vices, their preferences and peccadilloes, their bawdy escapades in and around Siwah, their business trips, financial positions, their relationships towards the local and visiting officials, their views on the economy, their obligations towards society and views on the state, the law, judges, police and politics.

When he'd heard enough of all this, Guido went off into the countryside: meaning that part of the main oasis which was not urbanized. There he would remain from morning till night amid nomads and travelling tribesmen, surrounded by hordes of small children and old people.

As he had done in the town, he proceeded to ask questions which at first seemed absolutely unrelated. He began by talking about, and initiating discussion of, their forefathers' way of life, then turned to the tastes and prejudices, the hopes and fears of the younger generation.

Did they eat any root vegetables or vermin, say, which were not generally known elsewhere? No. Did the Siwahs drink any unusual substances? No. Did they eat earth, then? They all laughed, Guido laughing louder than any.

Or he would spend hours not saying a word, sitting with them cross-legged on the ground or on a carpet, hearing them out or sharing their own silences and reveries.

He was not repelled by this constant togetherness. He was even glad of it. And Mehdi, because Guido was content, was happy too.

The strangest and most fascinating thing as far as Guido was concerned, was that this shameless intrusion and constant invasion of privacy didn't seem to surprise, annoy or embarrass those subjected to it. If he'd taken it into his head to go pestering an entire tribe or local populace anywhere else, were they Milanese or Pygmies, he'd very likely have ended up (he told himself with some amusement) mouldering in jail or a lunatic asylum – or maybe just in a hospital bed with a broken nose and a black eye.

He was received, however, without excessive demonstration of friendship or even of politeness: simply as if it were all part of the daily routine, with that same emotionless, passive fatalism which accepted the heat and aridity, day and night, trachoma and infant mortality.

Having observed all this, Guido and Mehdi travelled to the small neighbouring oases: the eastern ones were quickly disposed of; the ones to the north not very interesting; to the west, they were dotted along the Libyan border. In these they weren't so well-received – far from it. They even experienced considerable difficulties in staying there the minimum period required. After a few days Guido concluded that these uncouth people in no way resembled the Siwahs and left them to it.

He didn't himself relax, however. He seemed to need no free time, even to reflect and make mental notes upon the knowledge he had acquired. Everything swiftly filed itself, as soon as registered, in groups and types in that compartment of his brain destined to contain it.

Even stranger, the number of these compartments diminished as the acquisition of data progressed. One by one, categories were struck off. Subheadings disappeared, groupings were revised and gradually subsumed, until, like a thread stringing together a mass of pearls, there remained only one remarkable common factor.

What this was, though, the researcher kept to himself? For his part, Mehdi took no steps to find out what Guido's conclusion was, any more than he had ever asked him about the motives for and purposes of this Herculean investigation. Whenever, during a lull of some kind, the two men did exchange any confidences, these were upon only a single topic – sex. This, they both admitted, was inexhaustible, and consequently they were as thick as thieves. The oddest part of it was that they had almost no erotic predilection in common.

It wasn't long before Mehdi admitted he had come to Siwah to look for boys. He also revealed that he was finding as many as he wanted – and that was plenty, for he was as fickle as regards bedmates as he was constant in his platonic attachment to Guido.

Apparently, the temperaments of the young Siwahs wonderfully coincided with Mehdi's own. None of them, either, wanted the same partner twice. Their ardour when yielding to initial advances was only matched by their absolute indifference after getting their way. Were they to meet their lover of the night before, down some alley the day after their bout of passion, they wouldn't even greet them.

Mehdi recounted his exploits to Guido with as little restraint or embarrassment as the oasis-dwellers had displayed while satisfying the Italian's obscurer curiosities. As for Guido, he learned with considerable interest about mentalities and viewpoints as far removed from his own as the thought and morality of the Siwahs. He would tell all and sundry that homosexuality greatly intrigued him, but he would never say why, nor would he explain his reasons for not indulging in it himself.

He preferred to annoy Mehdi by maliciously wondering how a man on the whole as unseductive as his podgy little friend could have such success, with such ease, among young lads some of whom were handsomer than sculptures of *kouroi*.

Wishing to test (or try to disprove) the Cairene's attraction in this region in which he seemed to be at home, Guido had an idea whose perversity appealed to him. One day when they had just dined together and were returning arm in arm to their hotel, Guido said to him point-blank: 'My dear chap, you can do something for me.'

'Right away,' Mehdi assured him. 'What?'

'Screw your friend's son.'

'Whenever you like. Which friend?'

'Khaled Ayaddin.'

'Oh!' said Mehdi, his enthusiasm cooling considerably. 'And which son?'

'What do you mean, which son? The one who just got married, of course!'

'Oh fuck!' said Mehdi.

'Why? Don't you like him? He's a very good-looking boy.'

'That's not it. It's just not done.'

'What's just not done?'

'You know very well, you can't fool me.'

'You mean to say that once a Siwah marries he doesn't allow himself to be screwed any more, but screws other people's kids in his turn?'

'Precisely.'

'Oh well, not to worry,' Guido said. 'You suggest to him that he screw you.'

'That's not on, either,' said Mehdi with a sickly grin. 'You don't let yourself be screwed by someone younger than yourself. And I've already told you hundreds of times: I don't like being screwed.'

'So much the worse for you. Well, let's not discuss it any more. Once a bourgeois, always a bourgeois.'

Mehdi emitted a heart-rending sigh. He couldn't bear Guido's disillusionment over the whole business.

'You can imagine the trouble I'd be in if Khaled discovered what had happened,' he complained.

'Why should he find out about it?' Guido objected.

'Everything gets around here, especially things like that.'

'Really? What have you heard about me?'

'You? Nothing. Because you don't do anything.'

Guido smiled slyly.

'I have an idea,' he said.

'Which is?'

'While youre screwing Taha, I'll fuck his wife.'

'Oh really, come on!' Medhi groaned.

'What's wrong with that?'

Mehdi tried diversionary tactics:

'What do you see in that silly little creature which a hotel pageboy can't offer you?'

Guido didn't let himself be sidetracked by such a flimsy argument.

'I'll tell you that after the event,' he promised.

The teacher made an appeal to good sense:

'You know why I'm worried: I wouldn't like you getting into any trouble.'

'No danger, if you can help me out with it, You've got the knack. You lead Ilytis to me and the Siwah's natural docility will do the rest.'

'What makes you think they're likely to fall for that?'

'Nothing in particular. I know it because I've had the experience before.'

'It's not worth coming all this way to repeat what you do at home,'

'Correct. But what else can I do? You tell me the Siwahs only tolerate pederasty and incest. Fine, but I'm too old to learn to love men, even those who behave like girls. And I'm even less attracted to the other sort, whatever I may say or think. I once let myself be screwed, but it didn't change my sexual orientation. And please enlighten me: with whom can I be incestuous? So, I'm heartbroken to have to upset you, I don't have any choice: all that remains is the familiar joy of adultery. Praise be to Amon, whether such a sin pleases him or not!'

'You stick to your habits' Mehdi grumbled. 'But don't come trying to preach to me about the advantages of the new world!'

'I never preach anything, 'Guido declared. 'And please don't confuse what I do preach with Vanna's utopias.'

Meanwhile she too had been travelling around the oasis, but without such meticulousness or gusto. The visits she had paid to the Greek, Roman and Egyptian remains surrounding Siwah revealed nothing of real interest to her. She had found no new sites nor even a hint of any likely terrain where she could work. She had the impression that she was wasting her time.

She was trying to understand her disillusion, as she lay on the bed in her hotel room. One afternoon seemed much like another. What was she complaining about, though? It wasn't a passion for archaelology which had led her to Siwah. She had come here to find out if she was to regain a father, and because Guido had fucked her.

At present she preferred not to think about her father, and as for Guido, where did she stand with him? Were they getting bored with each other? His careful scrutiny of the town and its surroundings separated them during the day, but each evening she would be reunited with her lover and they would make love as well as ever.

Was it really as good? Why then was their physical understanding accompanied less and less frequently by those long, intelligently lewd conversations which had hitherto added spice to it? Even Guido was worried about this.

'It's as though I scared you, these days,' he remarked one night. 'You don't even dare shock me any more.'

'We used to play around more before, that's all. Now we've become more serious.'

'That's bad!' he said. 'Let's leave being serious to those who love to doubt.'

'We're serious without having wished to be so.'

'Worse still! We'll end up giving the world a message. I can just imagine its theme: living an ancient mirage in a contemporary desert.'

'Do you know why Siwah is so contemporary?' Vanna asked. 'Because the components of existance are more complex here than anywhere else. History has left its contradictory relics here, which all interconnect somehow without contradictions.'

'I don't think one can survive contradiction,' Guido said. 'Not for any length of time, anyway.'

'Maybe such lack of understanding is one of your limitations,' Vanna reflected. 'I have limitations, too. But yours and mine are different. We don't differ as regards our physical desires, our needs, or our ideas about

191

morality and society, but because we don't share the same politics.'

'What do you mean by politics?' Guido wanted to clarify.

'My politics are those of happiness,' she said. 'Learning, understanding, work, earning money, spending it, having nice things, dancing, travelling, gardening, getting to know others, respecting them, making love to them, and giving them pleasure – to me all these are ways of being happy. The same things are means to power, for you.'

She placed a finger against Guido's lips in order to silence his protests, and continued: 'No, I don't think you can understand what I'm saying – only precision and efficiency impress you. To you thoughts and acts are only interesting if accomplishing a preordained function; only permissible if concluding with the desired result. How could *you* bear my uncertain hopes, when you can only stand plans that leave no margin for error? How can you, who believe only in those stronger than yourself, fail to be irritated by my far less forceful faith?'

'I don't deal in power, nor do I wish to have any,' he said in his defence.

'That's as may be, yet power still impresses you. It has some intrinsic worth. When you yourself can't enjoy some sort of power, you enjoy that of others.'

'I don't recognize such a portrait of myself.'

Vanna couldn't conceal a sad smile.

'At least if the wish for real power motivated you, I could perhaps understand you,' she said. 'But to let yourself be influenced by the illusion of power!'

Another day, Guido recalled: 'You told me *nefer* in ancient Egyptian meant *beautiful*. I thought it meant *good.*'

'It has two meanings, like *kalos* in Greek. There was once a time when they knew beauty and goodness were the same thing.'

'And what does *titi* mean?'

'*She who has come.*'

She smiled wryly, adding: 'I really wonder what *I* came here for. I should know quite well by now that there's never anyone or anything you *can* find, anywhere.'

'Yet why do we go on searching, just the same?' Guido asked.

'Because we have no choice,' Vanna explained. 'What else can we do?'

'Is that why you still hope to find your father, weeks after having done so?'

'I don't know. Life's not a problem to be solved but an experience to be had.'

Exactly a month after their arrival Selim El Fattah asked them to lunch with him. It was the first time he had invited them together.

Guido had seen him again several times since the Ayaddin wedding. They had exchanged the usual platitudes upon these occasions: Guido, as ever, boning up on local customs, and Selim answering him with clichés. So the Italian was not expecting any great revelations from their next scheduled meeting. He was simply curious to observe how Vanna and her father would behave.

The latter's bearing was, as it turned out, neither embarrassed nor starchy. His manner was cool and formal, certainly, yet he was not arrogant nor obviously condescending towards his guests. He seemed mainly preoccupied with keeping some aspects of himself private, and Guido guessed this personal domain to be that of dream.

Their host sat them down and served drinks, without

asking them any questions. Guido felt he had to break the ice himself, and by talking about Vanna right away, without conversational preliminaries: 'Were you expecting to see her again?'

'Of course,' Selim said. 'I knew her archaeological researches would bring her to Siwah sooner or later.'

'Didn't you think she might come just for the pleasure of seeing you?'

'She didn't know I was here.'

'Why did you keep your job a secret?'

'Secret? That's the wrong word. What I'm doing doesn't deserve publicity.'

'Is it true to say that you're particularly concerned with keeping foreigners away?'

'If only that were true! I'd have the nicest of sinecures. No foreigner ever gets out here.'

'And don't you go anywhere else, ever?'

'What'd I do?'

'Do you like it here in this oasis?'

'Better than anywhere else.'

'Yet you're not a Siwah.'

'What is a Siwah?'

'One who thinks like a Siwah.'

'Then I am one.'

'That's not possible,' Guido said.

'Why not?' said Selim, evidently bewildered.

'Because you're in love with authority.'

'Does that prevent one from being a Siwah?'

'Yes.'

'I must confess, I don't see why.'

'Come on! You know as well as I do.'

Selim confined himself to a frown of disagreement which was really more of an expression of incomprehension.

'On that subject,' Guido joked, 'I believe you're only Vice-Governor.'

'That's right,' Selim said impassively. 'There isn't a Governor.'

'Since when?'

'There never has been one.'

Guido didn't bother to hide his amusement, but he let the matter drop. He wanted to hear Vanna talk. Yet the exuberant, talkative, brilliant young woman he knew seemed to be suddenly struck dumb. What had happened to that self-confidence and boldness Renato had so liked in her, before Guido had arrived on the scene? He really wanted to get things straight, but how? Could it be, he mused, that Selim too intimidated Vanna?

In the hope of hitting upon some subject which might loosen her tongue, Guido tried to steer the conversation towards the topic of women. But women clearly didn't interest Selim. Was that the reason for his coldness to Vanna? How could a man who doesn't like women love his own daughter? She was right to be afraid of him.

Guido remembered what Vanna had said: how twenty-five years ago Selim had been revolted by Iñez's lesbianism. Had he turned homosexual only after this conflict? Yet Guido could not believe that one could ever become other than what one already is by the age of ten. Maybe what the Egyptian secretly resented in his wife was that she had forced him to recognize in himself tendencies other than those he was then demonstrating?

Guido thought disgustedly that he must cease this facile psychologizing. What he had to do was hit out at Vanna's father's dryness, and in order to do that he needed to help her shed her filial respect – calling to his aid that very informality the Siwahs manifested towards their Governor.

'An administrator can resign himself to not being liked,' he said. 'But what an insult not to be feared!'

195

For the first time since their arrival, Selim El Fattah smiled. He'd understood what Guido was driving at, but he was going to let him do so unassisted. His guest, under the circumstances, deemed it inadvisable to waste any further time beating about the bush.

'They must have told you, I'm interested in history,' he began.

He was encouraged by the sly mockery in Vanna's grin, responding to his pedantry. Anything was better than the morose boredom which had enveloped her since the start of the meal.

'The historian's task is the most demoralizing there is,' he said. 'That's because the past doesn't seem to him so very different from the present. I mean, of course, in essence.'

Selim nodded sympathetically, without going so far as to utter a sound or show any sign of approval. Guido was thankful for small mercies, and so persevered.

'Now what *is* the essential thing? Just this: there has only ever been one kind of society on this earth. This society consists of men who wield power and those who dream of wielding it.'

A new gleam in Vanna's eye gave Guido, once again, the greatest pleasure.

'This set-up obtains everywhere,' he emphasised. 'With only one exception. The exception is Siwah.'

At this Vanna showed surprise, considerable surprise it seemed. Guido was delighted to hear her at last respond.

'Come on! There are bosses and slaves here too.'

'Those bosses haven't wanted to be in charge,' said Guido. 'Far from it! They've been forced to fulfill these roles, no two ways about it.'

'Don't their subordinates obey them?' Vanna asked.

'Absolutely. And they don't just stop there. They obey all and sundry. Real angels! But their reasons for

196

obedience have nothing angelic about them. If the Siwahs so complacently defer to orders received, it's because those orders seem to them quite without importance. In their eyes, any order seems so trivial that it's not even worth discussing, contradicting or disobeying. From this viewpoint, obedience is easier than disobedience.'

'Why such quietism?' said Vanna quizzically.

'It's to do with a basic disrespect for power, as I said earlier. A spontaneous, yet rational and considered disrespect. A smug sort of contempt, even. The Siwahs take delight in not enjoying any power, for power has no interest for them.'

'Not so stupid!' Vanna said.

'This way, they don't struggle for power with those who want to seize it, nor do anything about sharing power with whoever wields it. Everyone else may fret over not having such power, or at least not enough, yet the Siwahs think *they* have far too much of it. In short, you have to fight to stop them making you a present of their wretchedly few remaining rights – the ones they're still obliged to keep.'

'Why do you think that is?' asked Vanna.

'They never wanted power. The origin of their detachment or objectivity goes back to the dawn of time. Experience of slavery isn't enough of an explanation. Quite the opposite. Power is never as attractive and desirable as when one is deprived of it. I'm referring of course to the non-Siwahs! Every race except theirs has in turn been conqueror and conquered, oppressor and oppressed. This sequence of mutual devastation and continuing folly has still not disabused anyone of collective ambition or the practice of aggression. Everyone simply manages to alternate periods of submission with those of revenge.'

'But not at Siwah?'

'Not at Siwah. Here defeat has lasted for ever, because it's enjoyed. A Siwah only submits temporarily, in the expectation of a return to the status quo – just as a punchball wouldn't dream of winning the next round.'

'A punchball doesn't *like* being hit,' Vanna objected.

'Who knows? Since it doesn't get hurt. The Siwahs don't suffer from their resignation or even from their privation. They're poor without knowing it, because they're so happy not to have to rule. Yet in other ways, they're no less sensitive than the majority of mankind, nor more given to masochism.'

'Is their allergy to power hereditary?' Vanna wondered.

'How should I know?' Guido admonished her, as drily as if such a question constituted a personal offence.

After which he turned to their host, as if inviting him to contribute to the conversation more actively than simply perfuming it with cigar-smoke. Suddenly he addressed him without further formality, by his forename:

'Selim, how do you explain the fact that the Siwahs have never caused the slightest trouble for the central, regional or any other government?'

'The government takes care to govern them with the same concern and impartiality as it does the rest of the population of Egypt,' the administrator replied impassively.

'Allow me to put my question to you again,' Guido said patiently. 'I didn't ask you whether the government cared about the Siwahs, but vice versa.'

'Neither more nor less than their compatriots in the cities and the Delta,' their host replied.

'I don't get that impression,' Guido argued. 'It seems to me they care considerably less. To be frank, I'm sure they're totally unconcerned.

'That proves they have no cause for discontent,' Selim

said smugly. 'Most of the time, people are interested in the government only in order to criticize it.'

'I didn't put the words into your mouth. And not just to criticize, but to cause it all sorts of problems. Some people will go as far as plotting against the government, rebelling, overthrowing it, replacing it, installing a democracy upon the corpse of a dictatorship, a republic in place of a monarchy, and so on. That's happened even in Egypt, hasn't it? But not because of the Siwahs, that's for sure. Throughout their history – and here history really does go back a bit – this tribe has never caused the authorities, from Pharaoh to Sadat, the slightest displeasure. Do they ever complain about their modest salaries? Or gripe about taxation? Are they ever concerned about the insignificance of their role in national affairs, and do they ever make any trouble on that score? Do they ever revolt against decisions taken in high places, made above their heads without their so much as being considered, let alone consulted? Never! Frankly how could things be otherwise, since the Siwahs don't have any opinions – opinions, that is, on public issues, even though that public consists of themselves. I've never heard of such indifference anywhere else.'

'Are you sure you've come across it here?' Selim asked mildly.

'My eyes don't readily deceive me, Vice-Governor,' Guido replied sharply. 'And in that respect I don't believe the desert can produce mirages.'

Selim was silent, so Guido went on:

'The theory which springs naturally to mind is that the Siwahs aren't interested in politics because they aren't interested in anything. Maybe because they're born soft and stupid. That is, I must confess, one possibility I'd considered before coming here. My experience of the area, however brief, contradicts it.'

Selim seemed suddenly more intrigued than he had been earlier.

'This – what shall we call it? – *trait* you attribute to the locals, you already knew about it then, before making your journey?' he said with astonishment.

It took more than that to catch Guido off guard.

'My interest in history meant that I couldn't help noticing this peculiarity: for thousands of years society has been thoroughly inculcated with the conviction that might is always right.'

'Probably these oasis dwellers have always had reasons for being satisfied with the rightness of such might,' Selim again insisted.

'Maybe that's it,' Guido mused, not bothering to disguise his sarcasm.

But Selim seemed untroubled by both irony and insolence. He asked, in tones that put paid to the interrogation: 'So your stay here, Mr Andreotti, has led you to think that there might be some explanation for what is, in your view, the apparent placidity of my fellow Siwahs, other than the one you've just agreed to?'

Guido smiled bitterly, almost sardonically.

'Absolutely not,' he said bluntly. 'I haven't found one. None at all.'

'There you are!' their host concluded affably, rising to his feet to accompany his guests to the steps of Government House.

''Why does the Siwah's political apathy interest you so, Guido?' Vanna asked when they were alone together again. 'Is it that you'd like all men to be happy?'

'Do you think I might have other motives?'

'I didn't think you liked mankind all that much.'

'Maybe you don't know me too well.'

'Maybe I don't know you at all. And what you hide from me makes me afraid.'

'Vanna,' he asked her later, 'why don't you love your father? Didn't you come here to learn to love him?'

'Obviously you've convinced me that one can't learn any more, when one's outgrown childhood. Obviously it's too late for me to learn to have a father.'

'And what about him? Can't he learn any more either?'

'A father is someone who's there when one needs him. Someone who reassures his small daughter whenever she's afraid of night and death. Someone who doesn't leave her until she's able to manage without his strength. He's not somebody who smiles politely on seeing her for the first time in twenty-five years and says "How are you, Vanessa?'

'And yet Selim isn't a savage.'

'Not a savage. But a barbarian.'

'You're hard!'

'No Guido, not hard enough, for you have to be very hard on barbarians. So that those who abandon us at birth stop pretending to rule us.'

'How do you define a barbarian, you sophisticate?'

'I term barbarians those men and women who aren't ashamed of their ancestry nor afraid for their children,' said Vanna. 'Barbarians are those who believe that ideas fifty or twenty centuries old can still apply today and will still be valid in a hundred years' time. Those who maintain that the pyramid builders were necessarily more advanced than ourselves and that a masterpiece of cruelty and calculation is a timeless work. Those who see progress as unnatural and who model the future upon the idealized past. Those who always know best and always will. Those to whom the truth is revealed. Those who only think like their parents and gods. Those who ask priests to lead them or philosophers to reassure them. Those who swear by history alone, who are proud only of their own country or

201

race, who can support only their own party. Those who live in mystical ecstasy or according to superstition, and dream of plunging us back into all that. I call barbarians the executors of a heritage, the guardians of a tradition, the keepers of a faith. Barbarians are those who dress according to custom, those who don't tire of their habits or their fellows. I call barbarians those who meet in small groups, distribute insignia, invent their own secret language and code words – barring everyone who doesn't understand their fears and hatreds – so as to ensure that no outsider penetrates the exclusivity of their club or mafia. I call barbarians those who dip a rose in the blood of those men they've killed and place it upon the bodies of the men they've avenged. I call barbarians those who believe in 'keeping things in the family' – skeletons in cupboards, dirty linen and all. Barbarians are those who are sure of themselves, and can't trust anyone. Those with everything to lose and nothing to gain – who risk nothing. They've got where they are as though they're already dead. And like the dead, they won't change.'

'Here there are isolated yet supportive men and women, whose clannishness isn't directed against others,' Guido opined. 'Their isolation, rather than their gods, is capable of keeping us here. The desert doesn't always deceive.'

'I want nothing that holds one back. I'd sooner be deceived – and on the move – than static.'

'Don't you hope for anything more from Siwah?'

'For nothing more,' Vanna said.

Then, wide-eyed, and as though already far away, leaving a kind of explanation or last word before departure, she went on:

'I won't ask father or race to choose my fate for me, won't disguise my loneliness from myself with some

202

secret excuse. I won't build my future upon the past of others.'

3 The Unicorn and the Anti-Virgin

1

Brains Of Sand

The helicopter with the official fuselage roundel came down straight inside the almost obliterated circle that served as landing-mark.

Apart from the ground crew and two or three uniformed policemen who were cooling their heels in the waiting room, its arrival had only one witness. He went over to greet the man disembarking – Nesrin Adly.

A limousine drove them both to an hotel. The younger man was putting himself out to be attentive: 'I know you want to leave as soon as possible. I thought it best to book you a room anyway. You never know, these things can take time.'

'You've done well,' Nesrin assured him. 'That way we'll be more comfortable talking to our friend. If you like, you can join in the discussion.'

'I'd rather stay out of it,' the other insisted with an embarrassed frown which greatly amused the First Secretary.

'Are you afraid Mr Andreotti might resent your duplicity?' he said, stinging him to the quick.

His assistant seemed mortally offended, rather than standing on his dignity.

'Where he's concerned, I can't reproach myself for any lack of loyalty,'

'I wasn't suggesting anything of the sort, just joking.'

But the small man didn't want to let the matter drop without a further clarification: 'When you sent me off on this mission to Siwah, you thought this Italian had come here to harm us. Today, I know him better. I can assure you he's no enemy of ours.'

'Would I have bothered to talk to an enemy, Mehdi?' Nesrin Adly remonstrated gently.

Guido sat down comfortably in a Directoire armchair with a lace antimacassar. Nesrin had just had a bottle opened and he accepted the whisky poured for him.

'How many ice-cubes?'

'Three. Thanks.'

The Italian noticed, suppressing a smile, that his host had brought out his favourite brand. The crowning courtesy? Or was Nesrin hinting at the very start of the game that none of Guido's tastes and habits were unfamiliar to him? If that was it, thought Guido, the gesture was superfluous: he'd never been under any illusions about that.

By a tacit understanding they waited for the servant to leave the room before beginning the duel. It was a point of honour for Guido to fire the opening salvo.

'Have things in Siwah been labelled Foreign Affairs now?' he joked. 'Or are you on holiday? Looks like everyone takes nice long vacations in your line of work.'

'My dear friend, I might as well admit I'm a very bad diplomat,' replied the Egyptian. 'The proof of that is that I'm going to get right to the point. However, I won't do that before first offering you an apology.'

'Don't bother,' Guido said. 'I'm not easily offended.'

'The apology I owe you relates to an unpremeditated offence,' Nesrin continued imperturbably.

He too stretched out in an armchair, legs extended, stroking his beard reflectively. Guido simultaneously observed that Nesrin's beard was now fuller and that, amazingly, he was wearing old-style grey felt spats over his polished kid bootees.

'It goes back to our first meeting . . . That day I mistook you for someone else. I thought your name was Fornari. Maybe you know him? No, he's not the sort of man you'd know. Like you, he's employed by CIRCE, but in a humbler capacity than yourself. Which implies, naturally, that he hasn't your good breeding, either. My mistake is due to the thoughtlessness of that nice man Zannipolo Gatto, whose keen wit and single-minded devotion we both know and appreciate.'

'Devotion to what?' Guido wanted to know.

'To the future of Italo-Egyptian relations,' Nesrin was quick to inform him. And he lit his customary cigarette, making expansive gestures in the air before going on: 'CIRCE, we were led to believe, had entrusted this Fornari chap with a scarcely credible mission. He was supposed to go to Siwah to negotiate the clandestine acquisition of some private land. The purpose of this farce was to have been to lend credibility to the idea that under the oasis there was some hitherto undiscovered oil. Was this some sort of stupid diversionary tactic? One must admit that the project, if not trumped-up, would have been somewhat anachronistic. These days, if businessmen want to bargain on our territory they have to employ rather more adroitness than that. Therefore it was realized that CIRCE was setting up a smokescreen to disguise a more serious project. It's quite a well-worn tactic in itself, and we were interested in one particular aspect only. How could such a second-rate ploy be entrusted to someone of your ability? The question resolved itself when I realized you weren't Fornari. Or rather, that you weren't passing yourself off as him, if indeed you'd ever intended doing so. Anyhow, the episode has only a historical interest, that is, none.'

If a pointless preliminary speech had taken all this time,

Guido reflected, the main issue might last them all night. So much for his rendezvous with Ilytis . . . .

But as though unashamedly contradicting his previous affectation of languid contempt for matters past, Nesrin now apparently couldn't tear himself away from the ground covered.

'Whether on your own initiative, and at the last minute, you modified the original plan, or received instructions to do so, I don't know,' he went on. 'Maybe the devious cunning of CIRCE – in this scheme as in so many of its undercover enterprises – lay in perpetuating a front of incoherence, even nonsense. One's more likely to be forgiven a clumsy schoolboy prank than a carefully-laid plot, isn't that right?'

Guido saw no point in commenting at this stage, so his interlocutor continued: 'I myself am not averse to humour, or, shall we say, the occasional distraction. I recognized you only after you'd left my office.'

'Had we met before?' Guido politely inquired.

'Never. But I'd heard and read a lot about you. And while I think of it, before we get down to brass tacks, may I ask you one question? Why the hell did you tell me that lie?'

Guido did not flinch.

'You said you were the *engineer* Guido Andreotti. What was the point of that little joke? It wasn't any use to you, because you never once tried to act the driller secretly looking for deposits or the pipeline expert seeking a likely site.'

'I am an engineer,' Guido persisted.

Nesrin barely concealed an impatient sneer.

'Yet as you know quite well, your reputation is in another field. However, you certainly didn't realize I knew that.'

Guido emitted a sigh of obvious boredom, from which Nesrin inferred, with satisfaction he didn't bother to conceal, that he had just scored a point. He at once pressed home his advantage.

'It's possible you may be an engineer *too*, Mr Andreotti, but you're a chemist first and foremost, and, to be more precise – a biochemist. Biochemist of course implies molecular biology, but your specialist field isn't cytology as such, nor genetics – for which you yourself profess inexplicable scorn.'

'It's not genetics that's senseless,' Guido interrupted suddenly, 'it's geneticists.'

Nesrin seemed pleased that he had succeeded in rousing his man. He carried on drily: 'The branch of science you favour is neuropsychopharmacology. I'm sure your modesty won't be upset if I term you one of the most advanced researchers exploring this particular area. Yet only your colleagues can really appreciate your status, for the general public hardly knows what neuropsychopharmacology is.'

'Do *you* know?' asked Guido, with studied rudeness.

'Yes. Basically, it's the science of the substances governing the functions of the central nervous system and its related systems. These substances are usually natural secretions, but they can also be synthetic bodies, identical to or different from those spontaneously secreted by the organism. In this case, the effect produced is, shall we say, the reverse of natural.'

'Interesting,' said Guido.

'I won't be foolish enough to lecture you. I know who I'm talking to. I just want us to understand each other clearly as to the various implications of your science.'

'I have no personal science,' Guido joked once more.

'You do in a way! And it's probably just that element of personal obsession in your research that has so far excluded you from the Nobel Prize on which you'd otherwise have some claim. It'll go on excluding you from the reckoning.'

'I wouldn't stoop so low as to beg for that kind of trinket.'

'The fascination the high and powerful hold for you isn't in keeping with your arrogance. Yet it's not this aspect of your character that cuts you off from honours you'd otherwise receive: no, the use to which you want to put your knowledge does that. How could the Swedish committee, I ask you, dare put before the public the nature and effects of your most remarkable labours? I fear that our era isn't yet ready or magnanimous enough to value you at your true, surprising worth.'

Guido looked at him without showing the slightest interest. Nesrin didn't allow himself to be nonplussed.

'Rest assured that it's not my intention to give you a résumé of your career to date. Let's just take it (if you like) as far as the moment you succeed, by a dazzling economy of means and style, in synthesizing gamma-aminobutyric acid. Still more important, you show at the same time the process by which this chemical intermediary acts upon the synapses and hence the nerve impulses. Before your experiement, it wasn't established whether its effects were confined to encephalic matter or to the pyramidal system, which is, of course, your particular field of interest.'

Well put Nesrin! Guido reflected: such an exposition deserved some reward. The malicious twinkle in the Italian's eye did not pass unnoticed.

'Don't hold it against me, my dear colleague,' said Guido, 'if I correct you on one point of detail. The pre- and post-synaptic structures don't always synthesize the same intermediary. The fact of bringing out the nervous origin of one of these neuro-transmitters doesn't necessarily imply that the Gaba might be the fruit of a pyramidal activity *stricto sensu*.'

Nesrin didn't appear in the least impressed. He answered:

'If the act of learning is bound up with the cerebral cortex's producing *new* nucleic acids, proteins, polypeptides and polysaccharides, which prior to any given marshalling of data didn't exist in the batteries of chemical codes within our brains, don't we owe this process of information-gathering to the brain's pyramidal cells?'

'Balls!' Guido replied pleasantly. 'We only realize fresh molecular specificities in so far as we only learn what our genetic heritage renders us capable of learning. The bogus ability of inventing substances, which you instance, is really an embryonic procedure, genetically programmed. And genes will always escape our control. So we should let them operate freely and intervene elsewhere. So far, the learning process doesn't constitute progress for us, since the knowledge we acquire doesn't nearly compensate for the deterioration we start to suffer from birth onward. This deterioration isn't due to an impoverishment of our stock of information, of course, but to a post-natal incapacity to process such information intelligently. We're akin to the possessor of a computer, who must programme a growing mass of data, using a machine whose circuits are breaking down one after the other, immediately the warranty period – normally, two years – expires. Yet the owner would have only himself to blame for his misfortune, for the burnt-out circuits would only have been those he hadn't seen fit to service during those initial two years. He didn't do so because no one told him to, that's true. But let's be honest, his error and ignorance didn't change the situation much: his computer was anyhow obsolete, a primitive machine only suitable for a beginner. Let's give him another, instead of filling his head full of crap. Crap about how, through the operation of God knows what mutagen Holy Ghost or test-tube parthenogenesis, he'll give birth to superkids who'll justify his idiocies.'

'If I understand you correctly,' said Nesrin, stroking his

beard, 'you're saying first that the human race won't change through genetic mutation.'

'Not for the better, anyway,' Guido cut in.

'Secondly, that in order to modify the intellectual and even somatic capacities of human beings, they must be given artificial neuro-intermediaries as soon as their organisms are fully formed.'

'I wasn't just saying that,' Guido said sharply. 'At present not only are we not learning as much as we can from birth, but we're not using our cognitive potential to the full, still less our capacity for action. In fact, the older we grow the less we learn and the more inactive, impotent and helpless we become. Our much-vaunted growth is a progress of regression and loss, a continuous restriction of all that latent potential with which the foetus is endowed. It's not enough simply to enrich the organism by renewing and increasing its neuropharmacological heritage, this new equipment must enable it to employ to the *full* those already-supplied instruments which are promptly thrown away or which family or social structures erode or ossify after the traditional two-year guarantee period.'

'If that's your belief,' Nesrin coldly observed, 'I can't understand why your researches should be confined to an attempt to alter the human phenotype. With your sort of logic, why didn't you start by trying – as others have attempted to do psychologically – chemically to overcome those obstacles to the full realization of our inner potentials?'

'You don't actually understand at all,' Guido commiserated. 'One doesn't overcome a severed leg, one replaces it.'

'Should one assume that the vocation to educate, or rather re-educate, is less meaningful for you than the passion to alter creation?' Nesrin inquired. 'Hence you've left the job of activating or reactivating our cells as nature

214

made them to others less gifted than yourself, and you've retained the more Promethean ambition of providing man's brain with substances it doesn't normally secrete.'

Nesrin stopped, as if musing upon the arrogant portrait he had just painted. He reopened his eyes to compare this image with Guido's lazy expression as the latter slouched back in his armchair. The ways of science, he reflected, are impenetrable – or almost! With another insolent yawn, Guido replied: 'Nature does her best, but we do better.'

'That desire isn't obvious from your first discoveries,' Nesrin continued. 'It's not surprising that the tribe of biologists, far from being alarmed by them, hailed them flatteringly. But the praise ceased abruptly when your next master-stroke became known. Its scientific quality was in no way inferior to that of your previous work, yet the moral and social implications of your invention – for it involved a new substance, hitherto unsuspected until you created it – led to the considerable apprehension rather than the mere embarrassment of your peers.'

Guido had resumed his mask of indifference, but Nesrin paid no attention to it and went on: 'On that occasion you used beta-acetoxyethyl-trimethyl-ammonium, or, since too precise a terminology seems to irritate you, acetylcholine.'

'Absolutely correct,' Guido grinned.

Nesrin's face was unexpectedly jubilant.

'My dear Guido, I'm not at all the pedant you take me for,' he said directly. 'And I trust you'll do me the favour of allowing that I'm neither superstitious nor prone to detecting mystical links between people and things. But you must admit there's food for thought when it comes to your presence here and your choice of acetylcholine for your experiments. If I referred to this substance a moment ago by its full name, it wasn't in order to boast of my knowledge or my memory: to impress you I'd need far more of both. No, I just wanted to emphasize one of the most extraordinary coincidences ever ... This chemical term reminds us that the neuro-intermediary under discussion is an acetic ester of choline, and choline itself has a nitrogenous base derived from quaternary ammonium. *Ammonium!* Isn't it strange and astounding to be uttering that word here today with *you*, Guido Andreotti – here in this oasis! This oasis which at one time in its history went by the identical name, Ammonium. That was the name given it – yes, by your own countrymen's ancestors!'

'That's not what brought me here,' Guido assured him coldly.

'It's not just a matter of random homonymy,' said Nesrin. 'Ammonium chloride or "salts of ammonia" date back to ancient times. Ammonium was so named as specific homage to Amon. And not just to my Amon, but in particular to the Aghormi temple's Amon, the Amon of Hat-en-Shau and Siwah. Do you know why? Because the product was exported to Italy from that very region and none other. For two thousand years then, Siwah was known to the Romans. They went there not only because they believed its oracle and liked its dates, but in order to stock up with ammonium chloride. The desert dwellers of that era were merchants. They made it. How? By burning camel dung! In chemical terms this is called *sublimation* isn't it? You see, it all makes sense.'

Guido once again visualized the camel which had taken him and Vanna to those sublime and transitory heights where bodies sense themselves immortal. He remembered, too, the ruined temple of Ammonium inside which Vanna had quoted the Judgement of the Heart and Declaration of Innocence from *The Book of the Dead*, and had talked to him of justice and truth, goodness and the love of man. He tried in vain to link these disparate

216

images with the chemical formulae to which he'd dedicated his life.

He told himself there was no logical connection between these realities, nor was there a case for establishing mystical links between them. Everywhere in the world these amazing and absurd encounters flourished, those irrational marvels wherein men always seek to discern the indecipherable name of some god. Today as ever, the phenomena of life and inanimate matter enter the lists of chance, a realm in which everything that happens is both necessary and meaningless.

For a few minutes neither of them spoke. Perhaps they were trying to call a halt to the conversation they had to make and to cease the sardonic duelling they'd felt was obligatory.

Instead of flinging technical terms at each other like battle-cries, instead of scheming and obeying forces bigger than either of them, or yielding to hopes that might never be fulfilled, why didn't they simply talk of friendship and love, truthfully, honestly, gently? Or evoke the scented breeze rustling through the leaves of Siwah, poets together admiring the adventures of the Ancients, who well knew how to transmute the most stinking freight. Or link arms, as Guido and Mehdi had so often done, and go out for a stroll, laughing freely about those amazing adventurers who carried in their galleys jars full of precious essence of shit which they'd recycled in order to spread the fame of a god?

Guido finally broke the silence, shrugging as he said: 'It's true, ammonia doesn't smell too nice. But you get nice fertilizer from it, all the same.'

'And nice bombs,' Nesrin added. 'Men are like Amon and like ammonium: capable of anything. Of doing good and evil.'

217

'They do evil because they're not clever enough,' Guido corrected him.

Nesrin sighed in resignation:

'Here we are, back to the subject again. *Your* subject, I should say. Acetylcholine. And the use you wanted to put it to in order to alter human abilities you deem inadequate, or inadequately employed.'

He settled back once more into the velvet armchair, staring at the baroque ceiling, his fingertips touching – just like the professor he was. He addressed Guido without looking at him.

'I won't argue with you about the physiological origin of the neuro-intermediary in question, I'm not qualified to do that. Its existence and composition have been known about for some time. Its functioning, however, remains scarcely understood. We don't really know how or why acetylcholine works. So for the moment, as you like simplifications, let's just say that it's produced by the cholinergic cells of the cortex, and is somewhat related to the soporific properties of the opium dear to Molière's "*médecin malgré lui*".'

Here Guido had to intervene.

'Admit it, it's acetylcholine you really like. That stuff is cleverer than you think. It even affects its own synthesis, although that might shock the logician you consider yourself to be! Above all, it imposes its own freedom on the nerve-endings and upon the axons and dendrites of the neurons, a bit like Moses did when the time came to escape from the primitive pyramidal universe.'

Nesrin managed a smile again, and said: 'Is it this freedom which has won you over so thoroughly? Anyhow you weren't content, as you were with gamma-amino – sorry, Gaba! – to recognize its properties nor recreate this secretion as nature intended it. No, this time you couldn't be the first to synthesise acetylcholine: others did that

218

more than a century ago. Therefore you had to go one better. Which you did. You didn't, though, like Sganarelle "change all that". You changed only *one* element of the molecule ACh. Just one. One of the CH_3 groups attached to the nitrogen radical. This one.'

Without dropping his aristocratic imperturbability, Nesrin pulled a pen out of his breast pocket, tugged back his linen shirt-cuffs with their sapphire links and rapidly scrawled across the spotless tablecloth on the small table between them a complicated chemical formula.

Then he placed an elegant finger on the CH_3 symbol in the bottom right-hand corner and carried on: 'Had you confined yourself to this laboratory *tour de force:* your genius would only have aroused the eulogies (and maybe jealousy) of your peers.'

Nesrin nodded, as if in sympathy with both views. Then he launched off as was his wont, on a new digression: 'Before you came along, acetylcholine could be broken down, of course: but either completely or not at all. In more general terms, even inside our organisms doesn't acetylcholin esterase break down simply, yet relentlessly, into the vital ester in which you're personally interested? True, other rival inhibitors have less innocuous effects than this particular enzyme: for instance alkylphosphates whose action (as you couldn't fail to know) are lethal to animals. However, this in no way deterred you.'

Guido yawned politely. Nesrin smiled.

'I'll be brief,' he assured him. 'Anyway I don't know which nucleophilic activator you used to trigger molecular breakdown and the new formula I mentioned. Not atropine, of course. Nor noradrenalin, obviously. Maybe it was acetylarsan.'

Guido wasn't amused, as Nesrin continued: 'More important, what chemical agent did you substitute for the CH_3 element you succeeded in isolating? I don't know that

219

either, of course. To tell the truth, I hardly care. It's enough that I know the results of your labours.'

Guido nodded, as if encouraging some bright pupil's clever remark. Without showing what he thought of such an ambiguous response, Nesrin resumed his monologue:

'The new substance you thus created you called: EA 12 Unicorn. The letters and numbers are probably part of some private code, to which you alone have the key and which you certainly won't divulge to the likes of myself. I wouldn't even ask you, but I'm curious about the rest. Why Unicorn? Don't you think Chimera would have been more appropriate?'

Guido's expression remained inscrutable, and though Nesrin was left in the dark, he carried on: 'Forget about the designation you chose, the actual effects of your invention are mind-blowing. The substance you managed to produce seems to be imbued with prodigious properties.'

'To believe in prodigies is to lack imagination,' Guido murmured, looking down at his shoes.

'Let's hope the rats are brighter than I, as far as that's concerned!' Nesrin jibed, by way of dissent. 'Otherwise they'd still be wondering why they had the dubious honour of being selected by you to test your product. Unless they also know that their reaction towards acetylcholine is generally comparable to that of man's. For it is man you're finally interested in, isn't it, Mr Humanist? You don't think that rats are failures, do you – but that man is. Nature's failure.'

For once Guido deigned to smile as Nesrin went on:

'Before getting down to changing man, you began by altering animals. And what a marvellous change you brought about! If that fabled creature which protected virgins' chastity, that unicorn whose name your perverse fantasy invoked when christening your mixture, could have seen the indignities of which poor rodents were capable, he'd surely have stabbed himself with his own chaste horn! For no sooner had your rats been dosed with EA 12 than they started copulating incessantly. They could keep at it, ejaculating more than fifty times in succession. Fifty orgasms a day! What's more,' said Nesrin, 'they manifested utter lack of discrimination as regards their desires and choice of partners. Their erotic frenzy was such that they didn't only mate with females, but sprang upon any male available. If they'd left it at that, well maybe it wouldn't have been too significant, but they didn't. Their sex drive even impelled them to try and mate with cats! That might seem funny . . . . '

'Laugh then!' Guido said.

'There I'm afraid I'd show bad taste, Dr Andreotti,' Nesrin observed coldly. 'Since after their fifty fucks your Don Juans invariably drop dead. Whether from over-exertion or the effects of your drug I don't know. Obviously you don't either, because you've been testing and retesting your concoction, presumably varying the dosage and conditions. Hundreds and hundreds of rats of all types have thus known the intoxication of a single day of unlimited love. None has survived.'

Nesrin seemed to have concluded his speech, and he was surprised when Guido broke the silence that followed. Actually it was hardly broken, for Guido's voice seemed to come from a long way off, whispered and somehow disembodied. The voice uttered those words Nesrin knew:

> *I have committed no iniquity against men.*
> *I have wrought no evil.*
> *I have not raised my hand against man.*
> *I have deprived no man of what he desired.*
> *I have made none weep.*
> *I have not killed.'*

When Nesrin started talking again his voice also seemed to have changed.

'I'm not doubting the sincerity of your scientific intentions, Dr Andreotti,' he said. 'Had you remained an independent researcher, with no master but your own conscience; were you alone sole judge of the significance and direction of your work, I'd certainly never have dared bother you. But then, neither would you be here. You're at Siwah because you're not free. Someone sent you.'

Guido made as if to interrupt him, but Nesrin continued sharply and forcefully: 'You can't call yourself just a disinterested man of science when you're employed by private organizations whose objectives and activities are those of one particular government. That makes you a man of power – but, let's repeat, a power not of a State nor of a race. That's why I'm disturbed and why I'm disturbing you.'

Guido, however, didn't seem to be listening. For the first time a trace of weariness was detectable in Nesrin's attitude. He took on a gentler tone when returning once again to Guido's life and work: 'When you invented EA 12 you were subsidised by the Turin company Calandra. If one didn't know about the ambitions and morality of such monopolies one night be tempted to ask what they were doing, patronizing researches as far removed from their scope as biology. Could that have been why the celebrated Gianni Pecori cut off relations with you one fine day? Because he asked himself that very question? Or did he simply decide that your dangerous discoveries weren't commercial? How lacking in insight, eh? But even the shrewdest of industrial tycoons can sometimes have his lapses. How Gianni must have fumed when he saw the speed with which his arch-enemy seized upon the prey he himself had so foolishly abandoned.'

'People don't break off relations with me,' Guido said. 'I do that. I cut myself off whenever I like, from whoever I like.'

'From which I conclude that you also choose your

masters? That it was you who chose your new chains? When your newfound freedom, following your departure from Calendra, wore off, you (upon your own initiative, by what you've implied) threw in your lot with a group whose authority it's foolish to question. Quite voluntarily then – with all the other specialists and scientists already there reduced to playing second fiddle to your illustrious self – you became *the* top expert at CIRCE, otherwise known as the International Consortium for Research into Cyber-Energetics. Very few know of the existence of this monster, although it was officially registered as a subsidiary of the petroleum company Egida which, as everyone knows, is based in Milan, though its influence is worldwide. I'm sure the public would benefit from being informed about the considerable financial backing a firm as respectable as Egida has earmarked, through its intermediary CIRCE, for the undercover study of political science. Doubtless its directors consider the vexed condition of world affairs a major obstacle to self-sufficiency – to that of the multinationals, anyhow. For the latter are ripe and ready to be laws unto themselves. Irresponsible troublemaking from an uninformed public imposes unnatural restraints upon them and effects the smooth running of their operations. World administration requires calm. The serenity of political judgements, the big decisions – these can only be compromised whenever the weak take an interest in the affairs of the strong.'

'Are they taking an interest?' Guido asked.

'Very much so! Except at Siwah, as you know.'

Nesrin seemed to have recovered his previous high spirits and equanimity. He poured Guido another generous tot of whisky.

'We won't go back over all those ideas of which you gave the excellent Selim a clear picture. The Siwahs, as we all know, are basically uninterested in power. They let

223

the government govern them. They're content, and appreciative of what their leaders decide for them — meaning for their own good. They're wise. Cigarette?'

'No thanks.'

'The fundamental question we must ask is this: whence comes their wisdom? What's the reason for it? Nobody knows — not the Siwahs nor the powers that be, nor of course myself. No one's ever managed to find out. It's certainly not because they're soft in the head! The enigma remains, and that's why CIRCE sent you here, to get to the root of it.'

Guido was thinking about Ilytis:

'Breasts of a nymph! Thighs of an enchantress! What am I doing here when I could be the prisoner of your witchcraft? Turn me into your lion, daughter of Helios and Perseis! I'll drink your sun-brew, my ocean nymph! I'll get drunk on your deadly potion, my unicorn with stony hair! I won't take the gods' antidotes against your ether, my venomous virgin! I'll keep the intoxicating taste of your salty sex upon my tongue. I'll lick your new body all over, like a good lapdog. By your power, in your castle of sand, you'll turn me into the swine I am.'

'Why did CIRCE choose you?' said Nesrin, quite unaware of Guido's erotic daydreams. 'Why you rather than a real sociologist or a psychologist of some sort?'

Brought back to earth abruptly by these obscene sounds of speech, Guido grimaced disgustedly. But Nesrin couldn't let the point pass without pressing it home.

'Of course according to your views, you don't get to understand what's in anybody's head by stretching them out on a couch. No, you have to get people lying on the operating table, under forceps and scalpel, to find out what's inside their ill-formed skulls, those badly designed brain-boxes they inherited from their lizard, camel and ape ancestors. Dissection and chemicals, to you these are the means . . . .'

224

'I beg your pardon?' said Guido. 'Would you care to repeat that?'

'Did you come to Siwah to trepan its inhabitants? That's what I'm getting at,' answered Nesrin, impervious to all witticisms. 'Don't worry, though: I'm merely speculating. I know you're no surgeon. And yet how foolish and impudent to assume that such madness can be physically induced or analysed: that wouldn't be in keeping with your good sense and amazing self-control. Nor with that of your bosses. Although foreigners may not be worried by the prospect of indulging in vivisection at Egyptian citizens' expense, it's unthinkable that they do so without first obtaining permission. Or am I mistaken?'

'You're quite wrong there,' Guido replied abstractedly. Nesrin appeared somewhat put out, momentarily. He crossed and uncrossed his legs, displaying his anachronistic gaiters; carefully placed an unlit cigarette in a thick cut-glass ashtray, inserting another into his holder, and finally leaned over towards Guido, to enquire in a voice that betrayed a hint of annoyance:

'Am I to understand that that sort of experiment has actually been made?'

'You might do so,' said the other.

'Not here, though?'

'Obviously not.'

'Where then?'

'Ask your intelligence service. They've taught you so much.'

'And what were the results?'

Guido confined himself to a disgusted frown. Meanwhile Nesrin had reached his own conclusions: 'You certainly found out nothing. Otherwise you wouldn't have come to Siwah in person.'

'Good thinking,' Guido applauded.

'So, you've found no congenital difference in the Siwah

cerebral cortex that distinguishes it from the average man's? Nothing atypical?'

'Nothing.'

'And you're sure you've taken a representative cross-section? Under conditions which permit you to form valid and proven generalizations?'

'Of course.'

Oddly enough, Nesrin's intuition told him that for once Guido wasn't joking.

'In a word then, the Siwahs are no different from ourselves?'

'No.'

'And yet they are!' Nesrin exclaimed. 'The universal desire for and fear of power is unknown to them. They submit to political authority not only readily but with pleasure. Under the circumstances only one of two possibilities is feasible: either their eccentricity is inherited, or it's acquired. Right?'

Guido evinced neither agreement nor disapproval. Nesrin didn't let that worry him.

'The former hypothesis implies a genetic mutation. You don't like mutations, so let's leave that alone for the moment. The second possibility remains, and the question then arises: acquired *how?* Why should the Siwahs prove the the exception to the general rule? The answer that springs to mind is, because of their culture.'

'Springs to whose mind?' Guido asked.

'Have you read *Thus Spake Zarathustra?*'

'Why?'

'Because you'd know the parable of the lion, the camel and the child. This posits three possible states of maturity available to human beings. The first is that of the lion, which only understands violence and relies on its own strength alone. The second is the camel's, which bears its suffering patiantly and submits reasonably, waiting to seize the opportunity to get its revenge by kicking and biting. The third state is the child's, who doesn't yet know that it will gain strength. Meanwhile it doesn't waste each day trying to win or lose. It just doesn't think about power. It develops its intelligence, plays, creates, enjoys. Which of these categories do the Siwahs fall into?'

But Guido considered he had said quite enough. He was playing with a toad which had somehow got on to the carpet, tickling it with the toe of his shoe.

Nesrin answered his own question: 'Thinking about it, the Siwahs don't identify with any of Nietzsche's paradigms. They eat nobody, don't kick back slyly, and if their development was anywhere arrested, it certainly wasn't at childhood. The characteristics of children are curiosity, change, growth. They're perfectly aware of power – in order to disobey it. So therefore in one sense they're just the opposite to the Siwahs. The latter are exactly what I said, the pure product of a culture, and of a civilization more remote and less changeable than any other.'

Guido stared at him with the same impish curiosity he had bestowed upon the toad.

'Culture consists of renouncing change,' Nesrin went on, pursuing his line of thought, 'and renouncing change means, in practice, renouncing chances of growth. Progress implies continual innovation. Yet people don't really like the new: they like it less than they make out. Nor are they sure they'd gain anything by growth and expansion. They'd rather trust in the maturity and assurance of their own society. They don't wonder how it reached its particular level of culture. How else but by change? By what miracles have the innovations of ancient times now become worthy of conserving? Why are yesterday's scandals today's proprieties? Or yesterday's deviancy today's norm? Because conservatives are people with no memories who only preserve from the past what pays. And in their view, what pays best of all is prudence. It isn't logical, however, in a changing universe, to think that

227

immutability is any more sure than evolution. The trouble is that no society learns how to be, only how to have. And learns it as badly as everything else. By submitting to the obligations of one's society and by conforming to its conventions, one accepts being less in the hope of having more. Result: one is and has nothing at all.'

Guido was astounded to hear such ideas from someone like Nesrin. He smiled, unable to resist a reference to his companion: 'A pity Vanna can't hear you. She'd be pleased.' And couldn't help adding: 'You really owe her that.'

Nesrin in turn admitted: 'I like her a lot you know. I've known her since her childhood.'

He displayed the friendly informality of someone who's just had an idea:

'It wasn't just your real objectives and your methods of going about them which shocked me, Guido. You took the wind out of my sails by choosing Vanna to accompany you.'

There was a further offer of whisky, which this time Guido declined.

'How could an archaeologist have helped you?' Nesrin inquired. 'You arrived in Cairo quite well informed about her and didn't even look around to contact anyone else. It was her and her alone you wanted to take with you to Siwah. Why?'

Guido decided to do him a favour in return for his sincerity.

'It's really very simple,' he explained. 'I took her for a Siwah.'

'Oh come on!' said Nesrin sceptically.

'Not by birth, of course. Siwahs aren't only born, but can also be made.'

'Just supposing you're right, how could she have become one?'

'That I didn't know. One of those theories I wanted to test.'

'And did the theory prove false?'

'In every way.'

'Namely?'

'That's my business.'

'Well tell me about your other theories,' Nesrin encouraged him. But it didn't work.

'Don't bank on me to enlighten you, Mr Adly,' said Guido angrily. 'What you've been regaling me with for the last two hours should be quite enough to satisfy your superiors. I seem to remember that you're no more of an independent operator than I am.'

'You're right,' Nesrin said, showing not the slightest vexation at having had to endure such an outburst. 'The situation is perfectly straightforward. We've seen you rule out any endogenous origin as regards this Siwah peculiarity. There was therefore only one possibility left, which you came to check out: to see if there existed any *external* neuropsychopharmacological agent acting upon the brains of the Siwahs, without in fact being produced by their own organisms. Maybe the drug was a product of their native environment, or they made it themselves? Consciously or unconsciously, they were ingesting it somehow, and it was having the same effect on them as those neuro-intermediaries you're such an expert on. So it was quite natural to call upon you, to do the detection work and pin down the formula, operation, dosage, side-effects and so on, until, having isolated and identified the substance you could then synthesize it as neatly as you had done with Guido. That's the real reason for your presence here.'

Guido looked as though he was paying deferential attention now to a top-flight lecturer. Without further ado he poured himself a drink. Nesrin did not lose track of what he was saying: 'Why does the consortium employing you attach such importance to the Siwah syndrome? Because when you've identified the constituents of this substance, CIRCE, or rather Egida, has the technical and financial resources to produce the drug commercially. To what end? To offer it at a price to whichever governments and police forces are harrassed by agitation or unrest? To instill respect for the rule of law and order in the public at large and tranquillize the most volatile of its elements? To inculcate the eminently practical citizenship of the Siwahs into the population of the world?'

Nesrin didn't let himself be taken in by Guido's apparent drowsiness now. It made him suddenly vehement: 'Isn't that a naive idea? Governments and police forces themselves aren't stable elements. They can fall into anyone's hands. That's been known to happen, and sometimes it's just as well. A government, meanwhile, is an outworn superstructure. Real power is situated elsewhere than in council meetings and ministerial offices. Not in the choices the electorate has to make, nor in the visionary intuition of a seething mob. Nor is it in the revolutionary spirit of dominated races. The *polis* is now too populous to be policed. And politics too vulgar to be policeable. The big problems of this planet can no longer be dealt with by political man nor solved by politicians of the State. Such matters require a clearly defined technical competence that is available to the half-dozen CIRCEs at the disposal of the various large companies which acknowledge no country other than a cosmopolitan heritage they want to defend and expand. These real powers have begun to wax impatient with the tolerance shown by the 'false' powers to the powerless. This confused situation must be set right: computerized steps are under way, orders have been given, decisions taken. Only your go-ahead is needed, doctor, and the world's health will be assured for ever.'

Nesrin paused for breath, but he hadn't finished yet:

230

'What organization, I ask you, doesn't dream of workers and clients as easily satisfied as the Siwahs! Well, now it can have them! A drop of Hat-en-Shau elixir in the reservoirs or factory and office air-conditioning systems, and hey presto, no discontent, wage claims, strikes or demonstrations. Not even subversive thoughts. Everywhere desire and fulfilment will coincide. No one will ask for more than he or she already has. And since it's becoming increasingly difficult for the strong to give to the weak, the weak will ask for less and less. The whole world will revolve happily, its society in tune with the rhythms of the true masters of the universe, and as sweet and mild as a choir of archangels, with no more cries of complaint or suffering. The singing of those who are happy in their work will become as pleasant as the silence of outer space.'

'Siwah isn't a paradise,' said Guido suddenly, as if some deep compulsion had roused him from his lassitude.

'Yet you don't seem at all unhappy at being here,' Nesrin noted.

'I wouldn't be happy in an Eden.'

'I'm delighted to hear it. I'd distrust a fanatical believer. So much the better if you're only a scientist. It's the scientist I'm talking to.'

'What do you want to know?'

'Whether that scientist found what he was looking for.'

'He did,' said Guido calmly.

Nesrin showed no emotion: he already knew what was coming next. Guido didn't keep him waiting:

'The Siwahs judge things at their true worth. That's the secret.'

'How do you mean?'

'They're not interested in power because power isn't interesting.'

Nesrin exhaled deeply. He'd get to the bottom of all this, if it took all night. He returned to the point.

'All right,' he said. 'And where does this knowledge of the worth of things, this wisdom not shared by the rest of mankind, come from? The air they breathe or the water they drink? Is it some grass they chew, or a serum they inject without anyone's knowledge?'

'I really don't know,' said Guido.

'Not surprising!' Nesrin sneered. 'You spent exactly eight weeks snooping about here and no one disturbed you. Wouldn't you have been better occupied using some of your instruments, taking measurements or sorting out some samples? In short, pursuing your profession of chemist?'

Guido's manner became even more placatory.

'Poor old Nesrin,' he said. 'Don't get worked up over such trifles. Let your subordinates split hairs. I don't need to test the air or water of Siwah, nor its inhabitants' diets. I don't have to analyse their tobacco or *kif* or grain or whatever, for the very good reason that these measures have already been taken. A long time ago, and extensively.'

'Really?' said Nesrin.

'Not here,' Guido explained. 'In Milan. In CIRCE's fine new laboratories, and at great expense. All for nothing.'

'You mean no one found anything interesting?'

'Neither interesting nor uninteresting. Just nothing.'

For the first time Guido noticed a disingenuous expression upon Nesrin's face. The Egyptian crouched forward slightly in his armchair, muttering without much conviction: 'In that case, I don't really see how we can get away from that theory which seems to rile you so much – the inherited physical characteristic.'

'That theory has still to be discounted. Absolutely!' Guido declared.

'Why, may I ask?'

'Because if the Siwahs' indifference towards power was something genetic, I wouldn't have been able to contract it.'

'*Contract* it?'

'Yes, I wouldn't be showing symptoms of it today.'

'What do you mean?' said Nesrin, who now seemed distinctly perturbed.

'I now think like the Siwahs.'

Nesrin stared at him with obvious bewilderment: was Guido taking him for a ride or was he crazy? The Egyptian tried to treat the whole affair as a joke.

'Your consortium isn't going to like that!'

'From now on, my consortium doesn't count.'

Nesrin began to be seriously worried.

'Guido, you're a scientist. If you're not playing games with me, and this really has happened to you, you must want to know why and how? Surely you want to understand how something as odd as the Siwah syndrome has come to affect you too?'

'Maybe, yet its symptoms are too intangible to inspire such curiosity. Anyway, how could I be sure of guessing correctly? In my business, you can easily be wrong.'

'Tell me anyhow what you've observed,' Nesrin prompted him, as if addressing an invalid or a mental case.

'Observe is a big word,' Guido mumbled. 'I simply saw what anyone else can see. And anyone can have that particular trick of picking up a handful of sand and then slowly, almost grain by grain, letting it trickle out of one's fist. I don't even know if the habit is peculiar to the Siwahs.'

'Do *all* the Siwahs do it?' Nesrin asked.

'I've seen almost every man, woman and child do it. When I say almost ....'

'You mean everyone you've actually watched. I see,' said Nesrin patiently. 'And how do they do it?'

'What do you mean how?'

'Deliberately? Ritualistically? Devoutly? To soothe the nerves?'

'Not at all. I think it's more of a reflex action. An unconscious, impulsive, mechanical gesture. No importance or significance attached to it.'

'And how about you, did you test it?'

'I? Of course not! Someone caught me doing it. I wasn't even aware I was doing it.'

'But that someone ascribed some importance to the fact. Which contradicts what you were saying.'

'That someone isn't a Siwah and doesn't seem to want to become one. It was Mehdi.'

'Why didn't he tell me about it?'

'Quite simply, he thought it'd sound too stupid. He was afraid you'd kick his arse. How inconvenient not to have the thick-skinned Siwah posterior!'

Nesrin once again began wondering if he weren't the victim of an elaborate practical joke.

'So?' he said drily, in the tones of a superior who wants to get rapidly to the point.

'So that's it,' Guido concluded.

'That's what? Well, analyse the sand for God's sake, man! Instead of sitting there gawping! What sort of sand *is* it? Oasis sand or from the surrounding area? Logically, it can only be the former.'

'Well, for once logic hits the mark. What's more, it won't get you anywhere. The analysis you're asking for has already been made, and long before my arrival. The sand, like all the other substances in the region, was subjected to the closest scrutiny. With a fine toothcomb. I'll skip the catalogue, if you don't mind: it's a pain in the neck to list all the various tests. That's almost forgetting the psychological tests the company insisted upon.'

'All without any results?'

'Of course.'

For once Nesrin seemed close to being completely demoralized.

'What can one make of it all?' he said.

'That our methods of analysis don't permit us to isolate the element which determines the phenomenon.'

'Well find new methods then!' Nesrin cried, suddenly regaining impetus.

'No.'

'What do you mean, no?'

'No, that's all.'

Nesrin tried to rile his opponent by means of appealing irritatingly to his self-respect: 'Don't you have any scientific curiosity left?'

'CIRCE will send somebody else,' he warned Nesrin calmly.

'Much good may it do him! He won't find anything either.'

'And what if he did?'

'Your government would become CIRCE's first client.'

'Is that what you want to avoid?'

'You or anyone else, what's the difference, and why should I care?'

'At least we wouldn't experiment with our own citizens. Nor would we sell to the multinational outfits.'

'To whom then? One has to make a living.'

'We're a poor country Dr Andreotti. Is it fair that your discovery should go to the rich?'

'I've made no discovery.'

'But you still could make one,' Nesrin was quick to add. 'Don't restrict it to those who only encourage science the better to corrupt scientists. Those whose power enslaves you – and will enslave you still further, should you succeed.'

'Would I be any freer,' Guido asked him quizzically, 'if I agreed to work for you?'

Nesrin's expression brightened: he looked at his guest with what appeared to the latter to be quite sincere friendship, affection even.

'Try it,' said the Egyptian, 'and see.'

Guido got up, stretched voluptuously, and smiling as if a weight was now off his mind for good and all, let Nesrin know his decision, delivered in a flat, emphatic voice: 'You can go to hell. You're a government man. I ignore and despise you. I'm a Siwah.'

For a long while Nesrin seemed not to understand, so Guido went on: 'I'm returning to Hat-en-Shau. With the considered intention of spending the rest of my days there. But don't worry – not just yet!'

He put out his hand to say goodbye.

The Egyptian stayed in his chair, transfixed. He didn't respond to Guido's gesture. Then suddenly he leaned forward and grabbed the briefcase from the table in front of him: 'You're still married, Andreotti.'

His voice had changed tone: it was scarcely recognizable. Guido was neither surprised nor alarmed, he just smiled goodhumouredly.

'To be quite frank, old fellow, I'm not really sure!'

'I am,' Nesrin said brutally. 'Your boss hasn't had time to make use of that blank form of contract.'

'Not had time?' Guido repeated, with an expression now of cold suspicion.

'Yes. Your wife slipped between his fingers. No doubt she too has the elusive quality of your handfuls of sand.'

'Where's she gone?'

'Cairo, would you believe!'

'That surprises me, Mr Adly. Surprises me greatly,' said Guido grimly.

'I didn't expect you to believe me. I've never lied to you, however.'

Nesrin produced from his briefcase a set of 10 x 8 photo enlargements.

'You can check that these have been taken this very week,' he said, handing them to Guido. 'Note the name of the newspaper held by the person sitting next to our ladyfriend, on the terrace of the Cafe Groppi.'

The procedure was classic, and it made Guido feel sick. There wasn't a single kidnapper who hadn't used it! He almost retched when he saw how trusting and open Giulia's eyes were in the first photograph. She was wearing a summer dress that showed off her beautiful thighs. Her long black mane of hair covered her shoulders and her red lips seemed curiously full: she seemed entranced, ecstatic.

'You drugged her,' Guido said.

'Why me?' Nesrin said, affronted.

Guido turned to the next photo. In this one Giulia was nude, and her body was outlined by a strange light under which its every detail and even its skin-tones were clearly defined. The clear definition was more disconcerting than the fact that the young woman seemed to be floating among thick, barely penetrable clouds. Guido had no trouble recognizing the location.

'Your disgusting bath-house,' he spat out.

Guido rifled through the rest of the shots, fully expecting to see Giulia in a series of orgiastic poses, but to his surprise she was invariably alone. Here, she would be standing, like one of the Three Graces, oblivious of her sisters, or idly touching her stomach with a listless hand. In other shots she was lying full-length, either looking at herself narcissitically, thrusting out her loins or with one leg extended more like a gymnast than a seductress. Elsewhere, she was like Susannah in the bath, though Guido could discern none of the elders of antiquity.

So what were these clichéd artist's snaps in aid of? Did they aim to show Guido that Giulia was now in Nesrin's power? And if so, why? Guido felt his heart miss a beat: his Giulia! Had he always loved her so much?

'What have you in mind?' he asked the Egyptian scornfully.

'My country's best interests.'

Nesrin was silent momentarily before continuing:

'What exploits that beauty might accomplish if I were to inject her with the EA 12 Unicorn I've been saving up!'

There was another silence, before Guido at last asked numbly: 'How did you get a supply?' and answered his own question: 'From that bastard Pecori, I suppose.' Nesrin said nothing, and Guido went on: 'So this is the bargain – eitheir I work for you or you assassinate Giulia.'

'Assassinate!' Nesrin protested. 'Has such a concept any place in your own code of ethics?'

Once again, in style and tone, he was the perfect diplomat.

'For as long as it was some vast, featureless, stateless wealthy monster that asked you, you showed no scruples to my knowledge, in cooperating fully in the discovery of a toxin which would turn mankind into contented cattle. I suppose by doing that, you weren't assassinating anyone? Your conscience isn't offended until I suggest your putting this means of defence in the hands of an underprivileged nation. Your reservations about biological weapons meanwhile, are very recent, as I seem to recall. But haven't you invented one? This bewitching weapon whose deadly horn only pierces mythical virginities?'

'An erotic stimulant isn't a weapon,' said Guido.

'In that case, what have you got against me?' said Nesrin, surprised. 'Haven't I as much right to use it as

238

anybody else? Or do you now think that there might be some difference between myself and you?'

Guido stared back without any apparent hostility or emotion.

'Obviously you don't get erections too easily, Nesrin,' he finally said.

'I am, in fact, quite careful in my choice of partners.'

'Did you know Giulia, before you had her abducted?'

'Only by reputation.'

'You must have been pleased when you found she could give you a hard-on.'

'I'm not here in order to be pleased, Guido,' said Nesrin. 'I'm here to do a job.'

'Why not keep Giulia for your pleasure, rather than having her killed? You as good as admitted it: it's not so easy to find someone compatible. For once when the opportunity is offered you, take it! I'm telling you just what I think.'

He spoke with a detachment and objectivity which Nesrin sensed were unfeigned. Guido went on in the same vein: 'Desire counts for more than possession. The map survives the city.'

Once again they were silent. I like this man, thought Nesrin. Why do I have to fight him? Why must I do wrong, I who believe in the possibility of good?

'If I took you up on your idea,' he asked, 'what would your reaction be?'

'I'd stay free.'

Nesrin nodded, as if in approval. Or maybe he was just noting the fact. He got up, apparently very tired, almost exhausted.

'I'll inject Giulia with your product,' he said in a remote resigned, fatalistic voice that appeared suddenly to have aged. 'Not to pay you back for your refusal,' he added, 'but out of logic, as you're so fond of saying yourself.'

Guido watched him leave, but his mind was elsewhere.

His brain was functioning, inexorably, thoughts, emotions, plans, all evolving objectively, as if they had all originated within somebody else's brain, or were the product of a computer ... What fate, posited this machine, would he have preferred for Giulia? To be the slave-mistress – wife, that is – of a man like Nesrin, who lives without desire and belongs to a nation? Or what people often talk about but very few actually experience: dying of pleasure?

Through his hotel window Guido watched Nesrin cross the garden.

Before getting into the car that awaited him, the Egyptian stooped down to pick up a handful of sand. He held it for some time, then let it trickle through his fingers dreamily.

2

Beauty Arrives

'I've come to claim what's owed me' said Vanna, the moment she'd shut the padded door of the large, cedar-panelled office. Nesrin Adly had agreed to see her as soon as she'd shown up, without an appointment, on the very day he returned to Cairo.

'I don't want money,' she explained.

He offered her a chair she ignored. So out of courtesy he remained standing behind his table and waited for her to state her terms.

'I want the Unicorn,' she said finally.

He remained motionless, but for his hands, which toyed gently with his gold cigarette-case. At last he asked: 'For whom?'

'For me.'

Nesrin raised his eyebrows, which he did whenever something took him by surprise: this, it was true, didn't happen very often.

'But to do what?'

'To take it, for God's sake!' she burst out. 'Inject myself with it. You didn't really think I'd want to help anyone else get it, did you?'

He smiled patiently.

'You apparently don't know what this drug is, Vanna.'

She shrugged.

'What do you take me for? I know perfectly well what EA 12 is: ACh transmuted.'

'I mean you don't know about its effects.'

'And do *you*? Have you already tested the stuff on Giulia?'

He was silent. The hum of the air-conditioning was for a long time the only noise audible within the room, until it became almost hypnotic. Nesrin broke the spell: 'No,' he said. 'I haven't tried it yet.'

'Are you going to?'

'Yes.'

'Why?'

'Because I've decided to.'

'Has your own power taken you over, Nesrin?' Vanna said, half-pitying, half-sarcastic. 'Are you so servile now that you're no longer free to disobey yourself?'

He didn't respond, but answered another question, one she hadn't asked: 'I don't have enough EA 12 to share.'

'Really not enough for two? Well if that's the case, it's quite simple. Do without the experiment you want to subject youself to. Give me all your supply.'

He emitted a sigh of utter disbelief.

'My dear child . . . .'

'No Nesrin, I'm not dear to you, and I'm an adult.'

'If you were, you wouldn't come here with such an infantile request.'

'It isn't a request sir, but a demand.'

He smiled indulgently.

'Throughout this business, Vanna, I'm happy to acknowledge that you've been a loyal assistant. But you know as well as I that we haven't got anywhere. Neither of us is in a position to ask for more than we've achieved.'

'My stock in your political market doesn't interest me in the least, Nesrin. I've never been taken into your confidence, as regards what you were looking for, so I can't say whether you've found it. Nor can I judge your success or failure. What's more, I don't give a damn. On the other hand, I haven't found what *I* was looking for. In fairness, I have a right to compensation.'

'Didn't you see your father again? Didn't I keep my promise about that? The only one I made you . . . .'

'My life can't have room for two fathers: the cold father you sent me to and the warm one I'd invented over the years.'

'Is it reasonable to draw on imaginary funds?'

'Having a father who doesn't want to have a daughter wouldn't be any more real.'

'And what about Guido? He wasn't a myth to you. What's he been, then? A mirage?'

'You're the one, Nesrin, who made a myth of Guido,' Vanna said with irritation. 'Not I.'

'Had you noticed it always requires more courage to ask questions than answer them? Which of you – you or Guido – really questioned the other?'

'You wanted me to be a sort of siren where he was concerned,' Vanna said with some regret. 'I thought I was his Siamese twin. But I've outgrown him.'

'Your intransigence isn't wise, Vanna. Aren't you afraid your hard line will mean you're alone in the world?'

'I need the substance in your possession in order not to be alone among my fellow human beings.'

He shook his head wearily and slumped into his armchair.

'Tell me the truth,' he said sharply. 'You want to rescue Giulia, don't you?'

'I'm not Giulia's keeper,' Vanna replied. 'Anyway, I'm not losing any sleep over her: she has CIRCE to keep an eye on her. I told you, I want to try out this product myself. On and for myself. I want to test its truth, justice, goodness, its beauty, if only for one eternal day. Just one day of justice: do you realize what that might be like, Nesrin? I want to experience the change, to know and live

243

it. For one whole day I want to make no exceptions, not to differentiate between people. For one long wonderful day, I want not to do any of my fellow human beings the injustice of believing them to be worth less than anyone else. This day without discrimination, preference or privilege will really thumb its nose at eternity! It will redress the injustice of nature, which has separated the handsome from the ugly, the strong from the weak, the unfortunate from the lucky. If you only knew how I've hated injustice, Nesrin! I hated it enough to weep – I who never was a victim of it. It was the injustice suffered by others that gave me the will to change, to change in order to become fair and just. That's why you owe me the Unicorn, you see. Only that can really change me. That was what I was really looking for, everywhere, without realizing it. Now I've found it, nothing in the world could stop me doing what I must. Nobody could forbid me to become what I want to be. No longer will anyone suffer injustice that I have caused. This Unicorn has come for me, but through me it will work upon others. I'm here to share its unnatural nature. I've come to lend it my body, so it can make a new creation. And I'm telling you, Nesrin, you haven't the right to deprive me of its services.'

'It's deadly. Do you want to die, then?'

'Oh I'm not about to drop dead today or tomorrow!' said Vanna mockingly. 'I've got lots of years left to live. More than you yourself have. So don't worry about *that*, Nesrin. The Unicorn and I are made for each other: we won't harm or kill one another, you know ... Anyhow,' she continued, more and more cheerfully, 'a woman isn't killed so easily! A woman isn't a rat. Rats make love in order to propagate. If reproduction is so important to them, that's so they can die peacefully. *I* make love in order to learn how to love. As long as I know how to love, I won't die.'

Nesrin grew increasingly sorrowful and perplexed. He said gloomily:

'Even its inventor isn't sure of the effects of his invention. How can you claim to predict them, when you weren't even involved?'

'Who told you I'm not involved?'

'So you only needed a few weeks in which to turn into a biologist,' Nesrin said soothingly.

'Guido taught me that we are born capable of knowing everything. And I've always known we're also born capable of loving everyone. It's because we don't use this knowledge enough that our hearts close up, just like our brains do when they grow unable to imagine, understand or think correctly. Probably my desire to love is actually only a memory: I vaguely remember how I fell in love with all the world when I was born ... my first day ....'

For a moment Nesrin let his mind wander: 'Love everyone?' he murmured. 'Do you really think you have to love everyone? Don't intelligence and reason consist of making choices?'

'To be able to choose, you must first know how to hate. Must I waste my lifetime here on earth wishing ill upon ninety per cent of what I see? I'm not that stupid.'

'Isn't that just what you're doing when you hate injustice?'

'I'm not confusing people with what they're made to do. Behind men's unpromising appearances there are probably as many opportunities for love as there is unknown beauty in outer space.'

She flashed Nesrin a roguish smile.

'Do you know what Kepler shouted at the live stars and the dead planets, on discovering that the laws of terrestrial mechanics also explained the movement of the heavens – thus sounding the knell of divinity, without his knowing it?'

245

'I must admit I don't,' said Nesrin, who for once hardly appeared eager to be enlightened.

'This: "I exist, and I exult! I fly in space! I've learned what the clouds concealed. I see and understand. I've uncovered the golden secret of the Egyptians. I know! I am drunk with love because I know it! I want to abandon myself to my sacred drunkenness!"'

At this Nesrin gave a bitter little chuckle.

'Well that's it!' Vanna ended. 'I feel in just that frame of mind, even though I didn't succeed in making off with that priceless secret you coveted, and the drunken ecstasy I'm preparing for is resolutely profane.'

Nesrin had a distant expression, as if refusing to countenance visions that were not of his world; as if it pained him to hear hopes invoked which he had long since renounced in favour of very different utopias and illusory antidotes against death. He only abandoned his reverie in order to try to dissuade Vanna from her purpose.

'Why you rather than Giulia?' he asked tersely.

'Because you don't owe her anything.'

'If *she* took the EA 12 I could note its effects personally.'

It was as good as admitting that he didn't want to witness any such metamorphosis in Vanna. This surprised her and she was on the point of asking him his reasons. But she thought better of it, remembering his confession some time ago that he still cared about her. That was all she needed! A belated twinge of jealousy which might drive this man to refuse her what she was asking! She became blunter: 'Why should the effects concern you? That's not in your province, so stick to your own job. Don't waste your precious time with chitchat, because your time's not your own either. It, and all of you, belongs to the State. Except the EA 12, of course.'

He wasn't about to take this lying down.

246

'If I were to give in to this whim of yours, where would you go to take this poison? Siwah?'

'I never retrace my footsteps.'

'To which unexplored territory, then?'

'I'll know when the Unicorn's inside me.'

'You're mad.'

'That's what's always said of those who refuse to accept ancient boundaries. Those who try to go beyond culture and tradition so as to fulfil the promise of their birth. When the logic, politics and morality of others doesn't actually chop off their heads, they are so cunningly lobotomized that they and many other unconventional people end up thinking *themselves* wrong. Not me!'

'Is drugging oneself a good way of recreating the world?' Nesrin objected mildly.

'But I'm not seeking to recreate the world! It's myself I want to remake. I wasn't properly made.'

'You can console yourself at far less risk,' he insisted. 'Be content you're so much more than the rats.'

'The Unicorn doesn't console, it provides one with new methods. Don't you think I need new methods?' Looking him straight in the eye she added: 'And I don't want to be content. Nesrin Adly: I want to be happy. It's not the same thing. It's the opposite, even. When the time comes to die, I want to feel happy I've lived.'

Vanna realized that Nesrin's safe mental pigeonholes had received too great and sudden an upheaval for him to be able to make a rapid decision. She settled for a breathing-space and lay back comfortably, staring with some pleasure at her long bare legs. He remained speechless, motionless, his eyes half-closed. His fingers no longer toyed with cigarettes or his cigarette box.

'Nesrin, come on! Let's have the stuff!' she said sharply.

He came to abruptly. Apparently ignoring his visitor, he

leaned over and found the piece of metal which was the electronic key to his concealed inner sanctum. As though his limbs had suddenly turned rheumatic, he moved across half-hypnotized, to the light dot in the wall and went through the usual procedures to gain access, this time quite openly in front of Vanna, as if from now on all this security ritual was no longer important, rendered completely obsolete by some magic spell.

The young woman watched without interest. She knew as clearly as Nesrin that she would never come back here again.

The diplomat came back from the inner room that had once been so secret. He left the door wide open. He was holding a very small box, like a cube of light white wood, which resembled a jewel-box or those the Japanese sometimes use for tiny pieces of *curiosa*.

He placed it upon his leather desk-blotter and slid off its lid. It contained a minute syringe resting on cotton wool. The syringe was only a third full – of a liquid whose colour reminded Vanna of the turbid, opaque waters of the Nile.

'Where does one inject it?' she inquired.

'Wherever you like,' said Nesrin.

He closed the box and stayed where he was, looking at this object through lowered eyelids, like a priest contemplating the material and inconceivable host upon the paten.

Vanna leaned over the table, took the box and slipped it into her white linen handbag.

She gave Nesrin her hand and he shook it without emotion or any special pressure, a little abstractedly, as he doubtless did when taking leave of a visiting diplomat.

He sat down again and began leafing through a file in front of him, while Vanna crossed the long room and departed, leaving the door open behind her.

She descended the steps of the Adly mansion. A huge cloud of sand seemed to be drifting over the town.

'The war is over,' Vanna said, breathing deeply just the same, and added, 'the days of castles are dead and gone.'

A young man with the looks of a young girl came up to her. The tray he was carrying was full of marzipan pyramids and sugar camels.

'*Salaam!*' she said, without taking any.

He greeted her affably in turn.

She cast a penetrating, comprehensive glance like the beam of some lighthouse over the multitudes of men and women busily or idly thronging to and fro.

'I still find almost all these people disagreeable or boring,' she thought.

Through the material of her bag she felt the hard little box which contained the remedy, and smiled to herself tenderly.

She said calmly and for all to hear:

'Quite soon I shall love them.'

BESTSELLERS AVAILABLE IN GRANADA PAPERBACKS

Emmanuelle Arsan

Emmanuelle	95p ☐
Emmanuelle 2	95p ☐
Laure	95p ☐
Nea	95p ☐

Jonathan Black

Ride the Golden Tiger	80p ☐
Oil	£1.25 ☐
The World Rapers	£1.25 ☐
The House on the Hill	£1.25 ☐

Herbert Kastle

Hot Prowl	60p ☐
Cross-Country	£1.25 ☐
The World They Wanted	75p ☐
Little Love	85p ☐
Millionaires	75p ☐
Miami Golden Boy	95p ☐
The Movie Maker	£1.50 ☐
The Gang	95p ☐
Countdown to Murder	75p ☐
The Three Lives of Edward Berner	85p ☐

Calder Willingham

The Big Nickel	£1.25 ☐
Rambling Rose	50p ☐
End as a Man	£1.25 ☐
To Eat a Peach	75p ☐
Geraldine Bradshaw	40p ☐
Eternal Fire	£1.50 ☐
Providence Island	£1.50 ☐
Reach to the Stars	95p ☐

BESTSELLERS AVAILABLE IN GRANADA PAPERBACKS

Leslie Waller

The Swiss Account	£1.25 ☐
The 'K' Assignment	50p ☐
Number One	85p ☐
A Change in the Wind	40p ☐
The American	75p ☐
The Family	£1.25 ☐
The Banker	£1.25 ☐
The Coast of Fear	60p ☐

Patrick Mann

The Vacancy	60p ☐
Dog Day Afternoon	60p ☐

TRUE ADVENTURE – AVAILABLE IN GRANADA PAPERBACKS

Kenneth Ainslie
Pacific Ordeal   75p ☐

Henri Charriere
Papillon   £1.25 ☐
Banco   £1.25 ☐

Emmett Grogan
Ringolevio   £1.50 ☐

Clark Howard
Six Against the Rock   £1.25 ☐

William Laird McKinley
Karluk (illustrated)   £1.25 ☐

Miles Smeeton
Once is Enough (illustrated)   85p ☐

Nicholas Svidine
The Treasure of the White Army (illustrated)   85p ☐

FAMOUS PERSONALITIES YOU'VE ALWAYS WANTED TO READ ABOUT – NOW AVAILABLE IN GRANADA PAPERBACKS

THE MOST CHILLING HORROR STORIES –
NOW AVAILABLE IN GRANADA PAPERBACKS

Alfred Hitchcock (Editor)

Grave Business	60p	☐
Murder Racquet	60p	☐
Get Me to the Wake on Time	50p	☐
Death Bag	40p	☐
Bar the Doors	50p	☐
A Hangman's Dozen	35p	☐

Henry S Whitehead

Jumbee and Other Voodoo Tales	50p	☐
The Black Beast and Other Voodoo Tales	60p	☐

AGATHA CHRISTIE – QUEEN OF DETECTIVE FICTION

The Secret Adversary	95p	☐
The Murder on the Links	95p	☐
The Mysterious Affair at Styles	95p	☐
The Man in the Brown Suit	95p	☐
The Secret of Chimneys	80p	☐

C S FORESTER

Plain Murder	85p	☐
Payment Deferred	80p	☐

All these books are available at your local bookshop or newsagent, or can be ordered direct from the publisher. Just tick the titles you want and fill in the form below.

Name ....

Address ....

....

Write to Granada Cash Sales, PO Box 11, Falmouth, Cornwall TR10 9EN.

Please enclose remittance to the value of the cover price plus:

UK: 30p for the first book, 15p for the second book plus 12p per copy for each additional book ordered to a maximum charge of £1.29.

BFPO and EIRE: 30p for the first book, 15p for the second book plus 12p per copy for the next 7 books, thereafter 6p per book.

OVERSEAS: 50p for the first book and 15p for each additional book.

Granada Publishing reserve the right to show new retail prices on covers, which may differ from those previously advertised in the text or elsewhere.